AVENGING ANGELS: VENGEANCE TRAIL

A.W. HART

WOLFPACK
PUBLISHING
— EST 2013 —

WOLFPACK
PUBLISHING
— EST 2013 —

Paperback Edition
Copyright © 2019 A.W. Hart

Special thanks to Peter Brandvold for his contribution to this novel.

Published in the United States by Wolfpack Publishing, Las Vegas

Wolfpack Publishing
6032 Wheat Penny Avenue
Las Vegas, NV 89122

wolfpackpublishing.com

Paperback ISBN 978-1-64119-652-9
eBook ISBN 978-1-64119-950-6

Library of Congress Control Number: 2019950938

AVENGING ANGELS: VENGEANCE TRAIL

*But the coward·ly, the unbelieving, the vile, the mur·er-
ers, the sexually immoral, those who practice magic
arts, the i·olaters an· all liars—they will be consigne·
to the fiery lake of burning sulfur. This is the secon·
·eath."—Book of Revelation 21:8*

ONE

Most storms came to western Kansas from the south or the west, fueled either by moist air blowing up from the Gulf of Mexico or by the cooler winds blowing over the Rocky Mountains. This storm came from the southeast. It was a storm of men driven to rage and diabolical violence by the concession of the South to the Union Army at Appomattox Courthouse.

It was a tornado of battle-maddened ex-Confederate soldiers, mostly men from the lower ranks, but also of several officers who either had no home to go back to after their defeat or who no longer saw the battle-ravaged South as their home anymore. Theirs was a conquered land. They would not be conquered. There were Yankees still to be killed. They headed to the frontier West now to redeem themselves for their failings on the battlefield, and god have mercy on anyone who stood in their bloody path.

They were led by Colonel Eustace Montgomery known as "the Bad Old Man" and his senior, Major Robert "Black Bob" Hobbs, both men mounted on high-stepping cream horses, battle-bloodied bayonets waved high above their heads or angled low to cleave a beating heart.

Western Union had not spread its telegraph tentacles to most far-flung rural western settlements in the mid-1860s, so the people of the small towns of western Kansas and eastern Colorado, on which these wild human dogs concentrated their alcohol-fueled fury, had no or little warning that the storm was coming to their town next. Often the first indication that the apocalypse was imminent was a rumbling felt through the earth and a dark dust cloud churning against the southeastern horizon.

Minutes later the town would be on fire, its citizens lying dead or dying in the smoky streets, the killers whooping and yammering like coyotes on the blood trail.

"What's that?" asked Sara Bass one early-autumn afternoon along the grassy bank of Cottonwood Creek.

Her twin brother, Reno, lay on his back in the tawny wheat grass, twirling a wildflower between his fingers and thinking about their schoolteacher, Miss Cassie Bernard. They'd left her schoolhouse twenty minutes ago, after Reno had stayed late to help the pretty young teacher, only a few older than his own sixteen years, split firewood and clean and mop the floor.

"What's what?"

"That sound."

"I don't hear no sound."

Mounted atop their brindle mule, Otis, Sara turned her blond head to frown down at her dreamy twin brother. "That's because you're not hearing anything except the sound of Miss Bernard's voice in your head. Sober up, George Washington Bass, and listen to what I'm hearing."

That was his given name, all right, but he preferred his nickname, Reno, which his father had dubbed him when he was only three years old. It had been the name of one of John Bass's much-admired commanding officers during the Mexican War.

"You know I hate that name, and I ain't drunk. You know what happened to my backside last time I got into the Christmas—"

"Shut up. You're drunk on love, you moon-calf fool." Sara slung her right arm out, pointing across the creek toward the grassy, cottonwood-peppered embankment on the other side. "Look there!"

"You know, sweet sister," Reno said, sitting up and yawning lazily, "there ain't nothing wrong with tumbling for a gal as purty an' smart as Miss Bernard.

There wouldn't be nothin' wrong with you tumbling for a good-lookin' young man, neither. You'd probably have one or two coming around sparking you now an' then if you'd stop dressing like a boy and take a bath and brush your hair once in a while. Why, I got a suspicion that under that ragged sack shirt, burlap trousers, and tangled hair, under them frown lines and sunburn and dust, you might even be right purty."

"You know what ma says—'Purty don't get the cows milked'."

"Hey, where you goin'?"

Sara gigged Otis across the creek, batting the heels of her plain brown badly scuffed boots against the mule's ribs. "I'm gonna climb the yonder bank, see if I can see where that dust is coming from."

Reno gazed at where dust roiled beyond the creek's opposite bank. It hung in the air like a giant, charcoal feather, billowing slightly and moving slowly but steadily from Reno's right to his left. "Prob'ly just a dust devil, Sara."

Reno gained his feet—a solidly built, muscular young man even at sixteen. He sported broad shoulders, a lumpy chest, and arms thickened from years of running a plow behind Otis or one of his family's other mules, digging fence post holes, branding calves, and cutting firewood for the long Kansas winter. His eyes were the same cornflower blue as his sister's, his hair nearly the exact shade of strawberry blond.

George Washington "Reno" Bass well knew he was considered handsome by the fairer sex, for even at his young age he'd had more than a few neighbor girls and girls from school tumble for him. He wasn't sure, but he believed Miss Bernard was sweet on him, too, though she tried not to let on, her being his teacher and all. The truth was, he spent a lot of time thinking of his comely teacher, and was so fond of her, he'd even memorized the poems she liked best—most of them written by a dead British fellow named Keats. She'd given him a book by Keats, in fact.

"Hey, don't you go leavin' me out here on foot, now!" he called to his sister, who could be right colicky. Tiring of his company as well as what she saw as his intolerable vanity, more than a few times Sarah had ridden off and left him stranded somewhere afoot, with a long walk home ahead of him. John Bass was willing to spare only one mule, old Otis, for their transport to and from school, even though it was his and their mother's idea that they attend. The other mules and horses were needed for farm work.

"Sara!" Reno called.

Ignoring him, Sara and old Otis continued to the top of the opposite ridge. Sara stopped the mule and sat staring to the southeast. Reno watched her, ready to spring into a run and ford the creek if it looked like she was going to take off on him again.

"Sara, galldangit…!"

He stopped when the girl reined the mule around sharply and urged it down the bluff, heading back toward the creek and Reno standing on the stream's north shore.

"Go, boy!" Sara urged the mule, batting her heels harder against the big, heavy-footed beast's ribs. "Go, boy! Go, boy! Hurry!"

Reno watched her, scowling skeptically. "Sara, what in tarnation has gotten into you?"

He felt it, then, too—a trembling in the ground beneath his own worn boots. Distant thunder rumbled. Only he knew it wasn't thunder. At least, not the thunder of a natural storm. There wasn't a cloud in the sky.

Sara gigged the mule across the creek, its heavy shod hooves ringing against rocks, water spraying up and forming rainbows in the bright sunshine. When the mule had gained Reno's side of the creek, Sara urged it on up the northern bank, whipping the rein ends against the mule's right hip.

"Hurry, Otis, blame-it!" she yelled. "You heavy-footed crow bait!"

"Sara!" Reno bounded up the slope behind her, slipping on the straw-like, summer-cured grass and dropping to his knees.

Ahead and above him, Sara halted the mule on a gently sloping shelf jutting from the bank. She leaped lithely from the saddle, tied the reins to a tree, then climbed the last few feet to the top of the bank. She'd just dropped to her knees and doffed her floppy-brimmed hat when Reno moved up beside her, breathing hard and sweating from the climb.

"Sara, what in blazes…?"

"Get down!" She reached up to tug on his arm. "They'll see you!"

Reno dropped to his knees. She brushed his black, bullet-crowned hat off his head, letting it tumble into the grass. "Sara, who…"

She jerked her chin to the northeast. "Them!"

Reno turned to follow her gaze, and felt his lower jaw drop. "Whoa!"

A whole passel of riders was just then rounding a bend in the trail, heading from the southeast to the north. The trail passed about twenty yards away from where Reno and Sara knelt in the brush atop the stream bank.

"Down, Reno," Sara said, giving another tug on his arm and lowering her head close to the ground. "Don't let them see you!"

Reno lowered his own head until his chin raked the ground. He stared through the breeze-ruffled grass toward the riders coming hard and fast. There had to be two dozen of them. They were grouped close together, and their horses were really chewing up the trail. The ground shook beneath Reno's belly, and the din of the pounding hooves and the squawk of tack leather was all he could hear.

The first two riders galloped hard and fast along the trail. They were both mounted on pale horses. One of the two leaders, an older man, sported a long, gray beard. The other one, younger, wore a thick, black beard on his lean, angular face with a long, hooked nose.

What was most fascinating about them—in fact, what was most fascinating about all of them—was that most were clad in Confederate gray uniforms or bits and pieces of uniforms. Those who wore linsey-woolsey or wool or buckskin or broadcloth at least wore a Confederate gray campaign hat, or kepi.

Most, however, not only wore the hat but the tunic or a gray greatcoat, as well. Some, like the first two gents, were in full uniform right down to the bayonets dangling over their legs.

As the group thundered past Reno and Sara, Reno heard them talking and laughing. They seemed to be in fine spirits. One even tipped back a crock jug. Another man swatted him, and the man with the jug shoved the jug across to the other one. As the group passed to Reno's left, he followed them with his eyes. They rounded the next bend in the trail, curving away from the river, and headed northwest toward the little town of Kiowa Springs, on the edge of which sat the school.

Reno stared at the dust sifting over the trail. He still smelled the hot aroma of the lathered horses, the sweat of the men. Speechless, he wasn't sure he'd actually seen what his brain told him he'd seen. They'd been like ghosts in the night. Only, it wasn't night.

When he finally found his tongue, he turned to Sara and said, "I was gonna say sheriff's posse, but that ain't no sheriff's posse from around here. They was…"

"I know what they was, you fool," Sara said, mocking his poor grammar as she did everything else about him, as was her way. "What they was was Confederate soldiers. What I'm wondering is what they're doing up here in Union territory."

"You don't suppose the war's come clear up here—do you, sis?"

"The war's over, you simpleton. You'd know that if you actually listened to Miss Bernard instead of only followed her around the schoolroom with your mooncalf eyes. It ended last spring."

"Oh, that's right. I remember now." Reno glared at his high-headed sister. "Will you quit insultin' me, Sara Marie?"

Ignoring her twin brother, whom she considered beneath responding to, Sara stood and stared after the riders. They were disappearing into the sunny mist of the northern prairie, towing their dust cloud along behind and above them.

"What I want to know," she said, half to herself, because she was the only one worth addressing, "is where they're headed."

Slowly, almost reluctantly, she turned her head to stare to the southeast. "And where they came from."

Reno turned to follow her gaze. A ripple of dread climbed his spine. "Sara, you know as well as I do where the trail leads."

Slowly, fearfully, Sara nodded. "I know." She'd said it almost too quietly for Reno to hear. "It skirts our farmyard on the way up from Baxter."

They stared at each other in alarm.

Then they grabbed their hats and ran to the mule.

TWO

They saw the smoke not long after they'd left the creek and put the mule into an all-out gallop. Or at least as much of a gallop as old Otis could muster these days.

Thick smoke rose like a black chimney straight up into the air maybe three hundred feet before fanning out and waving gently like a summer kite in a gentle breeze.

Reno knew Sara saw the smoke at the same time he did. He felt her body tense behind him as she drew her arms tighter around his waist.

Smoke could mean only one thing.

Dread was a rusty knife piercing his heart, twisting.

No, he thought. No. It couldn't be. He'd heard the Confederates had raided and burned Lawrenceville only two years before, but nothing like that could

happen here. Not in his own home country. Not to
his family, for the love of god!

He urged more speed out of old Otis, but it wasn't
enough. He stopped urging because he knew the
old mule would likely drop to its knees, dead, if he
pushed it any harder. They covered the last half-mile
of the trail at what to Reno seemed a snail's pace. The
smoke grew before them—thicker and blacker than
before. When they'd climbed up and over the knoll
just north of the cattail-edged slough where they
shot ducks and geese this time of year and later, Reno
sucked a sharp breath of even darker dread.

From just over the next rise, where their small
farm nestled, orange flames licked up like a giant
tongue, shedding sparks and adding more and more
black smoke to the growing cloud. Otis shambled up
the rise. He wasn't going to make it all the way to the
top. Reno felt the poor beast's knees begin to buckle,
heard the raking of air in and out of its exhausted
lungs. Sara must have sensed it, too, because she
leaped off the mule's rump to the ground.

Reno hurled himself from the saddle and hit the
ground running, Sara right beside him.

They reached the top of the hill and stopped dead
in their tracks.

Reno's own knees buckled. He dropped to the
ground and knelt there, staring in wide-eyed, hang-
jawed shock and horror at the farmstead engulfed

in flames. Several bodies lay strewn about the yard, between the cabin on the left and the barn and corrals and stock pens on the right. Chickens lay dead, as well, while others ran crazily into the pastures and cornfield bordering the yard.

Horses and mules lay dead in one of the corrals. One of the eight pigs, which had not been killed like the others—shot in their pen, it appeared—was running in broad circles around the farmyard, squealing frantically. It must have leaped its pen when the others were slaughtered.

Reno's gaze returned to the human bodies lying twisted in the yard. Three of them. Reno knew who they were. They were his two older brothers, Ben and James and their sister, Mary Louise.

"Oh my god, Sara!" he heard himself wail.

Sara stood beside him, straight and unmoving, staring in expressionless shock and horror at the unbelievable sight before them.

The cabin looked like an orange torch. As Reno stared at it, some of the flames separated from the burning doorway and slid out into the yard fronting the cabin. Reno frowned, incredulous. But then he saw that the flames limned a human form. Two human forms, rather. The burning man walking out of the cabin held another burning body.

"Pa!" Sara screamed, and took off running.

At first, Reno couldn't move. His mind was slow

to come to the horrific conclusion that, inside those man-shaped flames, walked his father. His burning father!

A second later, he found himself running beside Sara.

Before them, their father, John Bass, staggered out away from the burning cabin and collapsed in the yard, dropping the body he'd been carrying. John Bass screamed an animal-like scream and rolled frantically in the dirt of the hard-packed, hay-strewn yard, trying to douse the flames incinerating him as well as the body in the yard, who Reno now saw with renewed horror was their mother, Alta Bass. He saw the white apron tied around her waist. Flames chewed at it, smoke rose from it. The rest of her body was black as ash.

Reno overtook Sara and flung himself atop their father, trying to douse the flames with his own body. Sara threw her own body atop their mother, screaming, "Mama! Mama!"

"Pa!" Reno cried, rolling on top of his father and swatting at the flames.

"Reno!" Sara shrieked and cast herself atop her brother, laying him out with his back against the ground, dousing the flames then clinging to his canvas trousers and checked flannel shirt. His flames then began burning Sara, and, sitting up, she extinguished them with her hat and her hands.

They both then turned to their father, whose charred body lay smoking before them, as did their mother's. Their mother didn't move. John Bass lay writhing and screaming, "Help...help your mother, chil—children! For the love of god, help your mother!"

Sara crouched over their father. She placed one hand on his quickly expanding and contracting chest, and the other hand on his cheek. He'd worn a beard, but now most of the beard had been singed off his once-handsome, craggy face now peeled and blistering and black. Most of his thick, salt-and-pepper hair was gone, as well. His old Colt Navy .36 resided in a holster strapped to his coverall-clad waist.

"She'd dead, Pa," Sara said, her blue eyes bright with consternation. "She's dead, Pa. There's nothing we can do for her."

"What?"

John Bass stared up at his daughter, his brow ridged with befuddlement. He switched his gaze to Reno as though sending the question to his youngest son. Reno turned to their mother. She lay unmoving, more burned that not. Her own blue eyes stared heavenward in shock, though a strange smile seemed to twist her charred mouth. Her gray hair, pulled up into a double bun atop her head, was charred and smoking.

"She's gone, Pa," Reno sobbed, returning his gaze to their father. "I'm so sorry, Pa. Ma...she's gone!"

"Oh, for the love of god," John Bass said. He grimaced against the pain in his burned body and stared heavenward, as though ready to follow his wife there. "For the love of god...we was set upon by the devil's hounds..."

Reno crouched over his father, sobbing with rage as well as grief. "Who were they, Pa? Who were they. Why...?"

John Bass wrapped his burned left hand around Reno's left wrist, and squeezed. "I don't know," he wheezed, spittle flecking from his lips, fury narrowing his eyes and causing veins to bulge and ripple in his charred forehead. "I don't know. You'll find out." He coughed, gritted his teeth. "Track 'em. Kill 'em. Understand?"

He slid his gaze to Sara. "You both understand?"

They both stared down at the dying man, speechless.

John Bass licked his lips. "Avenge your family. Do it in the name of god and all that's holy. Kill the devil and his hounds and rid this earth of his ilk. Do me proud, Reno. Sara. Do your family proud. Do god proud! You understand?"

"We understand, Pa," Sara whispered.

Reno's heart raced. "Yeah, we...we understand, Pa."

John Bass fumbled the old Colt Navy .36 from its holster. He shoved it at Reno.

"Put an end to my misery, son."

Reno looked down at the big Colt in his hands,

shook his head in disbelief. "We'll fetch the doctor from Baxter. You're gonna be—"

"I'm dyin', son. I can't bear the pain. Don't make me bear it."

Reno stared at him in shock.

"Please, boy," John Bass begged his son. "Your dear mother is waitin' on me."

"I can't, Pa."

"Yes, you can," his father said gently. "I'd do as much for you."

"Oh, Pa!" Reno wept. He knew his father was dying. He could imagine the pain he was in. But he couldn't kill him. Not his own father. "Please...don't ask me."

"I am asking you, Reno."

Reno looked at Sara kneeling beside him. She stared back at him. Her eyes were grave and dry.

Tears rolled down Reno's cheeks. He rose heavily, stared down at his father. Most of the poor man's clothes had been burned off his body. His skin was black and charred. Puss oozed from the bloody blisters.

"Please, son—put me out of my misery," John Bass begged.

Reno clicked the hammer back, aimed down the barrel at his father. Tears dribbled down his face. His lips trembled. His hand shook. He wanted to pull the trigger, but it was as though his finger was made of stone.

"Kill me," John Bass wheezed, sliding his pain-bright gaze between his two children. "Find Ty Mando in Julesburg. Old friend of mine. He'll help. You can both shoot...track. Killing men like those who killed your family is the same as killin' hydrophobic coyotes. You can two can do it...better than a whole army." His eyes flashed with rage, sharply reflecting the flames of the burning farm leaping around him. "Kill the rebel vermin who murdered your family!"

Reno's face twisted in misery as he aimed the Colt at his father's head. The gun shook like a leaf in the wind. Finally, he lowered the weapon to his side, and hung his head in shame. "I'm sorry, Pa. I can't do it."

Sara grabbed the gun out of his hand. She cocked the heavy weapon and aimed it at John Bass's head. "Goodbye, Pa." The revolver roared. "You will be avenged!"

She lowered the gun and turned to Reno, who stared at her in astonishment.

"Pull yourself together, brother," Sara said softly. "We have a job of work to do before dark."

✷✷✷

An hour later, shadows grew long, for the day was waning. Reno felt his strength waning, as well.

He carried his sister, Mary Louise, up the hill to the family's small cemetery plot north of the farm.

Mary Louisa had been shot but she'd also been ravaged terribly. Reno and Sara had found her with her torn day dress shoved up around her waist, her legs spread.

Sara had said nothing. Reno had gritted his teeth as he'd imagined how many of that crazy horde of devils had taken poor Mary Louise before one had finally shot her through her heart. Since their father had been the last to die, John Bass must have been rendered unconscious while they'd so terribly abused his oldest daughter. Or maybe he'd simply been restrained, unable to do anything but watch.

Had their mother been condemned to watch, as well? Maybe they'd savaged her, too, before they'd left her to burn to death in the cabin.

Reno shook his head, to rid himself of the images. Of course, it didn't work. The terrifying scenario continued to play in his mind.

As he topped the cottonwood-peppered hill south of the smoldering farm, he saw where Sara was digging the second grave beneath a giant cottonwood and near where another Bass child lay buried, killed by a milk plague twenty-some years ago, as well as the Bass grandparents. When John Bass had come out here from Illinois after the Mexican War, he'd brought his young wife, Alta Rasmussen, his first-born child, Benjamin Franklin, and Alta's parents, Oscar and Hilda. They'd both died when Reno and

Sara were very young.

The barn had not been totally destroyed by flames. Reno and Sara had found shovels inside. They'd also found a saddle blanket and burlap bags, which they'd cut up and used as burial shrouds. The Bass family deserved so much more. Reno had said as much to Sara, who had simply said, "Well, since everything's gone, it's all they're going to get."

He lay Mary Louise's blanket-wrapped body down beside the four similarly wrapped bodies of his father, mother, and two brothers. He dropped to one knee to compose himself. He hadn't shed a tear since Sara had shot their father. He felt little emotion now. Mostly, he felt numb. As hollow as an old tree stump. Deep down, he really didn't believe what had happened. Part of him wasn't convinced this was all just a dream.

A terrible nightmare from which he would soon awaken.

Still, his heart continued to thud heavily, painfully inside his chest.

He drew a breath, scrubbed his sweaty forehead with his sleeve, and turned to Sara. She stood about two feet down in the grave she'd been digging. She grunted as she tossed out another spadeful of dirt and gravel.

"Take a break, sis," Reno said, and spat to one side. "I have them all up here now. I think we should say a prayer over them."

Sara kicked the shovel into the ground again. "No time for prayers. These graves aren't going to dig themselves."

Anger burned in Reno. He straightened, hardened his jaws at his sister. "Sara, take a break!"

She turned to him, one brow arched curiously. She tossed away the last shovelful of dirt she'd dug, stabbed the shovel into the fresh pile, and sighed.

She stepped out of the grave and walked over to where Reno stood near the blanket- and burlap-wrapped bodies. She sighed and, standing beside Reno, looked down at the bodies of her family.

"Hurry up, then," she said. "It'll be dark soon."

Reno stared down at his family. Their father had taught his children prayers for all occasions; he'd made them memorize countless verses from both the Old and New Testaments. But for some reason, only one of those prayers found its way into Reno's grief-stricken brain now.

"I reckon we can just say the Lord's prayer for now."

"All right."

"I'll start," Reno said. He bowed his head and entwined his hands and began reciting, "Our father who art in Heaven, hallowed be thy name..."

Sara joined him.

When they finished, Reno lifted his head, cleared his throat. Suddenly, words came to him from his heart, not the Bible. Suddenly, he was fairly bursting with them:

"Goodbye, Ma. Pa. Brother Ben and James, Sister Mary Louise. I'm sorry what happened to you. Pa made us promise to avenge you in the name of the Lord and all that's holy, and that's what we're gonna do. But I sure am gonna miss you. Sara is, too.

"Ma—I'm gonna miss the way you always sang in the mornings when opening the curtains to the early sun, and filled the air with the smell of your great bacon and hotcakes. Pa, I'm gonna miss seeing you sitting in your rocking chair of a night, puffing your pipe and reading to us kids out of the Good Book, all of us sitting around on the hemp rug by the fireplace, Injun-style, listening, riveted to stories of Adam and Eve, Cain and Abel, Goliath, the Parable of the good Samaritan…Daniel in the lion's Den."

He smiled, swept a single tear that had filled his left eye and dribbled out of its corner. "I can hear the fire crackling and popping, and I can hear a winter storm howling outside, or a soft spring rain on the roof… Ma's knitting needles clinking together. The coffee pot chugging on the range for Ma and Pa's before-bed cups of coffee they'd drink together—just the two of them at the kitchen table, talking very quietly together—and nibbling some sugary snack."

He looked at a burlap-wrapped body before him. "Brother Ben, I'm gonna miss your hearty laugh. I'm even gonna miss those painful wrestling holds you always got me in, mornings up in the loft when I was slow to rise. I'm gonna miss how you could outshoot me when we hunted together, too. Yep, I'm even gonna miss that. Brother James, I'm gonna miss your quiet sincerity and gentle kindness. I'm gonna miss watchin' you sneak up behind Ma then grabbing her suddenly and planting a kiss on her cheek, and how she'd flush and slap you for giving her such a fright, though I know she loved it. I know she loved you most of all, and she should have because you were the best.

"Mary Louise, I'm gonna miss your salty tongue, though I know I shouldn't. I'm gonna miss how you always talked about Dennis Jordanstafff or the past year and a half, ever since you two decided to get hitched after he saved enough money from his law-reading job. You thought he was a saint sent from heaven to marry you." Reno chuckled. "I know he's gonna miss you, too, and I wish there was some way we could get word to him in Great Bend before we leave."

Reno drew a ragged breath, filling up his lungs then letting it out slowly, feeling his upper lip quiver. He sucked back another tear then said in a quaking voice: "I'm gonna miss you all more than you could ever know. You're passing has left a hole in my heart that ain't never gonna heal. All I can do is avenge you, and I don't know how in god's own hell I'm gonna do it—how we're gonna do it, Sara an' me—but we're gonna find a way. Just know that your memory will live on in both our hearts. Now…in the name of the Father, the Son, and the Holy Ghost, we bequeath you back to Mother Earth , even though I know you are already in heaven, sitting on the right hand of god the Father Almighty."

Reno cried against his beefy forearm.

He felt Sara step up close beside him. She slid an arm around his waist, pressed her left temple against his shoulder. He thought she might have even sobbed once.

THREE

"Reno, wake up!" Sara tugged on his arm.

Instantly, Reno awoke and reaching for the.54 Sharps carbine he'd found in the yard besides his brother James's bullet-torn body, as well as several paper cartridges for the breech-loading weapon—a relatively new gun and one for which James had sold game in order to earn enough money to buy.

Resting the rifle across his thighs, Reno turned to Sara kneeling beside him, near the cold ashes of the fire they'd built last night here on the hill where the cemetery resided. "What is it?"

He imagined the killers returning to kill anyone who'd managed to avoid their bullets and swords last time around.

"Someone's in the yard," she said very quietly.

"Who?"

"I don't know. Still too dark to see clearly."

Sara swept her thick, curly blond hair back from her face then straightened and walked away, stepping over her own crude bedding comprised of a single saddle blanket and a pair of saddlebags she'd used as a pillow. They'd dug all the graves and buried their family the previous night, not finishing until well after midnight. They still had to erect markers. By the time they'd finished filling in the graves, worried about predators, they'd been so physically exhausted, they'd both virtually collapsed.

They'd built the fire to work by and to ward off the night chill. They'd found flint and steel and a small metal case containing white phosphorus matches in Sara's saddlebags, which their father had used on a recent hunting trip and which still contained a few useful trail supplies, including a frying pan and a small coffee pot.

They hadn't eaten last night, however. Even if they hadn't been too exhausted to cook, neither had been hungry. They hadn't even brewed coffee, but only drank water from the well.

Reno tossed his own musty blanket aside, quickly stepped into his boots, and stumbled over to where Sara stood beside the big cottonwood, gazing down at the remains of the farmyard. It was dawn, but the hollow the burned buildings sat in was still murky with lingering darkness. Reno couldn't see much except the black lump of the burned cabin and the barn, about a quarter of which remained standing, as did the small stone blacksmith shop and tack shed.

What he could see, however, was a single horse standing switching its tail near the house, between the house and the barn.

Muffled voices rose from the ruins. Men's voices.

Reno took the Sharps in both hands. He'd loaded the rifle last night, and left it at half-cock. Now he worked the lever to fully cock it, and said, "Wait here."

He started down the hill, moving slowly so as not to spook the horse in the yard. Morning birds piped in the weeds around him. A mourning dove cooed. A coyote gave its fittingly elegiac cries from the prairie to the north.

Reno gained the bottom of the hill and angled to his right, heading for the cabin. Two walls remained standing, for their father and grandfather had built the place of sturdy cottonwood logs they'd gleaned from the woods along Indian Creek. The logs were badly burned, but they'd remained standing against the conflagration that had consumed most of the rest of the building aside from the stone hearth, which stood as proud and true as before.

Reno walked up along the cabin's still-sanding southern wall. He could hear the men's voices more clearly now. Two seemed to be rummaging around inside the cabin. He saw a third man as he edged a look around the cabin's front corner. The third man stood in the middle of the yard, holding the reins of two more horses. He was a slender, raw-boned man with long, coal-black hair. He wore white man's clothes, but he had some Indian blood.

Reno recognized him as Hawk Warren—one of several raggedy-heeled itinerant game hunters and small-time outlaws who haunted this neck of western Kansas, selling game or the cheap whiskey they brewed at their shack in the Limestone Hills country.

"Hey, look what I found," one of the other men yelled from inside the cabin. "Found it on the floor behind that sofa. I think it's still runnin'!"

The other man whistled.

Just then a man walked out of the cabin, through the burned front wall where a window had been and where only part of the charred frame remained. "Hey, look here, Hawk. Cabinet clock. It's still run—"

The man stopped abruptly as Reno stepped out from around the cabin's corner, revealing himself. Reno was so enraged that red lights flashed before his eyes. These men were scavenging his family's burned farm, desecrating the place of their deaths.

Kooch Carlisle stood staring at Reno. A tall, bearded man, he wore ragged clothes and floppy-brimmed brown hat. He wore a pistol low-slung on his right hip. A quirley dangled from between his thin lips. Those lips spread a slow, mocking smile as he dropped the scorched clock in his hands. It hit the ground with a thud and a ringing sound, the glass face breaking.

"Whups," he said.

The other man walked up from behind him. Lawrence Keneally—a short, stocky man with a freckled face and a red beard. A known lout and drunkard. They were all louts and drunkards. Hawk didn't say much, but he was a drunkard, as well. They'd all spent time in jails throughout Kansas and Oklahoma. Mainly, they were moochers and bullies.

And now they were looters, to boot.

"Hello there, young fella," said Kooch Carlisle. "We was, uh…" He glanced at Hawk standing in the yard, and smiled. "We was just ridin' through an' we, uh… we seen your farm. We was just wonderin' if anyone made it out alive, or, uh…if anybody needed help."

He smiled again, mockingly. He didn't care if Reno believed him.

Holding the reins of the two horses, Hawk grunted a laugh. "Yeah, that's what we was doin'," he said in the oddly flat inflections of his race. Reno had heard somewhere that he was part Creek, his father being a half-breed outlaw from Missouri.

"I know what you were doin'," Reno said tightly. "What you are doing."

"Oh?" Carlisle smirked at Hawk. "What's that? What are we doin'?"

Keneally cleared his throat and stepped up to stand beside Carlisle. He looked a little guilty but had a mocking set to his thick-lipped mouth. A silver watch chain dangled from a pocket of his grubby broadcloth trousers. That would likely be Reno's father's hunting case timepiece.

Reno held his angry gaze on Carlisle. "You're back-tracking those marauders and scavenging the farms they raided. You're carrion-eaters. You're human buzzards." He aimed the rifle out from his right hip, aiming at Carlisle's belly. "Get out of here or I'll shoot all three of you."

"Hey," said Keneally, feigning a concerned expression, beetling his brows. "We just came to see if everyone's all right, son. Noticed a lot of blood in the yard." He took a step forward, stretching a hand out toward Reno. "Why don't you just put the—"

Reno tightened his hold on the Sharps, aiming it now at Keneally's bulging belly. "I said get out. But you can leave that watch you got in your pocket."

"All right, all right." Keneally raised his small, freckled hands. "Just take it easy, son. I reckon you're doin' all right. Just a little edgy's all." He slid his little pig eyes toward Carlisle. "I reckon that's to be expected."

"Yeah, he been through a lot." Carlisle walked forward, as though heading for his horse. "We'll leave him alone. Give him time to get his drawers out of a twist."

As Carlisle and Keneally walked past Reno, Hawk

feigned a loud sneeze.

"Ka-chooo!"

Reno turned toward him with a start. Hawk twisted around toward Reno and grabbed the Sharps. As he pulled the gun, trying to rip it out of Reno's grip, Reno squeezed the trigger. He wasn't sure if he meant to fire the gun or if the move was inadvertent. Maybe a little of both, though he'd never shot a man before. He maintained his grip on the gun. Carlisle released the rifle and yelped as the bullet nipped his left side, just above his pistol belt.

"Whoa!" Keneally said, leaping back a step.

Carlisle looked down at his side. He looked at Reno, his face flushed with anger, then returned his gaze to his shirt. He raked a finger across the tear in the flannel cloth which marked the path of the bullet. The rip smoked from the burnt powder.

Carlisle gritted his teeth and glared at Reno again. "You damn near shot me, kid!"

"I'm sorry," Reno said, aghast at what he'd almost done. "I didn't mean…"

"You think you're gonna get away with that?" Carlisle lunged forward, bringing his right fist up and forward too fast for Reno to avoid the jab. The man's bare knuckles hammered his left cheek, throwing him backward. He tripped over his own feet and dropped the rifle just before he hit the ground on his butt.

Carlisle cursed roundly as he looked down at his shirt again. He stepped forward, pulling his right foot back before thrusting the pointed toe of his boot toward Reno's belly. Reno knew something about fighting. His older brother Ben had taught him to wrestle and fight with his fists. In fact, he and Ben had often cleaned up at the bare-knuckle fight competitions over the Fourth of July in Baxter. He wasn't about to let Carlisle break his ribs.

He shot forward, wrapping both of his brawny arms around the man's ankle. Grunting loudly, Reno hoisted himself up off his heels, lifting the man's foot. Carlisle gave a surprised yell as his other foot came up off the ground, as well, and he struck the ground on his backside. He landed with a resolute thud.

"So, the kid thinks he can fight, eh?" Keneally strode forward, swinging his fists and grinning, his fleshy cheeks glowing like small red apples in the growing dawn light. "We'll see about that; we'll see about that…"

He lunged toward Reno, swinging a haymaker.

Reno avoided the man's tight little fist easily by merely jerking his head back and to one side. When Keneally's fist had gone past him, the man grunting, Reno slammed his own right fist into the man's sooty face twice. He jabbed him a third time and then a fourth, making blood pudding of the man's mouth.

"Oh!" cried Keneally, stumbling backward and

then hitting the ground beside Carlisle, who just then bolted off his heels.

Carlisle came up swinging his right fist. Reno ducked it easily then buried his right fist and then his left fist in the man's soft belly. Carlisle jackknifed with a great chuff of expelled air. Reno smacked the man in his right temple. Carlisle grunted and dropped to a knee.

"Shoot him, Hawk!" Reno vaguely heard Keneally yell beneath the screaming sounds in Reno's own ears. In the corner of his eye he saw the short, red-haired man claw a revolver from his holster, but before he could raise the weapon, a black and white beast of some kind flung itself at him, growling.

A gun barked loudly and Sara yelled, "Toss the hogleg down, Hawk, or I'll drill you through your fool head!"

Reno moved forward toward where Carlisle had regained his feet and was gazing in red-faced fury at Reno, who gazed back at him in kind. Reno couldn't have stopped himself if he'd wanted to. He was not normally a casual fighter. He only fought for sport on the Fourth of July in Baxter, or to defend himself. But now he heard the deafening screams of his family inside his head, and the only way he believed he could get them to stop screaming was to beat Kooch Carlisle senseless.

Of course, Carlisle had had nothing to do with

the Bass family's murder, but only a sliver of Reno's consciousness knew that. The bulk of his brain had confused Carlisle and Keneally and the half-breed Hawk with his family's killers.

Carlisle cursed loudly and bolted at Reno. The man ducked under Reno's flying fist. Now it was Reno's turn to take two hammering blows to his gut. Carlisle's powerful fists knocked the wind out of Reno briefly. Before he could recover, Carlisle delivered a nasty right cross to his cheek, and then he thrust two left jabs against Reno's mouth, splitting his lips.

That enraged Reno further. He was half-consciously aware of the black-and-white beast—where had Apache come from?—still attacking Keneally several feet to his left and of Sara trying to call the dog off the man.

"I'm gonna kill you, sodbuster," Carlisle raged, brushing blood from his own split lips. "I'm gonna kill you and that dog and your purty little sister, but only after I've had my fun with her. Then I'm gonna send her and you and that flea-bit cur off to join the rest of your backwoods, hillbilly family in hell!"

He flung a haymaker at Reno, who dodged it, taking the brunt of the blow against his collarbone. Gritting his teeth, fury a wild stallion inside him, Reno hammered his right fist against Carlisle's right eye. The man grunted and staggered backward. Reno followed him, shuffling his feet and crouching and squaring his shoulders and smashing his left fist against the man's other eye.

Carlisle grunted and staggered backward, dropping his arms for balance.

Reno took advantage of the opening. He bashed the man's mouth and nose and jaw, and then both eyes again, and then his forehead...his ears...then back to his face. Suddenly they were both on the ground. Carlisle lay before Reno, wailing, trying to cover his face with his hands. Down on one knee, Reno hammered Carlisle's face through the man's hands until his arms dropped to his sides.

Only when Carlisle's head fell slack against the ground and his eyes closed, did Reno stop, for just then he realized he was beating an unconscious man. Carlisle's face looked like chopped beef. So did Reno's hands.

His heart still raced.

Blinking, he looked around. It was like waking from a dream that had seemed real. Sara stood ten feet behind him. Their dog, Apache, whom Reno had figured was dead since the dog hadn't shown himself until now, sat at Sara's feet, staring at Reno and mewling softly deep in his chest.

Sara stared at Reno, squinting her eyes slightly at the corners, an inscrutable half-smile quirking her mouth corners. She held their father's big Colt Navy .36 in her hand, the hammer cocked back. She held it straight down at her side. It must still have been enough of a threat, for Hawk stood with his hands raised shoulder high. The half-breed stared at Reno as though transfixed, his mud-brown eyes wide and round.

Keneally knelt several feet to Hawk's left. The red-head cradled his right arm—which was bloody, the sleeve in shreds—in the other one. He narrowed his little pig eyes at Reno, spat blood from his lips, and said, "You're crazy. Plum loco. You like to beat Kooch plum to death!" He turned to Sara. "You're both crazy! That dog damn near tore my arm off!"

Keeping her vaguely admiring gaze on Reno, Sara said to Keneally and Hawk in a voice pitched with quiet menace: "Take your friend and get out of here."

Hawk lowered his hands and looked at Keneally.

Keneally said, "Get him on his hoss. I ain't in no condition to do it." He glanced at Apache. "That damn mutt almost tore my arm off!"

Apache glared at him, showing his teeth and growling.

When Hawk had managed to wrestle Carlisle, who started regaining consciousness when the half-breed pulled him up by his arm, onto his horse, both he and Keneally mounted up, as well. Carlisle still appeared only half-conscious, but he managed to sit upright and to hold his bridle reins. His eyes were already swelling behind the blood masking his battered face.

He didn't even glance at Reno.

"The watch."

Keneally looked back at Reno. "Huh?"

Reno extended his hand. "You heard me. Toss it over here real nice or I'll pull you down off that horse and give you what your friend got."

Keneally cursed, pulled the watch from his pocket. He tossed it underhand to Reno, who caught it against his chest.

Keneally curled his lip at Reno then slid his glare to Sara. "Crazy. Crazy as coyotes on a full-moon night."

He put the spurs to his horse, and he and Hawk and Hooch Carlisle trotted off to the southeast, fast becoming silhouettes against the golden orb of the rising sun.

FOUR

"'Pache," Reno said, when the three looters were gone. "Where you been, boy? I thought for sure you were dead."

He dropped to a knee beside the shaggy shepherd dog, who was four years old and nearly all black except for white and a little fawn brown on his chest and paws. Instantly, the dog stepped up close to Reno, putting his head down.

The dog was shaking. Reno ran his hands over him, noting a patch of blood on his left hip.

"Oh-oh," Reno said, crouching low and parting the bloody fur to inspect the wound beneath. "You were hit, weren't you, boy? Not too bad, though. Sort of creased your hip a little." He noticed a curved cut on the side of the dog's head, behind the ear. The cut was in the shape of a horseshoe. "Looks like a horse kicked you, too—eh, boy? I think you'll make it, though."

The dog lifted his head to lick Reno's cheek, whining, likely still terrified by what he had seen yesterday when the lunatic Confederates had stormed the place.

Reno looked at Sara. She'd walked over to the well and was winching up a bucket of water.

"I bet he gave those killers holy hell—Apache did." Reno stroked the dog affectionately. "They tried to shoot him and it looks like a horse kicked him. He must have run off to lick his wounds. But you gave 'em your best, didn't you, boy?" He caressed the dog's ears and Apache looked up at him proudly, though with fear remaining in his liquid-brown eyes as well.

Sara walked over and set the bucket down in the dirt beside Reno. Apache sniffed the water then lapped thirstily.

"Hey, get away from there, dog." Sara shoved Apache aside with her boot. "That water's for Reno."

"What do you mean?" Reno narrowed an eye against the sun as he looked up at his sister.

"Look at your hands. They're all cut up. Soak 'em."

"All right, but Apache can have some first." Reno patted his thigh, calling the dog back to him. "Come on over here, 'Pache. Have you a drink, then I'll soak my hands."

Apache glanced warily up at Sara. For some reason, the shepherd seemed to like Sara best of anyone in the family though Reno didn't know why. She hardly ever petted him and usually acted as though he was in her way. Mostly, she ignored the dog. However, Apache followed her around like some love-struck suitor.

On the rare occasion she spoke to the dog, which their brother James had found wandering, seemingly lost, on the back streets of Baxter several years ago, and as skinny as a mange-stricken young coyote, Apache beamed up at her and laid his ears back against his head, wagging his bushy black-and-white tail with unabashed delight.

When Apache had drunk his fill of the water and wandered over to lie in the shade by the well, Reno shoved his bloody hands into the bucket. The water was cold as snowmelt. He sucked a sharp breath through his teeth and looked at Sara, who still gazed down at him with that funny half-smile on her lips.

"You should've stopped me, Sara. I might have killed him."

"There's no sin in killing evil, Reno."

Reno looked up at her, incredulous. He wished just once he could read his sister's mind. You'd think with her being his twin, and half him, so to speak, he'd have an easier time of it.

She seemed able to read his mind all the time. In fact, she always seemed to know what he was going to do before he knew himself. Rarely could he read her thoughts or even understand her in a general sense. When he thought he knew what she would do in a given situation, she almost always surprised him.

A mystery, this beautiful blue-eyed sister of his. A little frightening, too, if the truth were told.

Hoof thuds sounded to the south. Sara clicked the Colt's hammer back and whipped around, raising the weapon. Reno pulled his hands out of the water and stood. He looked around for the Sharps, but then he remembered he'd already fired the single-shot and would need time to reload.

Sara eased his mind when she said, "It's only Mr. Dodson."

She depressed the Colt's hammer and lowered the weapon to her side. Standing beside her, his hands aching from the cuts and the cold water, Reno watched Cletus Dodson ride into the yard on a husky black gelding. Beside him, on a mouse-brown dun, rode his son, Luther.

Luther had a bandage wrapped around the top of his head. The bandage angled down over his left eye. Blood had seeped through the bandage in several places. Apache ran out of from the shade by the well, barking, but Reno told him to heel, and the dog sat down beside him, growling throatily and watching the two newcomers with one ear almost pricked, the other one customarily standing at half-mast, which was about all it could ever muster.

Cletus and Luther Dodson reined in their horses before Reno and Sara. They both looked around with a darkness in their gazes that Reno knew was probably in his own, as well. A heavy-set man in his fifties, Cletus wore long, gray side whiskers. He was bald beneath his black felt hat.

He looked wary and nervous and deeply troubled. His son, Luther, appeared to be in shock. While Cletus didn't seem to be harmed—at least, not physically—it looked as though Luther hadn't been as fortunate. Blood stained the bandage over his eye.

"My god," Cletus said, slowly shaking his head. He looked from Reno to Sara then back again. "I see they got you, too."

Reno drew a breath and nodded. "How bad did they hit you, Mr. Dodson?"

"They killed Abigail, burned us out."

"I'm sorry."

"Your folks…?"

"Dead. They're all dead except me an' Sara."

Dodson drew his mouth corners in. He glanced at Luther, who was a couple of years younger than Reno and Sara, and said, "They took the boy's eye. Laid a bayonet across his head. They got him good. He hasn't said anything since."

Reno studied Luther, whose lone eye just stared off into space. His face betrayed no emotion.

"He will," Reno told the boy's father. "In time, he'll come around."

"I rode over here to see how you fared and to spread the word. The sheriff from Baxter is forming a posse. Those killers rode through town, shot up the place and burned a couple of buildings, then rode on through. They hit Mikkelson's and then my place and then yours. They killed a couple of Gypsies camped along the trail. They were mostly interested in the smaller places where they wouldn't get much resistance, seems like."

Dodson drew a breath and his eyes flickered angrily. "Anyway, the sheriff's forming a posse. He'll likely come through here tomorrow with a good dozen men from town. He aims to meet up with a couple of U.S. marshals at Millerville." He kept his gaze on Reno. "Will you throw in, boy?"

Reno glanced at Sara. She looked back at him and gave her head a quick, single shake, then returned her cold eyes to Dodson.

"I reckon not." Reno shook his head, too. "We'll be pulling out of here today, Mr. Dodson."

Dodson frowned. "Oh? Where will you go?"

Reno hesitated.

Sara said, "We have to finish tending to our dead now, Mr. Dodson. Thank you for the call, and please accept our condolences for your loss."

Dodson studied her skeptically, warily.

He switched his troubled gaze to Reno and said quietly, worriedly, "What do you two have in mind?"

Reno could only gaze back at him. He didn't know what to say.

Sara stared at the man, as well, a fresh morning breeze rising to jostle her hair and the neck thong of her broad-brimmed hat hanging down over the swell of her breasts.

Dodson turned to Reno again and said, "Those men were led by Colonel Eustace Montgomery and Major 'Black Bob' Hobbs. Montgomery is known as the 'Bad Old Man' for a reason. Neither one is anyone you want to mess with alone. They're leading a good twenty Confederates very unhappy about the outcome of the war, and they're heading west, killing Yankees along the way."

Reno felt a lump of fear grow in his throat.

Sara said quickly, smiling, "Good day, Mr. Dodson. Luther, I hope you're feeling better soon."

Dodson grimaced, shook his head. "All right, then." He turned to Luther. "Come on, son." He reined his horse around and spurred it back in the direction from which they'd come. Luther followed suit without so much as glancing at Reno or Sara.

Still feeling that hard lump in his throat, Reno turned to his sister. "Sara...couldn't hurt to join a posse. Pa never said anything about doing it all ourselves."

"No posse will run that horde to ground. They'll hear all those men coming from miles away. Dodson is a dead man if I ever saw one, and so are those marshals." Sara was gazing off to the west. Now she pointed and smiled. "Look there," she said. "Coyote's alive!"

Reno turned his head to look into the pasture flanking the barn. He saw the brown-and-white pinto gelding, Coyote, for which their father had traded another neighbor several wagonloads of hay two years ago, during a drought. Though many stockmen considered pintos fickle and high-strung, Coyote had proven to be a good, smart, reliable mount, and the best trained.

Of the three saddle horses the Bass family owned, Coyote was always the one the Bass children fought over when it was time to move their twenty head of beef cows around. Ben, being the oldest, had always been allowed to ride Coyote over to the small Shattuck ranch when he'd been sparking Miss Dora Shattuck, before Dora had taken up with a young man from the more prosperous Crosshatch Ranch north of Baxter.

It appeared that Coyote was the lone survivor of all the horses in the Bass corral. He'd either been let into the pasture before the attack, or he'd leaped the fence when the shooting had started. The other half-dozen mounts lay bloating where they'd fallen—a sickening scene. The whole farmyard sickened Reno, with its growing stench of death. He wanted to get away from here as soon as he could, even if it meant just him and Sara going after the massive gang of kill-crazy Confederates, a dubious task at best.

Despite what Sara had said, men more qualified

for the task would probably catch up with them first. Dodson had said the posse was to meet U.S. marshals in Millerville, in the northwest corner of Kansas.

"There's a couple of saddles in the barn that weren't burned too bad," Reno told Sara. "As soon as we finish up with the graves, let's ride on out of here. Head for Julesburg."

Sara was already walking around the barn and into the pasture to fetch the pinto.

***

"Look here, Sara," Reno said a half an hour later as he walked out of the burned cabin. "Pa's Bible!"

He raised the leather-bound tome, brushy with scraps of tablet paper on which his father had scrawled notes. "I found it on the floor by his an' Ma's bed. Everything else was burned in there. Even the table it was likely sitting on. It's hardly charred at all, just a little along the edges. Otherwise, it came through without a scratch!"

Sara smiled back at her brother but didn't say anything. Reno could tell she was in a hurry to strike out on the vengeance trail. Reno had gathered their gear from the family cemetery, having decided to leave the marking of the graves for later, once their grisly task was complete. The marking would take time, and he was afraid if he lingered in the cemetery, his determined sister would take off without him and leave him struggling to catch up to her.

It was hard to keep up with Sara even when she wasn't on a holy vengeance tear. Now he could see the fire of zealotry burning in her eyes.

"I'd say that's a miracle there," Reno said, chuckling and waving the Bible in the air. "Wouldn't you say so, sis?"

"I don't know, Reno."

"Well, I'd say it was."

"I reckon I'll know more about miracles after we've ridden down that 'Bad Old Man' Montgomery and 'Black Bob' Hobbs—and sent 'em to hell skewered on the devil's own pitchfork."

Reno chuckled uneasily as he stepped carefully down from the cabin's charred front porch. Sara had a way with words—he'd give her that. "Well, I myself call that a miracle. God meant for us to keep this Bible close and read out of it, just like Pa always did. He kept the flames from it, sure enough."

"I sure wish he would have kept those flames off Ma an' Pa, and those bullets away from our brothers and sister."

"Yeah, well..." Reno didn't know what to say to that, so he relied on one of Pa's old saws: "The Lord moves in mysterious ways."

He shoved the old tome into a pocket of his coat, and turned to Sara who sat astride Old Otis. The

brown-and-white pinto, Coyote, stood saddled beside her.

"What're you doing, Sara?" Reno said, frowning up
at his sister. "I was gonna let you ride Coyote. I'll take
the mule."

"The young warrior needs to ride the Indian pony.
Me..." Sara shook her head full of thick, strawber-
ry-blond curls and grinned, dimpling her smooth
cheeks that were the color of nicely ripened peach-
es. "I'll look good on whatever I ride...even this old
crow-bait mule of pa."

She smiled brightly at Reno, who chuckled as he
caught Coyote's reins from Sara, and swung up into
the old, partly scorched saddle. Otis had had a good
rest after yesterday's long run. The mule brayed then
lurched off his rear hooves as Sara touched spurs to
his loins, and broke into a run, heading north. She
didn't look behind her even once.

Apache barked then broke into a run, following
her.

As he gigged Coyote out of the yard, Reno looked
back over his shoulder at the charred ruins of their
farm, at the fresh graves atop the cottonwood-stud-
ded hill to the southeast of it. He choked back a
strangled cry of raw anguish. He turned forward in
his saddle, sleeved tears from his cheeks, and vowed
not to look back again but only ahead—toward their
family's killers.

FIVE

Reno felt a dark dread inside him.

He'd felt it just after they'd left the farm. It had started in his belly and spread up into his chest, like a growing pool of poison, like a cancer growing and growing inside him, making him feel sicker and sicker.

At first, as he and Sara followed the trail northwest toward Kiowa Springs, he didn't know what caused the ugly feeling. But then as they rounded the last curve in the trail that climbed the bluffs upon which the little settlement sat, and he did not see the bell tower of the school, which he usually did at this point on the trail, he understood what had caused the sickness was his trepidation about what he would find once he reached the school sitting on the very eastern edge of Kiowa Springs.

Until now, something had not let Reno think of Miss Cassie Bernard. He supposed he'd concentrat-

ed so heavily on his family, had been so horrified by
their murders, that his brain had not allowed him to
think about his sweet, pretty teacher, Miss Bernard.
He hadn't had room in his brain for anymore grief, so
his brain had simply shut out such speculations. Deep
down in the buried regions of his consciousness,
though, he'd known what he'd find once he reached
the settlement.

He and Sara rode side by side on the trail as it
crested the butte. They checked their mounts down
and stared at the charred and ruined school sitting
just off the trail's right side. The rest of Kiowa Springs
lay to the northwest of the school, a quarter-mile beyond—a dozen or so buildings including a few shops
spread out across the sage, prickly pear, and short
blond prairie grass. Most of those, too, had been
burned. Reno saw several bodies lying on the street
between the short double row of business buildings.
Horses and other animals lay dead, as well.

Some of the heaps of black ash still sent gray smoke
swirling into the air.

The school, too, still smoked.

Reno's heart kicked like a mule. It hammered so
hard, he thought it would burst through his breastbone. He stomach was a raw ache. It was the same
feeling he'd felt upon first seeing the farm all over
again.

He clambered heavily out of his saddle.

"Reno…" Sara said.

Ignoring her, he walked awkwardly, stumbling, toward the school. Apache started to follow him.

"Stay with Sara, boy," Reno ordered the dog, who instantly obeyed.

Apache sat near the mule, staring at Reno, whining.

The school's back wall still stood, but the rest of the building had been reduced to rubble. The bell tower had fallen forward to lie in a heap in front of the rest of the ruined building. The iron bell peaked out of the burned wood.

Reno negotiated his way through the debris of the tower and of fallen, smoldering timbers and lurched into the school itself, though it was no longer the school he remembered. The burned wooden floor was still warm beneath his boots, and his nose rebelled against the stench of charred wood and scorched varnish.

Very little remained recognizable—parts of a couple of student desks, the chalkboard at the back, near where Miss Barnard's desk had sat on its dais. Her desk had been reduced to gray ashes though, strangely, her black hat—the one whose crown was adorned with faux flowers woven into a black silk band and which she wore outside during recess—remained on the floor near the potbelly stove, which had been partly crushed by a fallen ceiling beam.

Reno reached down to pick up the hat. Flames had

chewed into the brim a little, but otherwise the hat
was pristine. It was like his father's Bible.

For some reason, it gave him hope for the fate of
Miss Bernard.

He looked around, heard himself foolishly call her
name.

"She's not there." It was Sara's voice from outside.

Reno swung around and retraced his steps until
he walked around the bell tower's rubble to find only
his horse standing where he'd left Sara. He turned to
his left. Sara sat the mule down the hill a hundred feet
to the east. She stared into the ravine that cut around
the side of the butte. Apache stood a little ahead of
her. The dog had his head and tail down, sniffing and
mewling softly.

Reno walked over to Sara and the dog. He looked
up at Sara, swallowed a lump of terror, and asked,
"Where?"

Sara dipped her chin and slid her gaze slightly
right. Reno followed her gaze and felt his belly tight-
en. Miss Bernard lay belly-down on the ravine's sandy bottom. From his vantage, he could see only her
head and her naked shoulders, one bare arm thrust
up above her head at an awkward angle. Her chestnut
hair was down. Reno had never seen it down before.
She'd always worn it up. One day he'd hoped to see it
down, but not now. Not like this. Now it was down
and badly tangled, and sand clung to it.

"I'm sorry, Reno."

"Yeah," Reno said, his heart drumming heavily, though not as painfully as before. "Me, too."

He turned to see the crude log shelter that served as a tool and buggy shed beyond the school to the north. It was nearly devoured by lilacs that had long since bloomed. The bushes had been scorched by the fire, the edges of their leaves black and wrinkled. He'd find a shovel in the shed. He started toward it.

"Do you want help?"

"No, thanks."

✱✱✱

It took Reno an hour to bury his teacher.

He dug the hole near the tool shed then retrieved her body, which he wrapped in a plaid blanket he'd found in Miss Bernard's buggy in the shed. She'd probably used it on picnics, for she'd once told him she'd had a fondness for riding into the countryside and picnicking along the bank of Porcupine Creek. She'd enjoyed identifying birds from a book. She'd been a curious and wholesome young woman. He'd hoped to join her on such an outing one day, but of course that would never happen now.

He gentled the body into the hole. He'd closed her staring eyes with his fingers, but they remained open and peering at him glassily through a fold in the blanket. He looked away until he could draw the fold closed. Then he climbed out of the grave and filled it in, feeling nothing now on the leeside of the horror of finding Cassie Bernard dead.

All he felt now was rage. His hands fairly shook with it.

As he'd worked on the grave, he'd kept seeing those two Confederate soldiers—one old and gray, the other black-bearded and younger, both fierce-eyed—riding at the head of that deadly pack of Confederate animals. He kept seeing himself shoot bullets into them and laughing as they begged for mercy then screamed as his bullets chewed their flesh.

He didn't know what made him think he and Sara could ever bring that pack of seasoned soldiers down, but apparently their father had thought they could, so that was enough for Reno.

Those men would die. And he and Sara would be the unlikely pair to kill them if, only for the simple but deadly reason that they wanted to so badly.

He said a prayer over Miss Bernard's grave, returned the shovel to the shed, and mounted Coyote. Sara and Apache had been sitting on the hill overlooking the ravine, but now Sara mounted old Otis, and Apache sat staring up at them, one ear raised, the other only half-raised, tilting his head from side to side, trying to figure out what his two sole remaining masters were up to.

Reno wished he could assure the dog that every-thing would be all right, but he was far from sure himself. He supposed the worst thing that could happen would be that he and Sara would join the rest of their family in heaven. He didn't think that out-come would give Apache much solace, however, so he tossed the dog a couple of bites of jerky he'd found in a pocket of his coat, and turned to Sara.

"Julesburg?"

"Julesburg."

She booted Otis back onto the trail. As they rode through the small town of Kiowa Springs, neither one looked at the death around them. Of course, they had friends here in the town. But death no longer held much interest for them. They'd seen the worst it had to offer.

As they rode through town, following the whining Apache, they kept their gazes straight ahead, staring west toward holy vengeance and the prospect of giv-ing the devils their due.

✳✳✳

They camped the first night about twenty miles west of Kiowa Springs. They'd managed to glean enough trail supplies from the cabin and the keeper shed be-hind it, which hadn't been burned, that they had plen-ty of food for several days without having to hunt.

They brewed coffee and fried steaks from the
chunk of beef hanging in the keeper shed. They
boiled green beans from one of the scorched cans
they'd found in the kitchen. Reno hadn't eaten in over
twenty-four hours. He'd had only water. He hadn't
been hungry until he'd smelled the steaks frying in
the cast-iron skillet. Then his stomach had groaned,
and his mouth had watered.

He ate several bites of the steak and beans hungrily, washing them down with the coal black coffee.
Eating and enjoying the food when his dead family
could not...when Miss Bernard could not...made him
feel guilty.

Why should he be alive when Pa and Ma and Ben
and James and Mary Louise...Miss Bernard...were
not?

He looked across the fire at Sara. She nibbled from
the plate cradled on her lap, her legs tucked beneath
her Indian-style, her tin coffee cup smoking on a rock
to her right. She didn't look up at Reno. She felt as
guilty about eating, about taking pleasure from food,
as he did.

Reno didn't feel guilty about Sara being alive. In
fact, he'd be eternally grateful he had his twin sister
by his side. He didn't know what he'd do if he didn't
have her here beside him. The world had become a
whole lot larger and more threatening in the wake
of his family's murder. If Sara were dead, as well, the

world would be so dark and ominous, he didn't think he could live in it anymore.

No, he didn't feel guilty about Sara being alive. He doubted Sara did, either. Her mind didn't run in those circles. But Reno's did.

He felt guilty that he was alive and that tonight he was sitting by this warm fire they'd built from blow-down and deadfall ash and oak branches, and that he was enjoying the taste of this beef, these greens, and the coffee Sara brewed strong enough to float Pa's big Colt Navy .36John Bass had bought from a former sheriff and which Sara seemed to have taken under her wing.

The gun rested beside her, tucked inside the holster she'd carried when they'd been riding, strapped to the pommel of her saddle. The accouterments bag con-taining the powder, caps, and balls for the unwieldy weapon rested on the ground by the weapon itself. It and the Sharps were the only guns they'd managed to salvage from the fire. Reno and Sara were adept with both weapons. Their father had taught all five of his children how to handle and shoot all the weapons on the farm, starting with old Kentucky flintlocks.

But the old Colt and the Sharps weren't enough. Reno had the folding knife he always carried in his pocket, but he'd lost his entire knife collection—two Bowie-style hunting knives and a Green River knife—in the fire, along with his Springfield rifle, the old .33-caliber breechloader he used for hunting rabbits and squirrels, and his prized Belgium-made, double-barreled percussion shotgun, which he'd used to bring down countless birds, deer, elk, and even bear. Soon, they'd have to find more weapons, but Reno didn't know how they were going to acquire such weapons when they had no money to pay for them.

He hoped the man named Ty Mando would help in that regard. Otherwise, their gooses were cooked.

They'd made camp by a creek whose name they didn't know. They were far enough from their home territory now that they didn't recognize many landmarks. They'd never been this far from home except on a few hunting occasions. They cleaned their dishes in the creek and then washed in the cool stream, as well. They hauled water from the creek to the horse and mule, which they'd tied to a picket line near the camp, close enough that the beasts could warn them of possible trouble.

As the last light left the sky and the stars grew more and more intense, Reno and Sara each poured a fresh cup of coffee then let the fire die. Reno read aloud from the Good Book in the fire's gradually weakening light, which fluttered and shimmered around them and shed sparks that resembled fireflies. He read from Romans, Philippians, and Isaiah—passages he remembered and which seemed fitting in the wake of losing loved ones.

Reno didn't read long—only ten or fifteen minutes was all. He was tired, and he knew Sara was tired, too. When he'd finally closed the Bible and wrapped it up in his jacket, to protect it from the weather, Sara gazed into the fire and asked, "Reno, do you promise me there's really a heaven and that Ma and Pa and our brothers and sisters are there?"

"What?" The question had shocked him.

Sara gazed at him directly, her sky-blue eyes glowing sharply in the firelight. "You heard me."

Reno gave a dry laugh. "Of course, there's a heaven!"

"How do you know?"

Reno frowned, hesitated, then shrugged and said, "I just do, that's all. The Bible wouldn't lie. Pa wouldn't lie, neither, Sara!"

"But the Bible's just words on a page. And Pa's just a man. He never saw heaven, I don't think. Leastways, not when he was alive. How could he have?"

Reno thought about her query. He'd never really considered such questions before. They troubled him now, and they irritated him a little, because he wasn't sure how to respond to them.

"Listen, Sara," he said after he hemmed and hawed a bit. "I reckon you just have to believe Pa and the Bible. No one would make up a lie like that. Besides, you feel it in your heart, don't you?"

"Feel what?"

"That the words are true. That Ma an' Pa an' James an' Ben an' Mary Louise are safe in heaven now, with the Lord and Jesus Christ looking after them." Reno paused, ground the heel of his boot into the sand near the fire ring. "I feel it right in here. It's a warm, good feeling." He ground his fist against his chest. "It's one of the last good feelings I got left."

"Oh." Sara nodded, looked down at her chest. "Yeah. You're right." She looked up and gave Reno a weak smile over the shortening, dancing flames. "I feel it, too. You're right. It's a good feeling." She peered at the fire then, after a while, she looked at Reno again. "I'm sorry, Reno. Of course, I feel it. Just like you do. I'm sorry if I made you mad."

Reno smiled, feeling better about the conversation. "You didn't make me mad, Sara. Just a little frustrated, is all. I think it's kind of a hard thing to relate to people. Faith, I mean. I think maybe it's just something you have or don't have, and I for one am sure glad I have it."

Sara nodded and her smile grew, making her eyes glitter. "Yeah. Me, too."

"I reckon we'd best get some sleep, huh?"

"Yep."

"Good night, Sara."

"Good night, Reno."

"I love you, Sara."

"I love you, too, Reno."

He rested his head against his pillow, but he lay for a long time gazing up at the stars. The fire had died, so it was impossible to see Sara lying in her own blankets across from him, but something told him she was staring at the stars, as well.

SIX

When Reno did finally sleep, it was a shallow sleep plagued by nightmares.

Several times he awoke to the screaming and shooting inside his head. Once when he woke, Sara was there beside him, wrapping her arms around him and gently shoving him back down against his saddle. She sandwiched his face in her hands, and smiled down at him. He could see the white line of her teeth in the darkness.

"We're gonna kill 'em, Reno," she said very softly. "We're going to kill every last one of them. Then we won't have nightmares anymore."

Reno wasn't sure what to say to that. He was sweating and his heart was racing. He was breathing hard.

Sara placed her hand on his chest. "Shhh. Go back to sleep. It'll be dawn soon."

He slept then, more deeply than before. In fact,

he didn't awaken again until he heard and smelled bacon frying. He opened his eyes and sat up. Sara was crouched over the fire, cooking. It was late in the dawn. In fact, the sun was beginning to fire several golden shafts up from between the low hills and haystack buttes silhouetted against it in the east.

"Come on, sleepy head," Sara said. "Time to rise and shine. We got devils to track." She poured a cup of coffee and, smiling broadly, sweetly, shoved it toward him.

They ate quickly, struck camp, and hit the trail, heading deeper into northwestern Kansas, heading toward Julesburg, but also following the killers' trail. They knew the devils had come this way because they'd seen death and destruction they'd left in their wake—more burned farms and dead homesteaders, a burned crossroads store and saloon, a couple of burned ranch supply wagons around which two young men clad in drover's gear lay dead, both sporting bullet wounds.

Reno wondered if the gang was heading for Julesburg, as he and Sara were, but then, late in the second day of their trek, they saw where the tracks of the twenty or so riders had turned off onto a secondary trail, heading straight north toward Nebraska. Likely, they intended to steer around towns of any real size, where they might run into more resistance than they thought they were capable of quashing.

And where they also might run into greater numbers of lawmen and perhaps even soldiers. Reno knew an army camp, Camp Rankin, had been built near Julesburg to protect settlers from the rampaging Sioux and Cheyenne. The Bad Old Man and Black Bob would likely not want to confront more Union soldiers, especially after the whipping they'd taken during their ill-fated War of Rebellion, Reno reflected snootily. He'd visited Julesburg a time or two with his brothers, when his father had sent them there to sell cattle to Camp Rankin's quartermaster.

Sara had wanted to continue following the Confederate devils but Reno had convinced her they needed supplies and a decent arsenal before they could confront them, there being just him and her against an entire horde.

"What if we lose their trail, Reno?" Sara had said. "What if they just disappear out west somewhere and we never find them again?"

"Men like that cut a wide swath, sis," Reno had said. "You've seen that for yourself. We'll find them again...when we're ready to find them. Now, let's do like Pa said, and go look for Ty Mando."

He and Sara continued along the stage trail that would take them a little farther west, then nearly straight north to Julesburg. Apache trotted ahead in the scout position, or fell back behind them. Often, he took off after rabbits to either side of the trail, and was gone for anywhere from a half hour to an hour, suddenly reappearing again either ahead of Reno and Sara, or behind.

Late that same day, not long before Reno thought they should start looking for another place to hole up for the night, two riders appeared on the trail ahead of them. Reno's gut tightened with apprehension. Apache saw them, too, and went running ahead, barking, until Reno called him back and told him to heel.

They hadn't met many riders out here, and under the circumstances, he was cautious. But then he saw the two coming toward him and Sara appeared to be as anxious as he was. They slowed their own mounts and canted their heads, squinting to get a better look at the two riders and the dog heading toward them.

Reno reached out with his right hand to finger the stock of his Sharps rifle, but now, as the two men approached, holding their horses to slow walks, he removed his hand from the Sharps and let it rest upon his thigh. Sara rested her hand over the walnut grips of the Colt Navy jutting from the holster strapped to her saddle pommel.

"Easy, Sara," Reno said under his breath.

"Yes, easy, miss," one of the two men said as they drew within twenty feet and checked their mounts down. "No need for the pistol. We're not trouble. Just a couple of lonely pilgrims out looking for ranch work."

As Reno stopped Coyote on the trail's right edge, beside Sara, who had halted old Otis, he studied the two men facing them. They indeed looked like out-of-work cowhands. They wore badly weathered and salt-crusted broad-brimmed hats and billowy neckerchiefs as well as linsey shirts, suspenders, and patched trousers, the cuffs of which were stuffed into the high tops of their stovepipe boots.

One was tall and wiry, maybe in his late twenties. The other was a few years older, not as tall, and he wore a brushy blond mustache with matching side whiskers. Both were unshaven, and they had the hungry look of men who hadn't eaten a full meal at a table in a month of Sundays. Each wore a holstered Colt Dragoon revolver, and each had a rifle jutting from a saddle boot, but neither made a move toward their weapons.

The one with the mustache had seen Reno inspecting their guns, and he said, "Don't worry, we're fresh out of bullets. Used the last one on the rabbit I shot last night for the supper fire."

"You hear about the trouble?" asked the other one, the taller of the pair. He had deep-set copper eyes and a prominent Adam's apple that showed above his soiled green neckerchief. "About them Confederates on a holy tear...?"

"As a matter of fact, we did," Reno said. "How'd

you hear about 'em?"

"Word spreads fast—neighbor to neighbor," said the man with the mustache. "We been on the lookout for 'em. Don't wanna get crossways with killers like that. Angry by the way the war turned out, we heard."

"Looks like they swung north a few miles back," Reno said. "I don't think you'll run into 'em if you keep heading east. I think they're heading north and west, killing and burning along the way." He hardened his jaws with that last comment, rage nearly overtaking him again.

The two drovers glanced at each other.

The mustached one looked at Sara then slid his gaze back to Reno. "If you keep along this trail, watch yourselves."

"Why?" It was the first thing Sara had said to the pair. She'd removed her hand from the big Colt. For that, Reno was grateful. He just never knew what Sara might do.

"We met a couple of riders a way back," said the tall man. "They wore Confederate gray and they spoke in southern accents. One was wounded. They asked us if we knew any doctorin', an' when we said we didn't, they both cursed us roundly up one side an' down the other, an' then rode on."

"I don't mind admitting I never been so scared of men in my life," said the mustached man. "I rode the trails up from Texas with some bad hombres, men who'd shoot you for spilling their coffee, but them two..." He shook his head darkly. "They had the meanest eyes of anyone I ever saw!"

"You best watch out for 'em," said the taller man. "If you see 'em, steer clear. It's gonna be dark soon, so they'll likely be makin' camp."

"Will do," Reno said. "We appreciate the warning." He glanced at Sara. She didn't say anything but only stared coldly at the two men.

They stared back at her, looking uneasy.

The man with the mustache pinched his hat brim, smiled at Sara, and said, "Miss..."

Sara only narrowed her eyes at the man.

Reno chuckled nervously. "We appreciate the help...don't we, sis?"

Still, Sara said nothing.

The man with the mustache frowned at Reno. "Somethin' wrong with her?"

"No." Reno smiled and shook his head. "She's fine. Just a little worried about them graybacks, is all. We'll be moseyin' on up the trail. Thanks, fellas. Like I said, we appreciate the information."

"All right, then," said the taller man, his own indignant gaze lingering on Sara.

When they'd ridden off to the east and Reno and Sara had continued west, Reno turned to Sara riding just off his right stirrup. "Sara, what was that all about? Did you forget your manners?"

"What do you mean?"

"You could have thanked those two men."

"I didn't feel like thanking them."

"Why not? Did you hear what they said?"

"Yeah, two of those devils might be near here. One's wounded. They're probably holding back from the others, lookin' for a sawbones. Good information, I'll admit."

"Yes, it was, so why the wooly eyeball, Sara?"

She turned to him, shrugged a shoulder. "I didn't like the way they looked. Mostly, I didn't like the way they were looking at Coyote. And me."

Reno was exasperated. "Huh?"

"They were lookin' at Coyote like they were wondering how much money the pinto might bring in a sale. And they were looking at me, like…well, like bad men look at a girl."

"I didn't see that."

"I know you didn't. But I did. Just take my word for it, Reno—those two men weren't as innocent as you think, and we'd better keep an eye on our back trail for those two. We might just see 'em again."

Reno looked over his shoulder, scowling. Could Sara be right? He turned his head forward again. No. Like he'd told the two drifters, she was just jittery about the graybacks. Sometimes Sara had an odd way of showing her true feelings. The men they had to look out for were the two devils the duet of drifters had told him and Sara about.

He had to keep a close rein on Sara. She could be ornery for ornery's sake. Out here, that could get them both into trouble.

He turned his thoughts to the two graybacks. One might be injured but, just like a wounded wildcat, that might make him all the more dangerous. He found himself studying the terrain around them cautiously, on the lookout for an ambush.

"So…it begins," Sara said quietly as she rode the mule beside him.

Reno looked at her. "Huh?"

Sara looked back at him. "This is our opportunity, brother. Our first one. One's injured. They're only two men. You know how the wolves always haze a single buffalo out of a herd so it's easier to bring it down? A young one, an old one, or an injured one?"

"Yeah…yeah…"

"Well, we're the wolves. Two buffs have separated themselves from the pack. One of the two is injured. Probably took a bullet in Kiowa Springs, or maybe even Pa or one of our brothers shot him." Sara turned to Reno again and smiled. "That gives us our first opportunity to go after those devils…whittle them down little by little. By two's…three's, and, when we get good at it…maybe even by fours an' fives."

"Boy, you sure do seem confident, sis." For his part, Reno felt the cold chill of fear deep in his loins. Sara made him nervous. That twinkle in her eyes put him on edge.

He'd be danged if she wasn't ready to go at them.

Was he?

"Well, I reckon we don't know where they are," Reno said, continuing to gaze out at the rolling, sage-stippled hills warily. He wouldn't have admitted as much to Sara—or even to himself—but he hoped he wouldn't see them. "They could be anywhere out here. It's a big country, Sara—western Kansas."

"They're close."

"Huh?"

"I can sense it." Sara smiled inside the dancing locks of her golden air. "I can smell 'em. They're out here…close. Just keep an eye skinned, Reno. We'll spy 'em soon, most like. Pa—he'll rest easier when we've killed the first two."

Reno swallowed.

SEVEN

There were few trees out here for shelter.

In fact, about the only shelter consisted of the infrequent dry watercourses that scored this relatively flat but gently rolling land like pale veins in a giant hand.

The washes had cut shallow ravines, and it was in one such ravine, where two watercourses forked, Reno and Sara set up camp about an hour before sunset. All they could find to feed a fire was sun-bleached wood that had drifted down the watercourse in past floods, some of which was half-buried in the chalky alkali between cutbanks.

When they'd tended the mule and the pinto, staking them near the camp with picket pins, watering and feeding and rubbing them down thoroughly, both knowing how valuable their stock was out here on this vast, dry prairie, they built a fire. They still had a couple of pounds of salted meat left, wrapped in burlap. While Sara scouted around, holding the Colt Navy down by her side in her right hand, Reno went to work throwing a stew together in their cast-iron skillet, adding tomatoes and beans from airtight tins to the beef.

As he stirred the stew, he watched Sara walking along the crest of the northern ridge, shading her eyes against the west-tumbling sun as she scoured the distance for the two graybacks. Apache followed close on her heels, leaving her side only to leap suddenly at mice or moles or to chase gophers. Deep down, Reno didn't want her to find the two Confederates. On the other hand, he did. Why not get the first two out of the way? That might make killing the others easier.

On the other hand, what if he couldn't kill a man? Not even one of the men who'd murdered his family and so cruelly abused his older sister as well as Miss Bernard?

Maybe he was a coward. He sure felt like one, his hand shaking slightly as he stirred the stew. In the abstract, he wanted very much to kill those murderers. But now, when the possibility was becoming real, he felt his guts tie themselves in knots. He wasn't even sure he'd be able to eat the stew he was making. Just the smell was making him feel sick to his stomach.

He looked up the rise again but Sara was no longer in sight. She'd moved away from the ridge.

He wondered if she sensed his fear. Probably. Sara seemed to know everything about him even before he did. The thought that she knew him to be the coward he feared he really was added humiliation to the nasty mix of emotions roiling inside him.

The sun fell, sucking the light out of the land and filling the ravine with cool, purple shadows. The small cook fire glowed brightly against the sudden night. Reno had dished himself up a bowl of stew, but he'd mainly been forking it around, taking only a few tentative bites, before he heard a footfall on the southeastern ridge. He dropped his fork in the bowl and sat up straight with a start.

"It's me, Reno—Sara."

He turned to see her slender silhouette move down the tawny slope, her boots crunching softly in the short, coarse grass and sage. Apache ran along beside her, a dead rabbit in his jaws. Sara moved swiftly down the ridge. Reno watched her, feeling a vague fear, knowing what she was going to say before she said it: "I found them."

She was breathless with anticipation.

"Really?" Reno said, hoping his voice didn't betray his reluctance. "Where?"

"Southwest. Not far."

"How do you know it's them? Did you see 'em?"

"No, but it's them, all right. Who else would it be?" Sara dropped to her knee beside the pan in which the stew steamed and bubbled gently. "Mmm—looks good. Smells even better. I'm famished!"

Reno glanced guiltily into his own bowl in which his own stew had sat so long it was nearly cold. He forced himself to down a few more bites, but Sara had finished her bowl in no time while Apache ate the rabbit he'd killed at the edge of the firelight, tearing at the hide, growling and snarling dramatically and breaking the bones with his jaws.

Setting her bowl aside, Sara wiped her hands on her trousers then grabbed a stick from the small pile of brush beside the fire.

"Here's the plan," she said, scratching a crude map in the dirt.

As Sara spoke, Reno watched her, wondering how in the world they could be twins. They might have looked alike, but how could she be so brave, even gleeful in the face of grave danger, when his insides felt like pudding?

✳✳✳

Reno crawled ever so quietly through the still night, dragging the Sharps along beside him. Every few yards he paused to lie flat against the ground. When he did, he felt his heart drumming against the earth.

He paused again now and lifted his chin to gaze straight out across the prairie before him. He saw the flickering glow of a fire dead ahead and beyond a thin screen of trees. The sight of that fire made his heart drum faster and harder against the earth.

That was the campfire of the two men he and Sara were after. The two graybacks. At least Sara was certain it was their camp. Reno had his doubts. Others might be camping out here. There was no way to know if the fire belonged to them, however, without checking it out.

And that's just what he was on his way to do.

He swallowed down his fear and, clenching the Sharps' forestock in his right hand, continued crawling on all fours, staying very low to the ground. He'd ordered Apache to stay back at the camp.

The plan was for Reno to get into position on the southern edge of the Confederates' camp. Doing that, he'd had to steal wide around it from the north, since his and Sara's camp was north of the graybacks'. That journey on foot, moving very slowly so as not to be seen or heard, had taken a good half hour.

Once he was in position on the backside of the Confederates' camp, Sara would make her move, which was a very dangerous one indeed, but it was one Reno had not been able to talk her out of. She was dead certain it would work.

"Well, I just hope you're dead certain and not dead, sis." Those had been his parting words, right before he'd climbed the bank south of their camp and set off across the prairie on this crazy mission he'd gotten himself involved in.

As he continued crawling, he started to hear the voices of the men around the fire. There were two, all right. Maybe Sara was right, after all. After he'd covered several more yards, he began to detect southern accents in the voices he heard. He'd been born and raised on the Kansas farm, and hadn't traveled much farther away than Dodge City and Julesburg, but enough southerners had passed through from time to time, even a few overnighting at the farm, that he knew what southerners sounded like.

The chill of terror enshrouding him grew. It was like lead in his joints, making it hard to move.

Oh, god, he hoped that when the chips were down, he wouldn't turn tail and run! He'd never be able to face Sara after disgracing himself so thoroughly.

Trying to will himself calm, taking deep breaths, Reno moved closer and closer to where the flames licked beyond the thin screen of cottonwoods. The men's voices became clearer and clearer. The voice of one of the men was pinched, as though with pain, and occasionally he broke off talking to let out a shrill curse.

As Reno gained a tree at the edge of the camp, he shouldered up against it and scrubbed a sleeve across his sweaty forehead. As he did, he heard one of the men say, "...yeah, she got you good, that's for sure.

Damn, that's a deep knife wound, Lonnie Ray!"

Reno edged a look around the tree, peering into the men's camp. They were both on the opposite side of the fire from where Reno hunkered behind the cottonwood. One lay on his side, clutching a bottle. The other knelt beside him, crouched over him. The one on the ground appeared lean and bony, and he had long, greasy red hair. The kneeling man had thick, dark-brown hair and a full beard.

The kneeling man dabbed a cloth at a wound on the other man—maybe on the man's left hip or on the inside of his right thigh. The dancing flames and shunting shadows made it hard for Reno to see them clearly from a hundred feet away.

"I know it's deep," Lonnie Ray snarled. "Galldangit, I'm the one sportin' it. The pain's been gettin' worse instead of better, too—I'll tell you that much, Ed!"

"Looks like it might be infected."

"Oh, lordy—don't tell me that!"

"I just hope she was worth it."

Lonnie Ray cursed and laughed shrilly despite his pain. "She was a purty little thing—wasn't she? That schoolteacher. If I'd had a teacher like her, that looked like her, even in her old-woman's dress, I might have stayed in school and learned somethin', sure as tootin'!"

A hot hand of fury wrapped itself around the back of Reno's neck.

The schoolteacher.

Miss Cassie Bernard.

"The thing of it is, too, Ed, she was swinging that knife at Gimpy, not me. Gimpy was holdin' her down for Hackamore Simms. But I'm the one she hit! And she stuck me deep, too!" The man cursed and sobbed, then took another deep pull from the whiskey bottle as the other man dabbed at the wound.

Reno looked down at the rifle. It now lay across his lap as he sat with his back pressed up against the tree. He squeezed the Sharps in both hands. Suddenly, before he knew what he was doing, he'd raised the gun to his shoulder. Fully cocking the rifle, he aimed around the right side of the tree and into the camp. He drew his index finger back against the trigger, trying to draw a bead on one of the men before him. He couldn't see them clearly because of the brush and weeds between him and them.

He shifted the barrel around, trying to line up the sights on the kneeling man, Ed. As he did, red lights of fury flashed behind his retinas, making it even more difficult to aim at the killers. He ground his teeth and hardened his jaws, fairly seething. His hands trembled, making the rifle shake.

No, he told himself. Don't take a hasty shot. You've got only one round. You might get one of them, but the other bastard will get you...or Sara...

Just then, one of the killers' horses whinnied sharply.

Reno jerked with a start. He saw the horse, dimly lit by the fire's flames, standing back in the trees beyond the fire. Both horses now stared off to the west, to Reno's left. A mule brayed in that direction.

Old Otis.

Both killers had jerked their heads sharply toward the horse that had issued the warning. Now they turned just as abruptly to peer west.

Sara's voice came sweetly: "Hello the camp?"

Pause.

The two killers looked at each other.

Sara's reed-thin voice again: "Hello?" Reno hadn't heard her sound that sweet and innocent in years. "My mule has lost a shoe and I was wondering if someone there might be able to help me get it back on. I'm lost and it's getting cold, and it's awfully dark out here."

She actually made her voice crack as though with fear. The fear of a sweet young lady lost and alone with her lame mule on a dark early-autumn night.

The two killers looked at each other again, wide-eyed with lusty expectation. They snickered goatishly.

Ed stood and stepped away from the fire. Staring westward, he stifled a chuckle then cleared his throat, brushed his hands on his grubby gray tunic, and said, "Come on in, honey. We'll be glad to help you with your mule. Come on in and make yourself warm here by our fire."

He beckoned heartily, staring into the darkness

beyond their fire's orange-gold wash.

"Sure, sure," said Lonnie Ray from the ground. "Come on in and let us get a look at you—er, I mean, your mule!" He wheezed a laugh into his cupped hand.

Reno aimed the rifle at the standing killer. He had a clear shot. His heart thudded. He wanted desperately to pull back on the trigger, but he couldn't do it. He had only one shot. He had to follow the plan. He had to wait for Sara to walk into the camp and, catching both men off-guard in their sordid lust, she'd drill Ed with her Colt Navy. Then either she or Reno would shoot Lonnie Ray before he even knew what had happened to his partner.

"Easy," Reno admonished himself under his breath. "Just...take...it...easy."

Sara had it all worked out. Just follow the plan.

Reno heard the slow hoof thuds of old Otis's approach to the fire.

"Come on in, honey." Ed glanced at the man on the ground, grinned, lifted a hand to his mouth and whispered something Reno couldn't hear, then moved into the darkness to Reno's left, toward where Sara was approaching the camp. "Oh, there you are! Come on over and get warm by the fire. I'll take a look at your mule in a minute."

"Oh, thank you, thank you," Sara said, pitching her voice with feigned relief. "I was so glad to see your fire! You're nice men, aren't you?"

"Sure, sure—we're nice men. Come on over here, honey. Let me get a look at you."

"All right. As long as you're nice."

Reno winced. Cripes, Sara—don't overplay your hand.

By the fire, Lonnie Ray chuckled. Reno drew a bead on the bald spot atop his head, caressing the Sharps' trigger, waiting for the Colt's roar. That would be his signal to go to work with the Sharps.

Suddenly, one of the two horses on the other side of the fire whickered deeply and lifted a shrill whinny. Reno switched his gaze to the horse. It was staring at him from the darkness beyond the fire, its eyes wide and round and bright with reflected firelight.

It had seen him or winded him! It stared right at him!

Lonnie Ray whipped his alarmed eyes toward Reno. "Trap! Look out, Ed—it's a trap!"

EIGHT

Reno's heart leaped in his chest.

He drew a calming breath, held it, and squeezed the Sharps' trigger and watched as the .54-caliber bullet, driven by ninety grains of black powder, smacked into Lonnie Ray's chest, hammering the man violently backward, blood from the exit wound in his back painting the tree behind him.

Ed cursed shrilly.

"Devil!" Sara screamed.

The scream was followed by the roar of their father's Colt Navy.

Ed bellowed. Reno heard the smack of a hand against flesh. Sara grunted and there was a thud as she apparently hit the ground.

"Sara!" Reno cried, and lurched to his feet.

He sprinted through the brush, crossing the distance between him and the fire in three seconds. As he ran, his heart leaped into his throat. A gun barked twice. He didn't think it was the Colt.

"Sara!" Reno shouted at the tops of his lungs, racing across the fire-lit camp and into the darkness where he'd seen Ed disappear.

Sara grunted then wailed angrily. Ahead, he saw two shadows moving violently. He headed for the larger of the two shadows and had just seen the white of Ed's eyes as Ed turned toward him sharply, before he rammed his body into Ed's without breaking stride. A gun flashed and barked in Ed's hand a quarter-wink before Ed hit the ground with a shrill wail, Reno on top of him. Ed squirmed beneath Reno. The man smelled like sweat and alcohol and sour wool. Ed cursed. Reno saw the man raise the pistol in his right hand. Reno wrenched the gun out of the man's grip.

Ed cursed.

Fury boiling through Reno, he flipped the gun in his hand, grabbing the barrel. He raised the revolver back behind his shoulder before whipping it forward and smashing the butt against Ed's head.

"Oh—ow!" Ed wailed, brushing a hand across his temple, which the gun had laid open.

Ed glared up at Reno and was about to yell again. But then the gun came crashing down on his head again, and he screamed.

Reno drew the gun up again, smashed it down.

Up…down…again…again…and   again…until
Ed no longer struggled beneath him. Again, Reno
slammed the butt of the man's own gun against Ed's
head.

When he looked down, he saw he'd caved the man's
head in. It was a bloody pulp. It didn't look human.
The man lay still, totally unmoving.

Reno turned to where he'd last seen Sara, called
her name.

"I'm all right."

She stood a few feet away, a shadow in the darkness staring at him.

Reno's heart still raced. "Are you hurt?"

"No. I'm fine, Reno."

Reno stood. Rage was still a wild stallion galloping through him. He flipped Ed's Confederate pistol
around, grabbing the bloody butt. He strode back
into the camp. Lonnie Ray lay gasping like a landed
fish. When he saw Reno walking toward him, his eyes
widened and he pressed his hands to the ground, a
still-born effort to flee.

He wasn't going anywhere.

Reno stood over the man. "This is for Cassie Bernard, you black-hearted demon!"

He clicked the hammer back, aimed down at the
man's head. Lonnie Ray opened his mouth to scream
but Reno's bullet plowed through the dead-center of
the man's forehead before he could make a sound.

Reno cocked again, drilled another round into the dead man's head. He cocked another round, fired again. There was one more round in the revolver.

He drilled it into Lonnie Ray's head.

When the hammer had clicked onto an empty chamber, Reno stood glaring down at his handiwork. He wished he had one more bullet. Just one more.

In fact, he wished he could kill both of these men all over again.

For her.

But there were more, he told himself. There were many more where these two had come from.

Sara walked quietly up beside him. Reno lowered the smoking pistol, drew a deep breath. Only now did his heartbeat slow. A vague chagrin washed over him.

He turned to Sara a little guiltily. She stood beside him, smiling at him. She didn't say anything. She wrapped her arm around his waist and planted a soft kiss on his cheek.

***

Later that night around their fire, Reno shuffled through his father's Bible. He came upon a passage in Deuteronomy John Bass had circled in pencil and marked with a star. He read the passage to Sara, who was taking apart and cleaning one of the Confederate pistols they'd taken off the dead men. They'd appropriated the men's horses, as well, hoping to sell them for food and ammunition.

"It is mine to avenge; I will repay. In due time their foot will slip; their day of disaster is near and their doom rushes upon them."

Reno frowned at his sister, vaguely incredulous.

Sara looked up at Reno, and shrugged. "We're helping Him." She smiled, winked. "Don't worry, Reno—we'll be rewarded one day. You'll see."

Reno smiled, nodded, and closed the Good Book. He slipped it into his saddlebag pouch, lay back against his saddle, pulled his hat down over his eyes, and drifted asleep.

He slept well that night—the first time his since family's savage murder.

***

In the afternoon of the next day they crossed the border into Colorado and rode into a small settlement known as Steinbach's Trading Post. Years ago, there'd only been the trading post itself here, but now there was a livery barn and a hotel, which sat side by side across from the sprawling log, wood frame, and adobe brick trading post.

The trading post was also a saloon, though the sign over the place only said "trading post." But it was even more than a trading post and saloon. Behind the

main building a half-dozen tent shacks crouched in
the brush and sage, some of them flanked by small
kitchen gardens as well as by privies and wash lines
strung with brightly colored female clothing, which
today, as Reno and Sara rode into the yard, fluttered
in the wind like low-flying kites. The feminine wash
lent the only color to the otherwise stark, earth-toned
environs.

When he and his brothers and father had ridden
here to sell beef one autumn, Reno had once asked his
father what those tents were for. John Bass had given
a dry chuckle and said, "Son, Mr. Steinbach uses those
tents for those men who partake of too much of the
devil's brew to ride back to wherever they came from.
Right charitable of him, wouldn't you say?"

Reno's brother Ben had laughed and then covered
the laugh with a cough. The milder James had turned
beet red.

Reno had known he wasn't getting the full story,
but he figured it out the next year, when a boy at
school had mentioned something about his ma having taken an iron skillet to his pa when she'd found
out he'd been "cavorting with fallen women" at Steinbach's Trading Post. Even now, seeing those tents and
the frilly underclothing blowing on the line brought
warmth to Reno's cheeks. He averted his gaze as
though the mere sight of such evidence of earthly sin
might blind him.

He and Sara rode past Eichendorf's Livery Barn as well as the three-story adobe brick hotel simply called HOTEL, which the last time Reno had visited had been run by an old Scandinavian, Edgar Johnson, and his half-Lakota wife, Flies-With-the-Wind.

Johnson had been a buffalo hunter, as had Joe Eichendorf. Emil Steinbach, a stout and fierce-tempered old German—many Germans had settled in these parts—had established the trading post here to trade with the Sioux and the buffalo hunters back before those two factions had become blood enemies. The cause of the clash, Reno knew, was the fact that the white buffalo hunters killed by the thousands the animals the Indians had relied on almost exclusively for both food and clothing for generations.

Worst of all, the whites took only the precious animals' hides for coats and hats to be made and sold back east, leaving the corpses to rot on the prairie. Meanwhile, many of the Indians starved or were driven off of their ancestral hunting lands to make way for the white invaders.

All of this Reno had learned from bits and pieces of conversations he'd overheard here and there, and the gists of which he'd stitched into his own narrative, knowing what he knew first-hand about the white man and the Indians. Miss Bernard had filled in the gaps of his knowledge at school. The fact of the slaughter was incontestable, and the Indians were naturally outraged.

The drift of Reno's thoughts had taken his mind into a sad back eddy from which Miss Bernard's pretty face smiled up at him, overlaid by the hideous visage of her bloodied corpse, making his heart ache. It took Sara's reaching out from her saddle to give him a hard shove to bring him back to the trading post.

"Reno!"

"What?" he said, annoyed.

They'd drawn their mounts up to the livery barn because they intended to sell the two dead Confederates' horses for enough money for ammunition and trail supplies.

"Look there."

Reno followed his sister's pointing finger to the brush ramada that ran along the corral on the livery barn's right side. Many horses were tied in the shade beneath the ramada, some with feed sacks draped over their ears, others drawing water from a stock tank. Their saddles' latigo straps dangled free beneath the horses' bellies.

There had to be well over a dozen horses tied there. A quick count told him twenty-two, in fact. Two of the twenty-two were cream stallions.

Vaguely, Reno heard Apache growling.

"That's a lot of horses," he said. He glanced around the yard. "Must be a passel of hands from one of the ranches…"

"On a weekday?" Sara said. "This early?" Judging by the angle of the sun, it was around three o'clock.

Apache growled louder. Reno and Sara both turned to see the dog sitting nearby, staring at the trading post, growling and showing his teeth. Reno looked at Sara. She returned his curious gaze.

Reno regarded the horses again then nudged Coyote over to the barn's right side, more closely inspecting the mounts tied before him. Sara followed him atop old Otis. Only three of the horses sported traditional stockmen's saddles. The others were outfitted with McClellan saddles. Most of the saddles were so badly worn that the wood shone through. Some of them didn't even sport leather stirrup fenders, but badly sun-faded canvas. Those horses had been ridden hard, too. Sweat still lathered most of them, making a streaky mud from the trail dust that caked them.

"Those horses aren't from around here," Reno said half to himself, ponderingly rubbing his jaw. "Military mounts of some kind."

"Reno?"

He glanced at Sara, who'd ridden up in front of him. She'd stopped the mule near the last horses in the line. "Look at that."

Reno rode over and again followed his sister's gaze to a cavalry sword poking up from a leather scabbard. It was a heavy war sword, not a dress sword. His mind flashed on the sabers he'd spied hanging from the sides of the two officers who had been leading the Devil's Horde away from his family's burning farm.

Reno felt his lower jaw sag with shock.

He turned to the trading post from which he now heard the low roar of men's laughter and boisterous conversation. Apache continued to stare at the place. Glare, more like. And growl...

"Oh, boy," he heard himself mutter, his heart quickening. "Oh, boy..."

He turned to Sara who had slid down from Otis's back. "Hey, now...now, just hold on, Sara. Sara, gall-dangit—where do you think you're goin'!"

NINE

Reno took the time to tie both the pinto and the mule to the corral, for the ramada was full. He ordered Apache to stay with the mounts, and the dog reluctantly complied, keeping his dark gaze on the trading post, growling.

Reno caught up with Sara just as she crouched beneath a hitch rack near the main building's front door. He crouched under the hitch rack and stepped up onto the boardwalk.

"Sara, hold on! You can't just go waltzing in there..."

But waltz in there was exactly what the crazy girl did, pushing through the batwings on the saloon side of the building. Reno stumbled in after her, reaching forward to grab her arm. He froze when the din of conversation died abruptly, so that nearly all he could hear was the clatter of the batwings slapping into place behind him. He had his left hand on Sara's arm.

She'd stopped just ahead of him and to his left, glancing around the shadowy, smoky room.

Reno looked around, then, too. He smelled the men around him before he saw them. They reeked of sweat and leather and horses and sour wool. He would have sworn they stank of death, as well, but maybe that was just his often-overactive imagination. As his eyes adjusted to the dim light, he saw them spread out to his right, sitting at round or rectangular tables.

They were a hard-looking, bearded lot, and the blue of the blue-eyed ones—and there seemed to be quite a few with blue eyes—stood out sharply in the dense shadows. There were some shaggy-headed ones and some with long, greasy hair. He recognized a few he'd seen in the pack that had thundered past him and Sara as they'd lain on the creek bank. He picked out the Bad Old Man right away, for the man's silver hair and curly beard the color of a soiled white rag stood out from the other, mostly far younger, men. Colonel Montgomery sat at a table near the far right wall. His Confederate gray campaign hat sat on the large, round table near his right hand, which held a fistful of cards. His silver hair, long from lack of barbering, curled down behind his ears and sat flat against his head, showing the lines of his hat.

Across from him sat another officer, the major called "Black Bob" Hobbs. He and Montgomery and three other men were playing poker, it looked like.

Hobbs had long, thick, coal black hair swept straight back over his head. It hung to his shoulders, clad in a linsey shirt and red neckerchief over which he wore a Confederate gray, blood-stained, sun-bleached, dusty jacket. His beard was thick and black, his face long and pale, and his eyes, nearly as black as his hair and beard, gazed out coldly from deep, shadowy sockets.

Smoke hung thick over the room.

A single, toneless voice broke the silence hanging over Reno like a hatchet poised for cleaving: "Help you?"

Reno turned to see a stout man standing behind the bar at the back of the room. He was old and bearded, with a bald head, and he wore an apron over his considerable girth. His face was very pale. Deathly pale.

"No, uh…" Reno hesitated. "We were just, uh…"

He looked around the room again. All the faces of the Devil's Horde were aimed at him and Sara, scrutinizing them through the smoky shadows, as silent and glassy-eyed as the animal heads mounted on the walls.

Sara regarded them coldly. Her chest rose and fell sharply. She wore two pistols behind a belt around her lean waist, on the outside of her faded sack pants. One of the pistols was the Colt Navy. The other was one of the Confederate revolvers she and Reno had taken from the men they'd killed.

Fear caused cold sweat to ooze from Reno's pores. If these men recognized that Confederate hogleg...

He wanted to flee. But he knew fleeing would only make him and Sara stand out even more than they already did. They were two jackrabbits that had sauntered into a rattlesnake convection, as the old saw went. They couldn't leave without stirring up the rattlers. Now that they were here, they'd have to stay for a while.

Reno hesitated again, then said, "I was just...I was just gonna buy my sis a cider is all...to cut the trail dust."

This evoked some chuckles from the killers around them. Colonel Montgomery even smiled a little as he lifted a fat cigar to his mouth, and puffed on it.

Reno gave a nervous laugh then squeezed Sara's arm. "Come on, sis...let's get that cider I promised..."

He stepped forward and tugged gently on Sara's arm.

Sara kept her feet in place, staring at the room teeming with the devils that had murdered her family. Reno looked at her hands, then at the pistols belted around her waist. He hoped to high heaven she did not reach for the hoglegs. No, Sara wouldn't do anything that crazy...

Would she?

"Come on, sis," Reno said again, smiling but putting a little more urgency into his voice. "Let's get us a coupla ciders."

Sara took another breath then said, "Ciders." She paused, keeping her eyes on the Bad Old Man, who regarded her in kind. For a few terrifying seconds, Reno thought she was going to skin those smoke wagons and start shooting, but then she said, "Right."

Reno breathed a sigh of minimal relief as she let him lead her forward. They walked down along the wall on the left side of the room, past the doorway, which opened onto the trading post part of the building and which was crammed full of goods of every kind.

They stepped up to the bar behind which the stout man stood, eyeing them expectantly, though his nervous gaze flicked frequently to the obvious cutthroats patronizing his saloon. The edgy look in his eyes, and the sheen of sweat on his pale face, told Reno the man—who must work for Mr. Steinbach, because Reno had met Steinbach, and this man was not him—knew exactly who his customers were.

"We'll each have a cider," Reno told the man.

"Cider, eh?"

Another killer laughed. The others began talking again. Talking and laughing. At least some did—enough that Reno felt as though some of the attention was being removed from him and Sara, and for that he was grateful.

The barman said, "Let me see if I have some."

He cast another glance at his other customers then stepped out from behind the bar and headed toward the door to the trading post part of the building. "Been awhile since anyone ordered cider. If I got some, it would be over here. I'll be right back."

Reno leaned forward, pressing his fingers into the edge of the bar. He was unarmed. He had two pistols he'd taken off the two jackals they'd killed in his saddlebags, and his Sharps still sat in the scabbard strapped to his horse. He'd been in such a hurry to stop Sara from doing whatever in holy blazes she had in mind to do—and he still didn't know what that was—that he now found himself in a saloon full of his family's killers without a single weapon except the folding knife in his pocket.

Sara was armed, however. In fact, as he glanced at her, he saw both of her pale, delicate hands were resting over the butts of the pistols wedged behind her belt. She looked at him, having to lift her chin a little because he was about three inches taller than she, and his stomach tightened at the fierce determination blazing in her cold blue eyes.

"Get your hands off them guns," Reno ordered her tightly.

Several of the killers were conversing, but there still wasn't enough noise in the saloon to cover anything but a whisper. Turning his head slightly to one side, he saw Colonel Montgomery sitting nearly directly behind him on the other side of the room. The man stared at Reno and Sara. So did the Major, Black Bob Hobbs. A heavy cloud of cigar smoke billowed around the colonel's gray head, but his blue eyes, every bit as cold as Sara's, blazed through it like twin lights on a foggy night.

Sara stared straight ahead now, at the dusty, mostly unlabeled bottles lined up on the back bar. Reno knew what she was thinking about. She had all the killers right here. She might have a good chance at killing the Bad Old Man and Black Bob.

But what then?

"Keep 'em holstered, Sara," Reno spoke again, his jaws hard, keeping his head forward but rolling his eyes toward his sister.

She didn't respond.

Reno knew that if he wasn't standing beside her, she'd do it. She'd spin around, skin both of her smoke wagons, and throw lead at Montgomery and Hobbs and then at the others...until she herself was dead. Her hatred for these men was suicidal. But she wouldn't get Reno killed. That was the only reason she kept both pistols wedged behind her belt.

"Here we go," the barkeep said, reentering the room from the trading post part of the building. "No cider, but I found three bottles of switchel. I brought over two." He held up the corked brown bottles and blew dust off of them. He set them on the bar before

Reno and Sara. He pried the cork out of each bottle and said, "That's twelve cents. Six cents each."

"Six cents each," Reno parroted the man, a fresh wave of anxiety rushing through him. He reached into his overall pockets and found only lint and dirt in one, only the folding knife in the other.

He had no money. Not even a half-cent piece. He doubted that Sara did, either.

He stood frozen with his hands in his pockets.

Sara rolled her eyes toward him and arched a brow expectantly. A gently mocking smile curled her mouth.

"What is it?" asked the barkeep.

"Uh…I don't, uh…seem to have any money," Reno said, hearing the shrill whine of his blood in his ears.

Suddenly, the saloon fell silent again. Reno could feel all eyes in the room on him.

The barkeep looked at him in disgust. "You don't have no money? You come in here an' order…"

"Barkeep." The voice had come from behind him. Reno recognized it as the voice of Colonel Montgomery. "The drinks are on me."

He tossed a coin. It caromed through the shadows and glinted in the shafts of light angling through the building's dirty front windows. It slapped against the barman's fat, open palm. He closed his fingers over it, lowered the hand, opened it, looked at the coin, and raised his brows in pleasant surprise.

"All righty, then," the barman said, and tossed the coin into a box beneath the bar.

Reno and Sara shared a look. Reno's expression was one of relief. However, Sara's blue eyes remained as cold as a mountain lake after the season's first hard frost. She looked at the flat brown bottle on the bar before her, her mouth pinched, her jaws hard.

Again, Reno knew what she was thinking. She was thinking she couldn't accept a drink bought by the man who'd led the gang that had butchered her family, raped and murdered her sister...

Again, Reno's heart thudded. We're not going to get out of here alive, are we? he silently asked himself. It was a rhetorical question.

As if in answer to the question, Colonel Montgomery piped up again, his deep, slightly raspy, throaty voice pitched with a slow, rolling accent cut through the low hum of conversation:

"Young lady?"

Reno's heart kicked like a Missouri mule. He felt himself wince.

"I say, there—young lady!" Montgomery said again, louder this time.

Reno turned his head to see the ramrod-straight, slender, gray-headed old man rise from his chair, the stogie smoldering in his left hand on which he wore a gold ring on his little finger. His eyes bored into the back of Sara's head.

She whipped around gracefully and shook her tangled hair back from her eyes. "Are you talking to me?" she asked haughtily, her voice fairly dripping with disdain.

Reno closed his eyes. Sara. Sara…oh, jeepers, Sara…

Colonel Eustace Montgomery strode toward her slowly, his long gray coat hanging from his slender shoulders, showing the dusty gray vest behind it, gold buttons glinting in the light from the windows. Around the man's wrinkled turkey neck was knotted a slender black tie. Three gold stars adorned the short neck of the coat's collar. A cavalry sword hung down the Colonel's right leg, swinging as he walked, taking pensive puffs from the half-smoked cigar. He stared at the guns wedged behind Sara's belt.

Well, that tears it. We're doomed. We've exacted all the revenge we're going to be able to exact for our family. We're going to die here in this backcountry saloon, shot like rats in a privy. All because Sara can't keep her wolf on a leash…

TEN

"Let me see that hogleg you got there," the colonel demanded, extending his long, bony right hand that had been burned by the southern son to the color and texture of old shoe leather. He'd lost the tip off his third finger, and the nail had grown down to curl over the end.

For some reason, it reminded Reno of the devil's cloven hooves.

"What hogleg I got where?" Sara snarled back at him.

"Don't sass me, child! That one there." Inwardly, Reno groaned as the Bad Old Man extended his talon-like hand toward the pistol Sara had taken off the dead devil, Ed. Montgomery snapped his fingers. "Let me see it!"

Sara gave a caustic chuff then pulled the hogleg out from behind her belt. She placed her thumb on the

hammer and for a second Reno thought for sure she was going to shoot him with the big Confederate horse pistol. He was so numb with dread by now, however, that he just watched with a strange detachment. He would be dead in seconds and there was nothing he could do about it, so that was that.

Sara removed her thumb from the hammer and shoved the pistol toward the man, not butt-first but not quite barrel-first, either. He snapped it angrily out of her hand, looked at it then let it hang down against his right side.

"This is a Griswold & Gunnison .36, young lady." Montgomery had said the words loudly enough for his brother killers to hear, and his voice had been pitched with none too little accusing. "Where'd you get it?"

Sara flicked her eyes toward Reno. Her face had turned a tad pale behind her suntan. Reno thought it was a good sign that she felt some fear. Maybe, just maybe, she wouldn't get them killed.

Maybe…

"I found it," Sara lied.

"You found it where, child?"

"I don't know—I just found it."

"I think I know where you found it."

Reno's stomach tightened again, the fear returning just after he'd begun to feel hopeful. The Bad Old Man had not only recognized the pistol as Confederate-made, but he recognized it as Ed's gun.

Montgomery glared at Sara as he said, "Your pa or brother likely brought it home with him from the war. He probably took it off a poor dead warrior of the Confederacy and kept it for a trophy. I suppose he hangs it above his mantel and tells over and over again how he killed that young grayback." He paused then blinked angrily. "Don't he?"

"Hey, Colonel?" one of the other men said. He was a tall, much younger, man standing at the window, looking out.

"What is it?"

"Take a look at them two horses tied with that pinto and the mule out yonder."

Montgomery kept his fierce blue gaze on Sara. "What about 'em?"

Another man, staring out the window with the first one, said, "That's Ed Gentry and Lonnie Ray Simon's roan an' claybank. I'd recognize that claybank anywhere, even if they wasn't both wearin' Ed an' Lonnie Ray's saddles an' rifles."

"That's Ed and Lonnie Ray's, all right," said the taller man.

Weakly, in crestfallen defeat, Reno silently said, "Ah, heck." These were the final nails being driven into his and Sara's wooden overcoats.

The colonel turned back around to Sara. His eyes were wide and his mouth was a broad slash across the lower half of his face, inside the nest-like mustache and beard. He looked down at the Confederate .36 in his hand and then narrowed his eyes curiously, gravely, and said, "Where…"

That was as far as he got before he furled his brows even more severely, then turned back around to face the front window. The old colonel must have had good hearing for his advanced years. It wasn't until several seconds after Montgomery had turned around to face the front of the room that Reno heard it, too—a low rumbling growing steadily louder.

All the men in the room swung their heads toward the front of the trading post to stare outside. Silence hung heavily over the room striped with smoky shadows.

Outside, the rumbling rose. Reno felt the reverberations through the saloon's floorboards. A couple of horses tied beneath the brush ramada whinnied anxiously. Others gave their tails agitated switches.

Reno shared a curious glance with Sara and turned back to gaze out the dusty windows. Just then, horseback riders galloped into the yard from the east, their own dust obscuring them. They checked their horses down in front of the trading post then rode on past the post and over to where the Devil's Hordes' mounts were tied beneath the ramada, with Reno and Sara's mounts as well as Ed and Lonnie Ray's mounts tied to the far western edge.

The newcomers milled around the tied horses,

conversing. Reno could hear their voices but not what they were saying. As the dust swirled, he recognized one of them. His heart turned a somersault in his chest. The man he'd just recognized—fat and middle-aged and riding beside a younger, sparer-framed man with a bandage over his head and one eye—was Cletus Dodson. Of course, the younger man sticking close to his side was his son, Luther, who'd lost an eye when the Bad Old Man and Black Bob had pillaged their farm just before doing the same to the Bass place.

Dodson talked to a man closely inspecting the horses tied beneath the ramada. Both Dodson and the other men turned their heads at the same time to look at the trading post. It was then Reno saw the deputy United States marshal's moon-and-star badge pinned to the wool coat of the man Dodson had been speaking with. The others in the gang, composed of roughly ten riders all sitting astride lathery, dusty horses, turned toward the trading post then, too.

They squinted against the sifting dust.

Reno saw badges on two more men. One of those men was Sheriff Bill Crowder from Baxter. The other man, like the man nearest Dodgson, was a deputy U.S. marshal. Crowder was dressed like an aging cowhand. The two marshals wore black suits. One wore a bowler hat. The other wore a cream-colored sombrero. Reno recognized some of the other men in

the group, too. At least, he'd seen them in and around
Baxter though in his shocked state of mind, he could
think of only one or two names. He thought one was
a blacksmith who sometimes worked as a deputy for
Crowder.

Inside the saloon, standing with his back to Sara,
facing the front windows, Colonel Montgomery said,
"Well, well, gentlemen—things are startin' to get right
interestin' around here. Yes, indeed...right interestin'." He spoke slowly, rolling his words out almost
musically, like the words in one of the many poems
Miss Cassie Bernard had read to the class, though
Miss Bernard had not spoken in a southern accent.
Reno had a feeling the Bad Old Man could making
cussing sound flowery.

Holding onto Sara's gun, the colonel took several
paces forward and stopped.

Reno stared out the windows beyond the man,
his mind a whirlpool of mixed emotions. When he'd
first realized who the newcomers were, hope had ris-
en in him. But then, after he'd hastily counted only
ten or so posse members, fear had begun to reassert
its stubborn foothold. The posse was outnumbered
two to one. True, the sheriff's bunch might be able
to surround the building, but that wouldn't do Reno
and Sara much good, them being stuck inside. Reno
wanted to grab Sara and make a run for the door, but
they'd be shot down before they could get halfway

across the room.

Outside, the conversation continued and the horses milled nervously while the posse members studied the trading post. Finally, the men dismounted their horses, shucking rifles from saddle scabbards. The two deputy U.S. marshals dropped their horses' reins, shucked their own rifles, and then walked toward the saloon. The one in the bowler hat came first, the one in the cream sombrero walking a little behind. The one in the bowler hat wore a mustache and a very serious scowl on his face. He was a man on a mission.

The man in the Stetson, a little taller than the one in the bowler, frowned hesitantly, almost grimacing in fear as he followed the shorter man up onto the boardwalk fronting the saloon part of the trading post.

Sara looked at Reno. He returned her gaze with a wary one of his own. As he did, he half-consciously reached forward and wrapped his right hand around her left one, to keep her from doing anything irrational when those two lawmen entered the saloon. She didn't try to pull her hand away. She arched a brow at him then turned back to the front of the room just as the bowler-hatted deputy marshal pushed through the batwing doors.

The other man followed him into the saloon.

They walked maybe four steps into the place and stopped side-by-side, each holding a Sharps slant-breech carbine. They both had a brace of Dragoon pistols holstered on their hips. Reno's heart picked up its beat as the two deputy U.S. marshals slid their gazes around the room. They both looked grim, but the one in the bowler hat appeared angry. His brown eyes were sharp, and one of his nostrils flared. Veins stood out in his sunburned forehead, beneath the narrow brim of his bowler hat. The hat and his mustache and his eyebrows were dust rimed. In fact, both men looked as though they'd rolled in the dirt.

They brought the fresh smell of sweaty horse into the room.

When the two lawmen had inspected the killers closely, the killers inspecting them back in stony silence—a silence so heavy and dense, Reno thought the room would implode from the sheer weight of it—they glanced at each other. An eye of the one in the bowler hat gave a nervous twitch. Then he turned around and started walking back to the doors.

The other one did, as well.

"Allow me to buy you a drink, gentlemen," the colonel said loudly.

That stopped both lawmen in their tracks.

Reno looked outside the windows. The other posse members now stood facing the saloon in a line about fifteen feet away from the building, holding their rifles up high across their chests and gazing through the windows. They all looked as though they'd rolled in the dirt, as well. Luther Dodson was the youngest of the bunch, and he looked terribly small and vulnerable, standing there beside his taller, thicker father.

"It's the least I can do," the colonel added, his voice echoing around the cavernous room, "before I blow your Yankee lights out."

ELEVEN

Those words stopped both lawmen in their tracks.

They stood staring straight ahead at the batwings. They glanced at each other as though in silent discussion. The one with the sombrero dipped his head slightly, then they both whipped around quickly, raising their rifles. They yelled as they snapped the Sharps' butt plates to their shoulders.

Neither got off a single shot. The colonel raised Sara's .36, and blew both of them back out through the batwings. The Bad Old Man handled the big Confederate horse pistol well enough that he managed to drill two rounds into each man before they did a bizarre death dance out through the swing doors to drop like pie-eyed drunks in the street just beyond.

The gunshots had sounded like cannon blasts in the cavernous room. Reno had leaped with each blast that had assaulted his ears like a hard cuff from an open palm, leaving them ringing in the ensuing silence. White powder hung in the shadowy air, smelling like rotten eggs left too long in the sun.

Reno squeezed Sara's hand in his own as he stared in shock and horror at the room before him. The only movement in the room was the colonel slowly lowering the smoking pistol. In the street beyond, the sheriff and Cletus Dodson and the other posse members stared down at the two dead federal lawmen lying dead in the street just beyond the saloon doors. To a man, they looked stricken.

When the colonel had lowered the smoking pistol to his side, he turned his head to stare out the window, lifted his chin and said, "Gentle-mennn!"

All the Confederates moved at once, bounding out of their chairs and running, kicking tables and chairs out of their way, to take up positions on either side of the colonel. They drew their own six-shooters—two apiece. They cocked them, raised them, and commenced firing through the glass, instantly shattering it, sending the shards raining onto the floor or out into the yard.

Reno stared in wide-eyed exasperation at the posse members standing twenty feet away. Several shouted curses and returned fire while others were hammered backward by the bullets tearing through them.

The posse's bullets screeched and buzzed through

the air around Reno and Sara, plunking into tables, shattering glasses or bottles, hammering into the bar to each side of them or into the back bar behind them. One of the Confederates yowled sharply and grabbed his arm while another wailed and dropped to his knees.

"Sara—take cover!"

As bullets swarmed like hornets, Reno grabbed his sister around the waist and launched both her and himself up and backward. Bullets tore into the top of the bar to each side of him and Sara as he rolled off a hip and shoulder and dropped down behind the bar, both him and his sister hitting the floor with bone-jarring, vision-blurring thuds. Glass from the back bar tumbled down around them; liquor rained from shattered bottles.

Reno lifted his head, groaning from the pain of the fall, his ears ringing from the deafening din around him, his hair wet from spilled liquor and peppered with broken glass. His gaze held on two brown eyes staring at him blankly. They belonged to the barman, who lay close enough that the man's cheek rested against Reno's right forearm. A puckered, quarter-sized hole shone above the man's left brow, filling that eye with spilled blood, which continued tracing a long, dark-red line as it ran down along the side of his nose.

Repelled by death and blood, Reno jerked away

from the man.

He turned to Sara who lay on the other side of him. Sara didn't move. She lay on her side, turned away from him, left cheek resting against the floor. Her hat had tumbled off, and her hair lay in a tangled blond nest around her head.

"Sara!"

Reno rose onto an elbow and squeezed her shoulder.

"Sara!" he yelled above the continuing fusillade, hearing several more bullets plunk into the bar, a couple showing their ominous-looking heads through the splintered wood. "Sara—you all right, sis?"

Again, Reno shook his sister. Her eyes remained closed. She didn't move.

Panicked, he rose to his knees and looked down at her. He ran his hands over her body, searching for a bullet wound, and stopped when he felt a sticky wetness just above her right hip.

"Sara!"

Suddenly, he realized the shooting had tapered off. His own voice now echoed around the near-silent saloon. Most of the sounds now came from outside— neighing horses, shouting men, a few more pistols fired sporadically. There was also a growing drumbeat of oncoming horses.

Reno rose slightly, lifted his head to peer over the top of the bullet-pocked bar. His eyes widened in shock. Colonel Montgomery stood at the very front of the saloon. In fact, he straddled the shattered window, one foot inside the saloon, the other planted on the boardwalk fronting it. He was aiming a revolver straight out from his right side, aiming at Reno, narrowing one cold blue eye.

Reno yelped and jerked his head down just as the Bad Old Man's six-shooter belched smoke and fire. The bullet carved a painful line across Reno's right temple. Enraged, Reno jerked the big Colt Navy .36 out from behind his sister's wide leather belt. He lifted his head up once more above the bar. As he did, he raised the Colt, cocked the pistol, and aimed it straight out over the top of the bar.

He took hasty aim at the colonel's silhouette, and fired.

The heavy shooting iron bucked and kicked in his hand. Orange flames stabbed from the barrel, instantly peppering his eyes with black powder. Montgomery screamed as he triggered his own revolver wide, flames lancing from the barrel toward the ceiling and the bullet plunking into the rafters. He lowered the weapon and stumbled on out of the saloon, clutching his upper left arm with the hand still holding the gun.

"Come on, Colonel!" one of his men shouted from the direction of the ex-Confederates' horses. "Appears to be more on the way!"

Montgomery took another couple of stumbling

steps into the yard, stretching his lips back from his teeth and glaring furiously into the saloon's shadows at Reno.

"Killer!" Reno yelled, his rage for the man cutting free inside him. "Murderer!"

He fired the Colt again, but his bullet plumed dirt in the yard several feet behind the man.

The colonel cast one more wicked glare at Reno then wheeled and strode quickly, clutching his wounded left arm, toward where the other Confederates were quickly mounting up and galloping west. Reno set the Colt atop the bar then dropped to a knee beside Sara. She was moving now, groaning.

Reno felt relieved for that much. He'd thought she might be dead.

"Sis, you okay? How bad are you hit?"

Sara pressed the heel of her hand to her head and blinked. "What?"

"How bad you hit, Sara?"

"Oh." She looked down at her side, brushed a hand across it, peered at the blood smearing her palm. "I didn't realize I was hit. Think it's just a graze."

"You were passed out."

Pressing her hand to her head, she glared at her brother. "That's your fault, ya big oaf. You picked me up and threw me to the floor like a sack of horse feed!"

"Oh, it's your head?"

"Yes, it's my head!"

He saw the goose egg growing on her left temple, and reached out to place a finger on it, but she brushed his hand away angrily. "Get away, fool!"

Her attitude rankled him. "I'm sorry, sis, but I probably saved your life, you hot-blooded catamount. You might thank me!"

"Did you kill that crazy old Confederate?"

"No, but I gave him somethin' to think about!"

"Thinkin' isn't good enough! I'll thank you when he's dead!"

"Sometimes you're just too damn much, Sara—you know that?"

"If Ma was still alive, you'd get a mouthful of lye soap for that 'damn'!"

"Damn you, Sara!" She could really get him riled. He didn't rile easy or often, but if anyone could rile him, it was his own sister. "Come on—get up. They're gone."

Reno stood then reached down and pulled her up by the hand. He led her around the end of the bar and into the bullet-riddled room. Beyond the broken windows, men and horses were milling in their own dust. Several lay dead in the yard. Several others lay wounded, and the other posse members as well as the newcomers—whoever they were—were tending them.

As Reno eased Sara into a chair, a man outside yelled, "I seen someone movin' around inside the saloon." Reno recognized the man. He was Emmett Stillwell, deputy town marshal of Baxter. He shucked a cap-and-ball revolver from a holster, and aimed through the broken windows, squinting his eyes against the sun.

"Hold on, Mr. Stillwell!" Reno threw his hands high. "It's Reno Bass! I'm in here with my sister, Sara!"

Stillwell frowned. He lowered his pistol slightly, then turned to Sheriff Bill Crowder, who appeared to have taken a bullet across his upper right arm. Two other men stood around Crowder. They were all peering through the broken windows and into the saloon's bleak shadows. Reno saw that two of the dead posse members—and there were several—were Cletus Dodson and his son Luther. They lay side by side, Cletus stretched out on his back, spread-eagle, Luther curled up on one side, his curly light-sandy hair sliding around in the wind. Little dust devils danced over them both.

"What the hell are you doing in there?" Crowder called. His face was taut against the pain in his arm, around which one man was wrapping a bandanna.

Reno looked at Sara. "Stay put, sis. Give yourself a rest."

He walked across the saloon to the front and stepped through the blasted-out window. He squint-ed against the harsh sunlight after the shadows inside the saloon. His ears still rang from the din of the gunfire. His eyes stung from the black powder smoke still wafting inside the building. His hands and knees trembled as though he'd been struck by lightning. He just then realized he'd lost his hat. The hot wind jostled his close-cropped hair as he looked at the scattered dead men.

He counted six dead, including Cletus Dodson and Luther, as well as the two dead federal men lying in front of the batwings. A couple more lay wounded, one cursing loudly from a belly wound and pounding the ground with his fist.

Apache, who must have made himself scarce when the shooting had started, now ran over to leap up against Reno, yipping anxiously.

"Sit boy, sit boy," Reno said.

"I asked you a question, Reno," Crowder said. "What were you and your sister doing in there?" He jerked his chin at Sara who, true to character, had disregarded her brother's orders to follow him out through the front window. Blood stained her pants just above her right hip. Her thick blond hair blew in the wind. She looked pale, worn out, and disoriented from the clubbing she'd taken when she'd hit the floor behind the bar.

"To tell you the truth, Sheriff," Reno said, glancing at Sara, "I'm not really sure what we were doing in there."

Sara looked around, holding her windblown hair

back from her face with one hand. She frowned in frustration and turned to Crowder, her eyes urgent, angry. "Where'd they go?"

Crowder stared at her. He glanced at Stillwell, who also gawped at Sara. Stillwell had tried courting Sara a couple of times and had occasionally followed her around, puppy-dog-like, when she'd been in town shopping for supplies, but Sara had always rebuked his advances—and not subtly, either, as was Sara's way.

"Miss Sara," Stillwell said, smiling fawningly. "I'm very glad to see you're still alive. We heard about your family from..." He let his voice trail off as he glanced guiltily down at Cletus Dodson. "...from Mr. Dodson, god rest his soul. "But...what...what're you an' Reno doing way out here?"

Sara kept her urgent gaze on Crowder. "Where'd they go?"

"West!" Crowder said, indignantly throwing his arm out to indicate west. "They've continued west."

"How many did you kill?"

"Wounded only a couple," Crowder said, sheepishly. He glanced at the two dead federals. "They caught us by surprise." He glanced at the dead men—his dead posse men littering the yard. "Cut us to shreds..."

He kicked a rock in defeat.

He turned to Reno. "What're you doing out here, boy?"

"We're going after them," Reno said.

"What?" both Crowder and Emmett Stillwell said at the same time, scrunching up their faces with incredulity. "Just the two of you?"

"That's right," Reno said, drawing a deep breath. "Just the two of us."

Crowder shook his head and walked over to Reno. "I can't let you do that, son. You come on back to Baxter with us."

"So you're giving up?"

Crowder looked at the dead men. Then he looked at the eight or nine men still living. To Reno, he said, "They ambushed us twice. We split up and followed them here."

So the second party of riders had been part of the posse before they'd split up. The second half had shown up in time to spook the killers just enough that they hadn't slaughtered all of Crowder's men, which they likely would have done if they'd been given another minute or two. They'd have slaughtered Reno and Sara, to boot.

"We've had enough." Crowder sighed, shook his head. "We'll go back to Baxter and I'll wire ahead to the authorities in Colorado. They're a federal problem now." His voice had trailed away slowly as his attention had drifted beyond Reno, and deep frown lines cut into his forehead. "Hey, where's that fool sister of yours goin'?"

He pointed to indicate Sara. She'd mounted old Otis and was galloping off to the west. Apache ran along behind her, barking.

"Ah, hell," Reno said, staring after Sara. He glanced guiltily at Crowder and Stillwell, and said, "Maybe see you around sometime, Sheriff. Deputy Stillwell. Or...maybe not..."

He ran over to the brush ramada, untied his three horses, mounted Coyote, and spurred the pinto westward after his sister. He trailed the two dead killers' horses along by their lead lines.

Crowder shook his head, staring after him. "That head-strong sister of his is going to get that boy killed."

"Yeah," Stillwell said, also staring after Reno. "She's as purty as she is loco...an' she's as loco as owls in a lightnin' storm."

TWELVE

"Excuse me, sir," Reno said two days later, after he and Sara had ridden into the bustling trading hub of Julesburg in the Colorado Territory, "but I was wondering if you could tell us where we might find a man named Ty Mando."

The man—a shopkeeper, judging by his suit and sleeve gators—scowled and flushed at Reno sitting astride Coyote just off the boardwalk fronting the man's dry-goods store at the eastern edge of the town. The skinny, bald, bespectacled man had been sweeping dung and mud off the sidewalk. Now he lifted the broom and wielded it threateningly, barking, "Go! Off with you! Both of you! Take that mangy cur with you, too. Git, dog! Git!"

Apache, who'd been sniffing for rabbits or perhaps mice beneath the man's boardwalk, growled and showed his teeth at the gent, hackles raised.

Reno and Sara, sitting to her brother's right astride old Otis, shared a surprised glance. Then Reno said, "Heel, Apache! Heel! It's all right, boy. Come on!"

He neck-reined the pinto around and booted the horse on up the street, Sara following suit beside him. Apache barked at the threatening shopkeeper then took off running after his master and mistress but glanced back at the colicky, broom-wielding towns-man, growling.

"What was that all about?" Sara asked, having to raise her voice above the midday hubbub. Horseback riders and wagons were clomping and wheeling along the broad, muddy main street, wagons rattling, men yelling and laughing, horses neighing, mules braying, and dogs barking.

"I don't know. Maybe he didn't hear me right. Aw-fully loud out here."

As Reno, Sara, and Apache continued westward, threading their way through the traffic, young ladies also appeared here and there about the street. Dressed as they were—if you could call them "dressed", for more bare skin than clothing shown on their curva-ceous persons—Reno didn't think they were any too respectable. At least, not the types that would sing in a church choir—or even be allowed inside to listen to the sermon, for that matter.

Most of the men were big and burly. They looked threatening in their buckskins and beards and wielding at least one brace of pistols, large knives, and big hunting rifles. There were Indians, too. And Mexicans. And black men. And a whole bunch of men who probably sported blood from various races.

There were soldiers likely from the nearby outpost, Camp Rankin. Most of these appeared drunk, as they were singing outside beer tents, their eyes glassy from drink.

The shops lining the street were constructed of everything from milled lumber to logs to tin to canvas to thin pine planks. Some were simple tent structures. One was merely a couple of large wagon boxes hammered together, set atop rain barrels, and covered by a sagging tarpaulin framed by unpeeled pine poles. A man in a top hat, long black coat, red foulard tie, pin-striped pants, and gold-buckle shoes held high a bottle while barking out the healthful attributes of the bluish-green liquid residing therein.

Some of the shacks looked as though they'd been here awhile. Others appeared so impermanent that a good breeze would pick them up and blow them into Kansas. Cook fires burned here and there along the street, muddy from a recent rain, and skinned animals—or those in the process of being skinned—hung upside down outside several shacks identified by crude shingles as meat or fresh game markets. Dead chickens, geese, turkeys, partridge, and prairie chickens were arranged on plank tables or in high-wheeled barrows tipped downward to give passersby a good view of their trappings.

An elderly Chinese couple in straw hats and ragged wool clothes were selling a barrow load of what appeared catfish probably caught in the nearby South Platte River. The old man sat in a rickety wooden chair, eating what appeared one of his cooked catfish, while the woman poked and prodded a nearby fire which she was having trouble keeping going after the recent rain.

Reno rode up to another man, this one on the street's right side and who appeared respectable, since he was dressed in a fancy suit complete with a bowler hat and a walking stick. He strode along forthrightly, clutching a newspaper under his arm.

"Pardon me, pardon me," Reno said, waving to get the man's attention on the busy boardwalk.

The man stopped and turned to him, frowning curiously, uncertainly.

Reno cleared his throat. "Could you possibly tell me where I might be able to find a fellow named Ty Mando?"

The man's face fell as though he'd suddenly lost control of his muscles. Behind him, an old woman in a fancy picture hat and gilt-edged purple gown gave a chuff of extreme displeasure, and said, "Ty Man—ohh!" She grabbed the girl in a frilly yellow dress walking along beside her, and said, "Come along, Bonnie. Hurry! We must get off the street this instant!"

They bustled on past the respectable looking man who merely shook his head reprovingly at Reno and continued walking, picking up his pace.

Reno turned to Sara, frowning, thoroughly befuddled.

"Let me try," Sara said, and rode ahead.

She swung toward the right side of the street again and to where a big, burly man in buckskins and with long dark-blond hair was skinning a deer, tossing chunks of the venison into a barrel. Sara swung Otis toward the man and said in a voice dripping with politeness and sweetness, "Pardon me, kind sir, but do you think you could direct my brother and me in the direction of a gentleman named Mando?" She winced slightly before adding, "Ty Mando?"

The man lowered his bloody hands from the deer's carcass, including the hand holding the knife. He stared blankly at Sara for a full fifteen seconds before sliding his gaze to Reno. He turned back to Sara and made slashing motions in the air with the knife, growling and snarling and writhing like a man in a fierce battle with some invisible opponent.

That got Apache all worked up, barking and growling at the man who then turned the knife on the dog.

"Come, Apache! Come, boy!" Reno followed his sister away from the still slashing and stabbing market hunter, and Apache ran along behind them, mewling and glancing dubiously behind at the madman in buckskins.

When Sara stopped at the mouth of a wide alley, Reno checked his mount down beside her and said, "Holy blazes, Sara—how are we going to find Ty Mando if we can't even mention his name without taking our lives in our hands?"

"I don't know," Sara said. "I'm starting to wonder if we should find him."

"Yeah, but…"

Reno's attention drifted to where several soldiers stood in a tight circle about midway down the alley. They were grinning and laughing. It appeared they'd surrounded someone, boxing him or her in, and they were jostling the person around. Studying the group more closely, Reno could see a head of brown hair inside the circle of four soldiers wearing the dark-blue, gold-buttoned tunics and yellow-striped slacks of the frontier army.

Long, dark-brown hair.

The girl turned her face toward Reno. Her coal-black eyes flashed angrily. She lurched forward, kicking one of the soldiers in the oysters. As the man stumbled back, groaning loudly and jackknifing over his privates, Reno got a better look at the girl. She appeared at least half-Indian. She wore a knitted blouse and a long wool skirt. A straw basket of eggs lay at her feet, on a bed of burlap. Some of the eggs had broken in the fall, and the yellow yokes shone in the sunlight angling over the rooftops into the alley.

The other soldiers laughed and howled.

One grabbed the girl's arm, leaned in quickly, and kissed her. The kiss was not wanted. The girl jerked her head back and, hardening her jaws, slapped the man across the face.

The other men laughed.

Sara frowned at Reno. "Reno, what are you…?" She followed his gaze to the assault taking place in the alley.

Reno swung his right leg over his saddle horn, dropping straight down to the ground. "Stay with the mounts, sis." He glanced at Apache who stood nearby, showing his teeth at the bluecoats in the alley. "Stay, Apache. Sara, keep him with you."

That wouldn't be too difficult, he knew. Apache was fairly glued to Sara's heels.

"Reno!" Sara called to him. "Let it go. It's none of our affair!"

Reno started into the alley. As he did, the young soldier the girl had kicked in the oysters leaned toward her, grabbed her knit blouse, and ripped it down the middle. He ripped the white cotton chemise beneath it, as well, leaving bare a good bit of copper-toned skin.

The girl gasped and pulled up the torn flaps of her blouse and chemise to cover her bosoms.

"Little squaw witch!" shouted the soldier who'd been kicked in the privates. "How dare you kick me like that? Who in hell's fires do you think you are?"

He was red-faced angry and shoving his head up close to the girl while the other three soldiers laughed, passing a crock jug.

Sara called again, placatingly, but Reno ignored her.

He smelled the whiskey sweat on the soldiers, see the glaze of drink in their eyes. It was time to step in, since other men passing through the alley in both directions did nothing but ignore the soldiers and the girl they were assaulting. Some glanced at them and merely smiled or chuckled and elbowed each other.

Reno could tell Julesburg hadn't become any more civilized since his last visit a couple of years ago. In fact, it had nearly doubled in size and seemed a whole lot rowdier and nastier. Now, a poor Indian girl was being assaulted right out in public.

Not for long.

"Hold on there, friend!" Reno grabbed the arm of the soldier who'd been kicked, and pulled him away from the girl, swinging him around to face him. He was a tall, gangly redhead with close-cropped hair under his leather-billed forage cap, and a thin little mustache mantling his pink lips. Pale and freckle-faced, his eyes were large, cobalt blue and opaque from all the whiskey he and his pards had probably been swilling all day. Maybe for a couple of days. "Can't you see the girl ain't exactly welcoming your attentions?"

The man stared at him, aghast, as did the others. One held onto the girl from behind, pinning her arms behind her back. She struggled against the man, but he only laughed and nuzzled her neck. The redhead looked Reno up and down, his face forming a sour expression.

"Don't touch me, sodbuster!" the redhead fairly screamed, taking a belligerent step forward.

Reno held his hands up, palms out in supplication. "I don't want any trouble, friend. I don't think the girl does, either. Why don't you fellas just leave her alone and go find one a little more willing?"

"Why don't you go to the devil, sodbuster?" screamed the raging redhead.

He took another step forward and swung his right fist at Reno's face. He was drunk and slow, and his fist merely glanced off of Reno's left cheek. Reno barely felt it.

"Hey, now," he said, backing up another step and keeping his hands raised. "I don't see any reason why we can't—"

But then the redhead was on him again, moving forward and swinging his right fist again. This time, Reno easily ducked the blow and, straightening, smacked his right fist into the redhead's mouth. He followed it not a half-second later with his left fist—straight jabs delivered from the middle of his own chest.

They were not hard blows. Reno wanted only to give the soldier a taste of what was to come if he and the others didn't pull their horns in.

The redhead stumbled backward into one of the other soldiers, who pushed him back upright. The redhead stared in astonishment at Reno. He touched two fingers to his lips, and looked at the blood smeared on them.

He spat the blood away and said, "You're gonna die, sodbuster!" He glanced at two of the others. The fourth man, the largest of the bunch, still held the girl, who struggled against him, fighting him, screaming while he pawed her body and nuzzled her neck. "Get around him," the redhead told the other two, both wearing corporals' stripes on their tunic sleeves. "We're gonna show this sodbuster what happens when he sticks his nose in where it don't belong!"

"Reno!" Sara cried behind him.

The three soldiers surrounding Reno took a second to swing their gazes toward where Sara knelt at the alley mouth, holding taut to Apache's rope collar. The dog was glaring and snarling at the soldiers and would have come running if Sara didn't hold him back.

"That your sister?" asked the redhead, turning back to Reno. He shaped a lascivious grin with his bloody lips. "She's right purty. We'll take her next!"

THIRTEEN

That cinched it for Reno. The man's threatening words directed at his sister turned Reno's wolf loose.

A red curtain of raw fury billowed before his eyes as he hurled himself forward, smashing the redhead's mouth again with his fists—two brutal jabs. He ducked as he sensed another soldier bounding toward him on his left. He rammed his right elbow into the belly of the man who'd swung at him from the side. Straightening quickly, he bulled into the third soldier before that man could swing the fist he had cocked, ready to let fly.

The man flew backward, screaming, the back of his head and his shoulders striking the ground hard.

"Reno, behind you!" Sara shouted.

Reno whipped around in time to see the redhead stumbling toward him, his lips bloodier than before, one brow ripped. The redhead had picked up a stout oak post he must have found in the weeds at the alley's perimeter. The other soldier was climbing to a knee, snarling and spitting blood and unholstering the Army Colt 1860-model from the holster on his right hip.

Sara must have released Apache; the dog came running into the alley in a black and white snarling blur. Apache leaped up and grabbed the arm of the soldier retrieving the Colt. The man screamed and dropped the revolver as he tumbled backward, the growling and snarling Apache on top of him.

"Ow—you witch!"

The bellowing wail had come from the big soldier accosting the girl. She must have bit his mouth, because he brushed a hand across his torn lips. When the hand came away bloody, he leaped forward and backhanded her. She screamed and flew to the ground.

Reno stormed over to him. Just as the big man, wearing sergeant's chevrons on his sleeves, turned to Reno, Reno grabbed the front of the man's tunic, whipped him around, and slammed him into the side of the building abutting the alley's east side.

The man cursed and shook his head as though to clear it. He looked at Reno with rage in his eyes, and used both his thick arms to shove Reno away from him.

He glanced at where Apache was still snarling atop

the soldier who'd tried to draw the 1860 Colt, then stepped toward Reno, raising both his big brown fists. Reno bolted at the man. He wasn't afraid of him. He'd fought men larger than this bully before. The man outweighed Reno by about thirty pounds. Most large men were slow. The sergeant was drunk, to boot, and he wasn't half as angry as Reno was. The only thing Reno hated worse than men abusing women was men threatening to abuse his sister.

Reno gritted his teeth and faked a left jab at the big sergeant. Just as the sergeant pulled his head back and to one side to avoid the blow, Reno delivered a savage haymaker that connected with the left side of the sergeant's face.

"Oh!" the man said, lurching backward and covering his face with both hands.

Reno punched him twice in the belly.

The man grunted and bent forward, playing right into Reno's hands.

Fists, rather.

Reno delivered another fierce blow to the man's left temple, then to his right temple. When he straightened partially to stumble back against the side of the building again, Reno hit him three more times. As the man slid down the wall behind him, his eyes rolling up in his head, Reno finished him off with three more punishing blows to his face and both ears.

The man dropped into the brush at the base of the

building, groaning.

Reno turned to where Sara, having pulled Apache off the other soldier, knelt with the dog still showing his teeth at the soldier sobbing in the brush nearby. Reno turned to the girl the men had been trying to savage. He felt a pull in his heart when he saw her on her hands and knees, her blouse badly torn.

Angled away from him, she looked at him over her right shoulder. Her coal-black hair was badly mussed, but enough of her face was exposed that he could see how pretty she was. Her face was vaguely heart-shaped, her mouth broad and firm, the lips full. Her nose was long, tilted ever so slightly up at the end. Her lower lip was cracked and bleeding.

What caught the brunt of Reno's attention, be-sides her rarefied beauty, was that her eyes were not brown as he'd at first thought. Almond-shaped, they were a hauntingly clear blue-green. The soft hazel of a mountain lake in the morning as the very first soft rays of the sun glinted on the water. The girl's eyes were a stunning contrast to the smooth radiant copper of her skin and the perfect sculpting of her high, gently tapering cheekbones. She wasn't really beautiful, though most would probably call her that. But beauty was common.

This girl was at once earthy and exotic.

"What in the bloody tarnation is goin' on back here?"

The thundering voice had come from the mouth of the alley.

Reno and Sara both turned to see a thick-set, middle-aged man in a three-piece suit and bowler hat enter the alley, a long-barreled shotgun in both hands. He wore two pistols on his broad hips. Walking severely bull-legged, he came on down the alley, looking as gruff as the sky before a severe summer storm. He had a large, round, red face framed by thick pewter side-whiskers; his knife-slash mouth was mantled by a full walrus mustache.

"Bloody hell—I should have known Peppers and King would be involved. And Mortimer and Coffee, of course. Where those four tread, trouble follows. Never fails." The man, who wore a five-pointed star pinned to his brown wool vest, raked his bespectacled gaze across the four half-conscious soldiers then looked from Sara and Apache to Reno. "But yours— your mug is new around here, bucko. Fresh trouble, are ya?"

The lawman spoke with a thick accent Reno believed was Irish. Possibly Scottish. Anyway, he more than likely came from a place called Great Britain and which Reno had learned a little about from Miss Cassie Bernard.

"No, sir, I didn't mean for there to be any trouble," Reno said. "I was tryin' to prevent trouble, in fact. These four brigands were harassing the girl over there, and I was just tryin' to discourage them, is all. They didn't discourage easy. And when they threatened my sister, well…"

"What girl?" asked the lawman.

"What's that?"

"What girl you referrin' to, bucko?"

"Why, the girl right over—" Reno stopped as he turned to the girl—who was no longer there.

Sara turned, as well, and frowned.

"She was right over there," Sara told the lawman.

"Honest," Reno said. "There was a girl here. They were harrassin' her, probably would've…well, you know."

"Oh, I know, me laddy. I know what they would have done. Happens often enough in this canker on the devil's arse. I reckon I should thank ya for doin' my job for me. She was probably one of the girls from the line. You know, workin' girl. Doesn't like to be seen with the law even when she needs our help. Bad for business. Prob'ly ran when she heard me comin'." The lawman tilted his head a little and narrowed his eyes behind his glasses, scrutinizing Reno closely. "Tell me, though, what business is it of yours?"

"To keep a girl from gettin' savaged by four drunk soldiers?" Reno asked, incredulous. (Or kill-crazy Confederates? Reno remembered his sister's badly abused body lying in the Bass farmyard, and his anger flared again.) "Isn't it everyone's business?"

The lawman chuckled, showing a gold front tooth. "Well, not everyone would think so." He glanced at Sara and then at Apache sitting beside Sara and giving the lawman the wooly eyeball. "Who are you two, anyways? Three, I should say. I take it the dog's with you."

"I'm Reno Bass," Reno said, extending his hand to the rugged lawman. "This is my sister, Sara. The dog's our pal, Apache."

"Apache, eh?"

"That dog bit me somethin' terrible, Marshal O'Donnell!" shrieked the soldier Apache had lain into. He sat up, groaning and holding his arm. It bled through the torn blue sleeve. "Why, he like to rip my arm clear off and would have if that girl hadn't finally pulled him off'n me. I'll be hanged if it don't hurt somethin' terrible!"

"He did, did he?" said O'Donnell. "Why'd he do that? You wouldn't have been tryin' to shuck that hogleg there, would you, boyo?" The marshal had walked over to the man named Coffee. He crouched to pick up the 1860 Colt .44, and shoved it inside the waistband of his broadcloth trousers.

"That's exactly what he was trying to do," Sara said.

"Bringing a hogleg to a fistfight." O'Donnell clucked reprovingly. "Anderson Coffee, don't you know that ain't fair? Maybe in Deadwood or Abilene, but this ain't Deadwood or Abilene."

"Diddle fair!" Coffee spat blood and dirt from his lips. "That kid's got a haymaker on him like I never seen before. And he moves quick for a big ole sodbuster."

"Yeah, it appears to me he cleaned up right well." O'Donnell chuckled then put some steel in his voice as he leveled his shotgun at the other three soldiers who lay groaning as they regained consciousness. "Rise and shine, soldier boys. You're gonna pay another visit to Sandy O'Donnell's jail, me thinks. How many times do I have to tell Major Canby out to Camp Rankin to stop furloughing you four wretched no-accounts? You're trouble with a capital 'T' and I'm bloody tired of having to put you up and feed you. I got enough civilians who need jailin' and not enough deputies to help me jail 'em."

He frowned as an idea dawned on him. As the soldiers slowly, complainingly regained their feet, O'Donnell turned to Reno. "Say, now…how 'bout it, son? You needin' a job?"

"A job?" Reno said.

"Sure, sure. I could use a capable young deputy. I'll admit, it's dangerous—I just lost a man two days ago. A drunk gambler stabbed him at Curly Kate's. But with your size and strength, and seein' as how you know how to handle yourself…"

"We're just passin' through, I'm afraid."

"Passin' through, are ya?" The marshal glanced at Sara then at Apache, who was showing his teeth at the three groaning and moaning soldiers, looking as though he'd like to chomp into another one for kicks and giggles. "Where you three from, anyway?"

"Little farm near Baxter," Sara said.

"Near Baxter, eh? You wouldn't happen to have run into a little trouble over that way, would ya, sis?"

Reno gave a caustic snort. "If you mean a lot of trouble in the form of that Devil's Horde led by 'Bad Old Man' Colonel Montgomery and Major 'Black Bob' Hobbs, then you'd be right, Marshal O'Donnell." He drew a deep breath, clenching his scraped and bloody fists at his sides. "They burned us out, killed our whole family, most of our stock."

"Ah, bloody damn!" O'Donnell spoke softly, grimly, sucking in his mouth corners as he inspected the two weary-looking towheads and their black-and-white shepherd dog in a whole, new, sad light. "I'm sorry to hear that—purely I am. I got a telegram about them, warning me they might head this way. Happened they turned north just before they crossed into Colorado, and swung up into Nebraska.

"Last I heard they were headed west now, avoiding most towns of any size, mostly riding roughshod over farms and small ranches, don't ya know. They likely avoided Julesburg on account of its size and its bad reputation. If they'd taken on Julesburg, they'd have met their match, and I reckon they were smart enough to know it." He grimaced, shook his head. "Bloody devils is what they are. Black angels it was who sent them, for sure."

While he'd been speaking, two of O'Donnell's deputies had shown up. The marshal turned to them now and ordered them to take the four soldiers off to the jail and then to send word of their incarceration to the commanding officer at For Rankin. As the four bluebellies walked away, the deputies' pistols aimed at their backs, they cast glares at Reno and lusty leers at Sara. The girl had to hold Apache's rope collar to prevent the dog from chomping into an ankle.

Now, with the soldiers and deputies gone, O'Donnell shouldered his shotgun and turned to Reno again. "Where you headed, then? You and the fair lass." He gave an admiring smile, sliding his gaze back to Sara. "You must be twins, or I've missed my guess."

"Twins, all right," Reno said, adding with a grin, "I'm the better lookin' one."

Sara snorted.

Reno continued with: "We're on the trail of those…"

"Ty Mando," Sara cut in quickly, apparently thinking it best they don't relate their grisly aspirations to the lawman, who'd likely try to talk them out of it. "We're on the trail of Ty Mando, my brother means. As he lay dyin', pa told us to look up his old friend Mando in Julesburg. Told us Mr. Mando would help get us back on our feet."

"Mando?" O'Donnell said, incredulous.

"Not you, too!" Reno cried.

O'Donnell canted his head to one side and narrowed his eyes at Reno. "Just who was your father, boyo?"

Reno glanced at Sara, frowning curiously. "John Bass," he told the marshal.

"Ahh!" The marshal smiled broadly, knowingly. "Of course. I should have recognized the surname. John Bass, was he? Well, that explains it."

Sara looked at Reno again then returned her puzzled gaze to the bandy-legged lawman. "Explains what?"

"Uh…never mind, never mind." O'Donnell brushed a fist across his blunt nose. "I tell ya what, I'll tell you where to find Ty Mando if you remind him he's still banned from Julesburg proper for another two weeks it. Do we have a deal?"

"Why is Ty Mando banned from Julesburg proper?" Sara wanted to know.

"Do we have a deal, my two tow-headed avenging angels?" was the lawman's only reply.

Reno looked at Sara. They both flushed. The marshal was onto their plan.

"You got a deal," they both said at the same time.

He told them where to find Ty Mando then strolled away, calling over his shoulder in a tone none too ominous, "You two go with god, if you're goin' after the Devil's Horde. Indeed—go with god, and not even he may be able to help ya!"

Sara rose from where she'd been kneeling beside Apache. "Come on, Reno." She started walking back to where they'd left their horses and mule then stopped to frown at Reno, who stood gazing toward the alley's end. "Reno? What's wrong?"

"That girl." Reno couldn't help remembering the almond-shaped eyes, the hazel of an early-morning, high-country lake, peering out from the face of a Sioux princess. "Who do you suppose she was?"

FOURTEEN

"I wonder if this trail really does lead to Ty Mando's place," Sara said after they'd ridden south of Julesburg and through some prickly pear- and rattlesnake-infested buttes for close to an hour.

"Where else would it lead?"

"Your guess is as good as mine. Maybe it doesn't lead anywhere."

"It leads somewhere, sis. The trail we're followin' has been well-traveled. Recently, too."

"Still..."

Sara had a point. They'd been riding a good forty-five minutes since leaving Julesburg, and they now found themselves in gnarly buttes threaded by old, dry watercourses. The only thing that grew out here was cactus and Spanish bayonet. They'd seen a couple of coyotes—scraggly, wary-eyed beasts skulking off behind cover.

Tired-out from all their traveling, which he wasn't used to, Apache had leaped up to ride behind the cantle of Reno's saddle. The dog liked Sara best, but Sara wouldn't let him ride with her, just like she hadn't let him sleep in her bed back home on account of how she didn't want to get fleas. Apache would sneak into her bed, anyway, after Sara had gone to sleep, and slip out just as she awoke so's not to get a boot or a hair brush thrown at him.

"It's gotta lead somewhere," Reno assured his sister, giving a little inward shudder when he spied what appeared wildcat scat lying on a low, flat rock just off the trail's right side.

Riding just behind Reno and the two horses he was leading, tied tail to tail with Coyote, Sara said, "I'm wondering if Marshal O'Donnell wasn't just trying to get us good and lost and perhaps spare us a grisly end at the hands of 'Bad Old Man' Montgomery and Major Hobbs. I think it was Pa himself who said you can never trust an Irishman."

"Pa never said that."

"He sure did. Don't you remember Mr. Kavanaugh in Baxter?"

Reno laughed. "Yeah, but he's a banker!"

"An Irishman first and foremost, to Pa's eyes."

Reno thought he'd heard a tremor in his sister's voice when she'd said those last two words, "Pa's eyes." He turned his head to gaze back at her. She was staring off, blinking, and by the softening rays of the westering sun, Reno could see tears in her eyes. She was blinking them away to beat the band, and when she turned her head forward to see Reno gazing back at her, they rolled down her cheeks.

She flared her nostrils and hardened her jaws as she said, "What in blue blazes are you lookin' at?"

"It's all right, Sara," Reno said gently.

"What's all right?"

"To miss Ma and Pa and Ben an' James an' Mary Louise."

An angry pallor climbed into Sara's cheeks, shaded slightly by her floppy-brimmed felt hat. "No, it's not! Not until Montgomery and Hobbs and all the rest of those grayback devils are dead!"

The fury of his sister's words rocked Reno back on his proverbial heals. He turned his head forward and heaved a weary sigh. "All right, Sara," he said quietly, mostly to himself. "Have it your way."

Coyote took three more strides, then Reno drew back abruptly on the reins. "Whoa!"

"What is it?" Sara said, stopping the mule behind the pinto and the two spare mounts it was trailing. She must have heard it, too, then, because she said, "Oh..."

The sounds rose from ahead along the trail. Reno stared up the chalky hill they were climbing, listening to what could only be the din of rollicking men.

It sounded similar to the way Baxter sometimes sounded from a distance during some civic festival or a national holiday like the Fourth of July.

Somewhere ahead, men were whooping and hollering and laughing in celebration—a good dozen or so, Reno judged.

Reno glanced back at Sara, one brow arched with speculation, then booted Coyote on up the hill. As he crested the hill and started down the other side, he saw they were entering a brush-choked river course. The bottom was muddy. Off to his left, to the south, stretched the broad, brown-green expanse of the South Platte River. It traced a broad curve over there. Because of the buttes cropping up all around, only a short stretch was visible.

Reno urged Coyote into a trot, crossing the muddy ravine quickly. Meanwhile the voices raised in revelry grew louder from dead ahead. Reno and Coyote crested the next butte, and again Reno reined in the horse.

As Sara rode up to stop the mule beside him, he stared down into a flat area inside a broad horseshoe of the South Platte and up a rise from the broad glistening waters, which lay maybe a half a mile away. Several age-silvered plank or log buildings, including pole corrals and barns and smaller shacks were arranged around a windmill.

The largest of these buildings was a sprawling

notched log and stone affair. Divided into two sections by a foxtrot running down the middle, it proudly announced itself in red letters painted across a large sign stretched across the building's high false facade:

TY MANDO'S GENERAL STORE.

Reno smiled at Sara. "See? I told you we could trust the Irishman."

Ignoring the comment, Sara frowned at the crowd gathered inside a large corral off to the right side of the main building. Many saddled horses were tied outside the corral, and a few wagons sat nearby as well, horses standing hang-headed in the traces. "What do you suppose all the hullabaloo is about?"

"I don't know," Reno said, batting his heels against the pinto's sides. "Let's ride down and find out. And find Ty Mando, to boot."

He rode down the low hill and into the yard. As he did, a shaggy brown and white dog came running out from beneath one of the wagons parked outside the corral inside of which all the commotion was occurring. The dog appeared a mixed-blood collie; it was dusty and burr-ridden. It also looked to be older and a little gone to seed. In other words, it was fat. She was fat, rather, Reno saw.

Behind Reno, Apache gave a yip then leaped down from Coyote's back. He ran over to greet the brown and white dog running toward them with a slight arthritic hitch in her gait. The dogs stepped tentatively up to each other, tails stiff. When they each had agreed to be friendly, they went to wagging their tails and sniffing each other's behinds, which was the dogs' way of shaking hands.

Reno stopped the pinto beside the round stone stock tank ringing the base of the windmill and swung down from the saddle. He released the saddle thongs on all three mounts, so they could drink freely at the trough, then walked toward the corral. When Sara had given the mule the same treatment Reno had given the horses, she fell into stride beside him.

They peered curiously at the men sitting atop the corral fence, facing the others gathered in a circle inside the corral.

Reno climbed the fence near a couple of gray-bearded old-timers and a young Indian man who held a wad of money in one hand, a small leather notebook and a pencil stub in the other hand. The old graybeards were talking and laughing with the young Indian man, who was dressed like a white man in denim trousers, calico shirt, and broadcloth jacket. A beaded thong hung around his neck. His inky-black hair hung in twin braids down his back, and as Reno climbed the rails to the young man's right, feeling a little awkward and hesitant, being a stranger here and not knowing what kind of bailiwick he'd ridden into, he saw that the young man wore small, round spectacles on his long, fine nose, which gave him a sensitive, learned look.

Reno peered into the corral and saw two men facing off against each other inside the circle of men surrounding them. The two men were fighting with their bare hands. They were both big men, and older—Reno guessed mid-fifties.

One had long, thick gray hair and a gray beard, and he stood a little over six feet tall. The other man was maybe a little younger; he was also taller by four or five inches, giving him the advantage over the other man. He appeared a full-blood Indian, and his long, greasy black hair was threaded with silver. He wore deer leggings, moccasins, and a collarless poplin shirt under a beaded buckskin vest. A medicine pouch dangled down his chest from a braided leather thong around his neck.

The white man was clad in a calico shirt and fringed buckskin trousers, the whang strings of which danced as he and the other man punched and feinted as they shuffled around a hole in the ground. They each chomped into an end of a leather strap maybe eight feet long. The competition, Reno saw, was to see who would release his end of the leather strap first while being assaulted by the clenched fists of his opponent as they danced around the hole.

Reno wasn't sure what the hole was for. Wasn't the strap enough to keep them within striking distance of each other? Or was another aspect of the competition to see if they could pull the other one into the hole?

The hole was roughly three feet in diameter. Something appeared to be moving around inside it. Moving quickly. Occasionally, as the men kicked up dirt around the hole, punching and feinting and landing solid, smacking blows on their opponent's face, Reno saw something inside the hole darting suddenly toward the men's moccasin-clad feet and ankles. Reno couldn't make out what that thing was, for late afternoon shadows had stretched across the yard of the general store, and the hole was a murky brown blur.

The dust rising around the men's ankles caught the late light, and glowed with a mix of butternut and copper.

While the fighters punched and feinted, delivering quick uppercuts and nasty hooks and crosses, the men on the corral or in the crowd surrounding the fighters insulted the fighters' bloodlines and the propriety of their mothers until Reno felt his cheeks warm. The spectators laughed and cheered, great volleys of bawdy mirth rising from the crowd when one of the spectators cut loose with a particular colorful bit of insolent wit.

It was obvious to Reno that the men in the crowd were trying to rattle whichever fighter they'd bet against, trying to distract him, thus helping the other man win.

Neither appeared to have the advantage, however. The crowd's interests seemed equally split.

Despite the savagery of the battle, the overall tone of the competition seemed to be one of good cheer...until the Indian let out a sudden shrill grunt and reached down toward his lower right leg. He crouched forward, exposing his face, and the white man took advantage, hammering the Indian's fleshy, pockmarked left cheek with a solid right cross.

Half the crowd laughed and cheered. The other half booed.

The Indian straightened, narrowing his dark eyes at his opponent, who grinned jeeringly around the leather strap clamped between his jaws. The white man's long, thick gray hair danced around his craggy, bearded face sun-burnt to the chestnut of a full-blood Sioux but set with one blazing green eye. The other eye was hidden behind a black patch.

Enraged, the Indian swung at him from the other side of the hole. The punch missed, and the white man grinned around the strap in his teeth and delivered an uppercut to the red man's chin.

That enraged the Indian even more, and he leaned farther over the hole, carelessly swinging a haymaker. He'd gotten his large fist only halfway over the hole, however, before he jerked his left leg back suddenly, giving another startled and injured grunt. That time, Reno saw the flat head of what could only have been a snake leap up out of the hole and sink its fangs into the red man's leg, just below the knee.

As the tooth-gnashing sound of an enraged viper's rattle emanated from the hole and which Reno could hear in the fleeting ebbs in the crowd's din, Reno realized with a crawling feeling in his own belly that the two men were fighting over a hole writhing with rattlesnakes.

As the snake pulled its head back into the hole, the Indian's jaws loosened and the strap nearly fell from his mouth before he dug his teeth into it once more.

Grinning delightedly, that one green eye glowing like a chunk of pure jade, the white man hit him again.

Again, a snake darted up out of the hole, flinging its head toward the Indian's left leg. Reno saw a slender, curving shadow, like the silhouette of a tossed lariat. A lightning-fast lariat. The sand-colored head winked briefly in the waning sunlight as the snake again dug its fangs into the red man's flesh before dropping back into the hole.

That was enough for the Indian, who dropped his end of the strap and leaped back, falling to the ground on his butt and clutching his left leg, yelling and writhing.

The white man dropped his end of the strap, as well, and raised his bloody fists high above his head in victory. Half the crowd roared while the other half groaned and punched the air in defeat.

The young Indian man sitting to Reno's left clambered down off the fence and limped into the crowd. He appeared to have a bad leg. Consulting his notebook, he counted money out of a hat and distributed it to the winners while the losers slowly quit the group and headed for the corral fence where they'd tied their horses and parked their wagons.

The happy gamblers patted the white man's back and shoulders, congratulating him on his victory while three others crouched over the red man who sat up now, his left leg stretched out before him. As the crowd continued to disperse, the winners now having gathered their winnings from the young Indian's hat and also returning to their horses and wagons, Reno leaped down from the fence and touched the shoulder of one man counting the gold coins in his palm and laughing with the man walking along beside him.

"Excuse me, sir," Reno said, "but is Ty Mando out here somewhere?"

The man stopped and scowled at Reno. He looked the young man up and down and then glanced at the girl standing beside him, and said, "Who's askin'?"

The man beside him, a fat man with a red beard and a leather slouch hat, leaned across his friend to rest the point of a big bowie knife against the underside of Reno's chin. Reno tilted his chin up, wincing, as the red-bearded man snarled, "Land o' Goshen, pup, don't you know it ain't polite to ask questions out here? That question right there's likely to get your ears cut off, dried, and hung around the neck of men less polite than Boyd an' me are!"

"S-Sorry about that," Reno said tensely, staring down his nose at the knife kissing the tender flesh beneath his chin.

Red Beard pulled his knife away from Reno's chin, sheathed it on his voluminous waist, and walked off with Boyd, laughing as they climbed heavily over the corral fence.

FIFTEEN

"Ty!" The cry had come from outside the corral. "Ty Mando, you incorrigible old catamount!"

The invective had been nearly drowned by the drumming of hooves and the clatter of a wagon's wheels. Reno and Sara swung their heads to peer over the corral.

Most of the men who'd enjoyed the festivities here at Ty Mando's General Store were leaving by two's and three's on horseback or in small ranch supply wagons. A buckboard wagon drawn by a steeldust pony, however, was just then entering the yard at a spanking trot. It was driven by a woman in a plain gingham dress and with a thick curly bush of silver-gray hair blowing behind her head in the wind.

She fairly crackled with fury as she brought the steeldust to a halt just outside the corral, near where one man was opening the corral gate while two others helped the big Indian, the loser in the fistfight over a rattlesnake hole, out into the yard. The Indian was moaning, his head lolling back on his shoulders. He could barely put any weight on his left foot; each time that foot merely touched the ground, he loosed an agonized wail at the sky.

"Ty Mando!" the woman cried again, pausing to regard the big red man being carried out of the corral. She turned to glare, bayonets of raw fury glinting in her eyes, at the big white fighter standing inside the corral and whose cut and bruised face was being tended by the young Indian who'd been holding the kitty.

"Sakes and devils!" bellowed the gray-haired white man as both he and the young Indian man with braids turned to regard the enraged female. "Who in the Sam Hill told Colleen?"

The woman leaped down off the wagon and strode angrily through the corral gate, glancing at the two men helping the Indian and jerking her chin at the wagon behind her. "Get him in the buckboard. I'll be back shortly!"

The woman looked especially frightening with all that curly silver hair blowing around her head like a tumbleweed in the wind. Sort of crazy-like, witch-like. Her blue-eyed face was long and bony, pretty at one time but careworn. Reno could see her clearly as she passed him and Sara from only a couple of feet away. She fairly reeked of unbridle rage.

Reno, Sara, the white man, the Indian boy, and now the enraged woman were the only folks left inside the corral. All the others seemed to be making an especially hasty retreat now with the angry woman's sudden appearance.

"What have I told you, Ty?" She stopped before the big, bruised white man, whose battered face was framed by his long, thick gray hair. She looked up at him, fists planted on her slender hips. "What have I told you about encouraging him to fight over that viper pit?"

"Now, hold on, just hold on, Colleen!" said the one-eyed man who was obviously none other than the elusive Ty Mando himself, backing up a couple of anxious steps and holding his battered hands out defensively. "I didn't encourage Black Owl one whit. The fight was all his doin's. He was crowin' around about how he could lick me after all these years and—"

"I told you not to fight anymore, and I meant it, you stupid old devil!" With that, she brought up a haymaker from her knees and smashed it against Mando's left cheek. Stepping back, she hitched up her skirts with both hands, cocked her right foot clad in a black side-button leather boot, and thrust it up and forward, landing the kick in the worst possible place a fella could have one land.

Ty Mando bellowed a coyote-like wail and jackknifed forward over his injured privates. He dropped heavily to his knees, groaning.

"Pa!" the young Indian man said, dropping to a knee beside his father. He looked up at the woman, who'd swung around to march back in the direction of her wagon, and said, "You had no call to do that, Aunt Colleen! Pa didn't encourage Uncle Black Owl. Black Owl got likkered up and started bragging about—"

Swinging back around, Aunt Colleen cut the young man off with: "You keep him on his leash, Peter, or what I just gave my stupid wretch of an uncivilized brother here today will seem like fresh cream in his coffee!"

She dipped her chin to stamp the threat.

She swung around once more and strode forthrightly, head in the air, to the wagon.

Ty Mando lifted his face, bloated and red with misery, and shouted, "Any good Lakota oughta be able to take a couple of rattlesnake bites. Black Owl's gone soft, and that's why his folks is goin' the way of the buffalo!"

Aunt Colleen climbed into the wagon, ripped the reins from where she'd tied them around the wagon brake, and spoke loudly in what Reno took to be some Indian tongue. Probably Lakota, though he didn't understand a lick of it. When she was finished, she whipped the reins over the pony's back, turned the wagon around, and headed back in the direction from which she'd come, not slowing to ease the pain of the howling Indian reclining against feed sacks in the back.

"Oh, you mean old she-lion!" Mando bellowed at his sister's back, still red-faced with fury, that lone jade eye fairly glowing.

When the wagon was gone, the young Indian man, Peter, said quietly: "You all right, Pa? She didn't hurt you too bad, now, did she?"

"She's hurt me worse."

"Can you stand?"

"Sure, sure. I can stand. Hell, I don't got me a lick of Injun blood, but I'm still more Injun than that wretched uncle of yours."

"Ah, come on, Pa," Peter said, gently. "Uncle Black Owl's an all right sort. He just got into the squeezin's is all, just like last time. You shouldn't have let him fight over the pit."

"No. No, I shouldn't." Mando turned to his son and grinned. "I reckon I got into the squeezin's myself. And we had a high old time, didn't we? Just like the old days. Me an' Black Owl over the viper pit."

"Yeah, I could tell you were enjoying yourself."

"Never could take the poison, though—Black Owl. That always bothered him somethin' terrible. Not even when he was a younker. Still felt he had to prove himself after all these years."

Mando stared speculatively at the viper pit that had gone ominously still and quiet. All at once, he turned to where Reno and Sara stood near the corral's open gate, feeling suddenly out of place and wishing they'd come at a different time. Not on the heels of a family squabble, though the viper pit fight had been a thing to see...

"Hey, you two," Mando said.

Reno glanced around as though believing the man might be calling someone else. But there was no one else in the corral except himself and Sara. Reno placed his thumb against his chest.

"Yeah, you..." He glanced at Sara. "And you." He beckoned. "Help me up. Peter's got a bum hip regards a bronc he tried to bust when he was ten years old. Help me up and over to the cabin and I'll set you on your way."

Reno and Sara shared a vaguely puzzled, speculative glance.

They strode over to where Ty Mando sat on his butt in the corral dirt, his bespectacled half-breed son standing over him, regarding the two towheads quizzically but with an affable smile on his clean-lined, handsome face.

Peter's light-brown eyes were intelligent behind his round-rimmed spectacles. He seemed particularly interested in Sara. Reno didn't find that peculiar. Most boys took particular interest in his sister, comely despite her dressing like a boy and sorely lacking in hygiene.

Reno didn't find himself bristling at the young man's attentions. He didn't favor her with a leering, hungry look like most males did. The young Indian smiled at her admiringly, warmly.

Reno looked down at the big, gray-haired, one-eyed man. "So...you're Ty Mando..." For some reason he hadn't pictured him this way—wild, rugged, half-drunk, foul-mouthed, bloodied from battle. Complete with a rattlesnake pit. In short, a curly wolf of the long-coulee variety. His father had been a pious, taciturn man who'd lived his life by the Good Book and the Golden Rule. This man...well...from what Reno had seen so far of him, did anything but.

Mando narrowed his lone eye curiously, suspiciously. "Boy, you're lookin' at me queer. Purely, you are. She is, too. Yes, indeed, I am Tiberius Ezekiel Mandrake, 'Ty Mando' for short an' ever since I was knee-high to a jackrabbit. This is my son, Peter."

He canted his head to the young Indian, who offered both Reno and Sara a warm smile. He dipped his chin to Sara and left his gaze on her. "Pleased to meet you."

"Peter, don't fall all over yourself." Mando raked his eye across the two big pistols bristling from behind Sara's wide, brown belt. "That girl looks like she could eat you alive and suck the marrow from your bones." He extended his hand to Reno. "Help an old man with sore oysters up, now, will ya, an' I'll point you wherever you're intendin' to go."

"What do you mean?" Sara asked. "We came here to find you."

Reno wrapped his hand around Mando's. The older man set his boots in the dirt, and Reno pulled him to his feet. Mando grunted, cursed, stumbled back a step, then got his own high-topped, mule-eared moccasins set in the finely churned dung and dirt of the corral.

He scowled at Sara. "You did? I thought you was lost. Maybe strayed from one of the immigrant trains that pull through here from time to time. Too many folks bleedin' into this land, an' more'll be comin' now that the War of Southern Rebellion is over. I even heard they're makin' plans for a railroad way out here." His lone, suspicious eye shifted to Reno. "Who are you pups, pray tell?"

"Reno and Sara Bass," Reno told him.

Mando just stared at him, a grim understanding flickering across his eye. "You don't say..." He spread his arms. "Help me inside. I'll be hanged if sweet ole Sis didn't kick me hard. And I didn't land right, neither. Gettin' old..."

Reno ducked under one of the man's arms; Sara ducked under the other arm. Peter hovered nearby, looking concerned for his father, who stood a good foot or so taller than the slender young half-breed who looked like a full-breed to Reno's inexperienced eyes. Peter had found a carved wooden cane, and was leaning on it. Mando rested most of his weight on his two benefactors, and they turned him around and headed for the open corral gate. Peter followed, using the cane and swinging out his stiff left leg.

The yard had cleared out now. Only the two dogs remained. Apache and the brown and white shepherd bitch were cavorting crazily over by the windmill and circular stone stock trough. Shadows had slid down the buttes and into the yard, casting an early twilight over Ty Mando's General Store and its accompanying corrals and outbuildings.

"That was your sister?" Reno said, incredulous.

"Yep, yep."

"Boy, she sure treated you harsh for a sister. Sara's never even…"

He glanced across Mando's broad, lumpy chest at his sister. She gave him a snide look and said, "Just keep mindin' your P's an' Q's, brother."

Mando chuckled throatily. "Colleen loves her older brother, she does. She just likes to remind me from time to time who's boss. Ain't that kinda the way it is with you two, Master Bass?"

"Oh, I don't need remindin'," Reno said with an ironic snort.

"Bass, Bass," Mando said, wincing against the pain

in his various regions, likely from blows delivered by both his brother-in-law as well as his sister. "That's a name I ain't heard in a while. A name from back deep in the years." His voice was pitched with dark speculation as he aimed his lone eye at Reno and Sara in turn. "Tell me, children, what happened to bring you here? I know it's bad, because your ma never woulda let…"

He stopped when a buckboard wagon clattered down the southeastern buttes and into the yard. "Oh, don't tell me she's back for another…" Mando stopped. Reno, too, had first thought Mando's half-crazy sister, Colleen, had returned to deliver another round of punishment to her older brother. But just as Reno saw that the driver of the wagon was a younger woman with dark hair, Mando said with relief, "Oh…Isabelle…"

"Pa!" the girl cried as he galloped the fine black Morgan in the traces over to where Reno and Sara were helping Mando toward the General Store hulking on the north edge of the yard. She set the buckboard's brake, leaped to the ground, her calico skirt rising enticingly before settling back down to her slender ankles rising above beaded moccasins.

She ran over to Reno, Sara, and Ty and Peter Mando. A purple scarf with white polka dots disguised her face but could not restrain her thick, coal-black hair. As she ran, the jouncing tresses assaulted the scarf until the knot beneath her chin pulled loose, and the scarf fluttered off her head to sail away on the breeze.

As she approached the group standing just outside the open corral gate, she halted, swept her hair back from her face with one hand, and opened her mouth to speak.

She stopped when her eyes met Reno's. Reno gaped at her in open-mouthed shock. Her own lips parted as she stared back at him.

The waning light found the girl's eyes the luminous blue-green of a high-country lake in the early morning.

SIXTEEN

Ty Mando looked between the young woman with
the amazing hazel eyes and who was apparently,
improbably, his daughter, to Reno. Mando's craggy
features creased with as much befuddlement as was
likely on Reno's face, and said, "You two've, uh...
met...have ya?"

Reno hesitated.

Staring at him gravely, the girl gave her head a
quick, covert shake. Before either one of them or
Sara, who appeared as astonished to see the young
Indian woman here as Reno was, could say anything,
Mando reached forward, cupped the girl's chin in his
big hand, and tipped her head back and to one side to
get a look at the blood on her lower lip and the slight
bruising around her left eye, where the big sergeant
had smacked her in the alley back in Julesburg.

Mando hardened his jaws. Anger glinted in his

lone eye, which owned the same almond shape as his daughter's, and said, "Isabelle...?"

"It's nothin', Pa." Isabelle glanced from Reno to Sara, quietly shushing them both, then turned back to her father. "I tripped over a boardwalk in town, is all. You know how clumsy I am. Broke a whole dozen eggs I was trying to sell, too, galldangit."

She cast another furtive admonishing glance at Reno.

Mando wasn't buying it. "No, you didn't! Tell me what—!"

"What happened to you, Pa? Have you been fighting over that viper pit again? Oh, Pa, tell me you haven't!"

"He has," Peter put in.

Isabelle's angry-bright gaze shifted to her brother, and her lips pursed with even more anger. "And you let him?"

"Well," Peter said, giving a sheepish shrug. "He did bring in twenty dollars..."

"Peter!" Isabelle gave her brother a good half-dozen slaps about the head and shoulders. Peter raised his hands and lowered his head to avoid the brunt of the blows. Something told Reno it was a maneuver he'd become good at by necessity over the years.

"Here, here!" Mando objected. "Pull your horns in, chillens! You were not raised by wolves!"

Was it the same with brothers and sisters of every race and generation?

Glancing at Reno and Sara, both crouched with a thick arm of her father around their necks, Isabelle said with disgust, "Bring him on inside and I'll start tending to that face." She turned to start toward the main building but stopped and glanced curiously back at Reno once more, wondering who he and Sara were and what they were doing here, most likely. Her curiosity could be satisfied later.

She swung around again and hurried off to the main building, aiming for the door on the right side of the dogtrot and which more than likely opened onto the family's living area.

"Oh, boy, gonna be hell to pay now," Mando said fatefully to Peter, as Reno and Sara began leading the injured man toward the main building once more.

"I told you, Pa."

"Yeah, well, I live for the moment." Mando chuckled deeply, almost silently. "Anything to shut up than insufferable rock-worshippin' brother-in-law of mine. Say, look there." He glanced toward where Apache and the shaggy brown-and-white collie were playing tug of war with a bloody rabbit carcass. "Looks like our sweet old Sabrina has finally found herself a man. Is that dog yours, children?"

"We're his, more like," Reno said.

"That's Reno's dog," Sara said. "I have no time for the flea-infested varmint."

Mando chuckled, then cut loose with a string of

curse words that brought deep flushes to Reno and Sara's recently sunburned cheeks as they led him up the painful half-dozen steps to the porch fronting the general store.

"I apologize for my father's blue tongue," Peter said, pulling his mouth corners down in shame as he held the door open, leaning on his cane. "You get used to it after awhile. Don't even hear it."

He smiled at Sara.

She shook her hair over her left eye, ignoring him, as she and Reno helped the young man's father over the threshold and into the house.

"Set him down at the table," Isabelle said as she ladled water from a warm reservoir on the giant black range that sat in the kitchen part of the big house yawning before Reno and Sara.

The lower floor was a large open area divided by a stairway running up the middle of it, roughly twenty feet straight back of the front door. To the left sprawled a large parlor area outfitted with heavy wood and leather furniture—mostly hand-hewn, it appeared—as well as a great fieldstone fireplace abutting the rear wall.

Animal heads stared blankly down from the pine-paneled walls; hides and skins served as rugs. The kitchen lay to the right, dominated by a heavy wooden table scarred from much use. Open cupboards were stuffed with all manner of staples in the form of tin cans, small boxes, and burlap pouches and such. Pots, pans, kettles, and sausages hung from the ceiling. Old muskets and accouterment bags leaned in shadowy corners. Coats, scarves, hats, and leather tack hung from wooden pegs.

The place had a heady, almost intoxicating aroma of old leather, molasses, pine smoke, coffee and cured meats.

While Peter shoved the clutter of dirty dishes and a coffee grinder to one side of the table, making way for his father, Reno and Sara eased Mando into a stout wooden hide-bottom chair.

"That's it, that's it," Mando grunted, stretching his lips back from long, crooked teeth as he settled his weight in the creaking chair. "Thank you, children. Thankee. Appreciate that."

He swept some of the clutter, including part of a loaf of crusty brown bread on a cutting board to another part of the table, and said, "Have a seat your ownselves and tell ole Ty what brought you here." He glanced at his son. "Peter, bring a jug of wine. These two need a taste of my chokecherry wine to cut the trail dust. They've come long an' far an', by the green showin' around their gills, they been through somethin' purty prickly."

He leveled a grave look at Reno and Sara. "Am I right?"

"You don't need any more drink, Pa." Isabelle carried a bowl of steaming water and a couple of cloths over to the table. Even scowling reprovingly, Reno thought she was about the most beautiful girl he'd ever seen. Young woman, rather. He guessed she was right around his and Sara's age. "Looks like you and your cronies have been partying it up in the store, and that's what led to the fight over the viper pit."

"No, what led to the fight over the viper pit was your uncle Black Owl getting into the squeezin's an' braggin' about how many times he beat me over the pit an' that I couldn't fight anymore because I was an old white man now, an' white men went to seed earlier than his people. When white men get old, they got soft, he said. Ha!"

He slammed a big hand down on the table, knocking a tin cup to the floor.

"Just the same, you shouldn't drink anymore and you shouldn't fight Uncle Black Owl or anyone else." The young woman clucked as she drew her own chair up close to her father and began dabbing at his cut lips and cheeks with a steaming cloth. She must have poured some root medicine into the warm water, for the steam climbing from the bowl smelled of boiled bark and mint.

Mando smiled fondly at his daughter as she cleaned a cut on his right cheek. "Don't mind Isabelle, children. She's just tryin' to fill the shoes of her mother, gone now these three years." He shifted his gaze to

Reno and Sara, who now sat at the table, too. Mando caught Reno staring at his daughter, and said, "Ain't she a beauty?"

He slid a lock of black hair from Isabelle's radiant cheek. "A rare one, my half-breed princess."

Reno's cheeks warmed. They grew hotter when Sara peered at him and rolled her eyes as though to say, "Here we go again. Reno's tumbling."

Isabelle glanced at him. When her eyes met his, she looked quickly down at the cloth she was wringing out again in the pink-tinged water, and went back to work on her father's cuts and bruises. The reproving scowl returned to her lips. Mando leaned forward and pecked her forehead with a father's affection, and said, "Won't you tell me what happened in town, my butterfly? You know I don't like you going into Julesburg alone. You're young and beautiful, and there's bad men there."

"Yes, there are bad men there," Isabelle said, in her alluringly raspy, slightly husky voice. "Bad men like you. That's why you've been banished for the next two weeks. Don't forget. But, then, there are bad men like you everywhere, Poppa"—she pressed her lips with genuine affection to his forehead—"and someone has to sell eggs and restock the larder."

"You could take Peter."

"He dawdles in the gun store when we have enough guns here. Or at the bookseller's wagon." Isabelle shifted her admonishing gaze to her brother, who had just set two small glass goblets filled with blood-red wine on the table before Reno and Sara.

"Besides, there's worse men than me in Julesburg now," Mando said, glancing at Reno and Sara. "Did you two children come that way? You must have. Around here, all trails lead to Julesburg."

"Yes." Reno glanced at Isabelle. This time she did not return his look.

"We asked for you, Mr. Mando," Sara said. "It was like asking for a jug of whiskey at a seminary." She glanced at the glass of wine sitting before her on the table, and the skin above the bridge of her nose creased. She slid glass away.

Mando had cut up at her comment, laughing and making it hard for Isabelle to tend him. "My reputation precedes me in Julesburg, it purely does." He seemed proud of that fact. "I have my friends and I have my enemies."

"Pa cuts a wide swath," Peter said from the rocking chair beside the range and in which he rocked gently, holding on his lap a small badger he'd plucked out of a box behind the chair. The badger, maybe half-grown, purred like a cat as the young half-breed stroked it with his long, oddly feminine fingers.

To Reno, Mando said, "I used to get roaring drunk and tear the place up. Practically the whole darn town. And I cheat at cards. I also used to run a little wide of the law. What's worse—I married a full-blood Lakota. The good men and ladies in Julesburg don't approve." He sipped from his wine glass. He glanced at Sara's glass and then at Reno's and frowned. "Don't imbibe?"

"No," Sara said primly.

"We were taught that spirituous liquids are Satan's tonic," Reno said.

"Ah." Mando smiled. "That would be your dear old ma. She saved him."

Sara frowned. "Saved who?"

"Why, your pa, of course."

"What did he need savin' from?" Reno asked, feeling his hackles raise a little, defensively.

"Why, from himself, of course." Mando chuckled deep in his throat and studied Reno and Sara each in turn. "You don't know."

"Our pa was a good man," Sara said with quiet defiance.

Mando opened his mouth to speak but stopped when Isabelle pinched his furry chin between her thumb and index finger and gave him a direct look, shaking her head. "Pa..."

Mando wrapped his hand around his daughter's hand, and lowered it from his chin, holding it.

To Reno and Sara, he said, "Your pa was the best man I ever met. He saved my life in Mexico twice. The first time he carried me to safety behind a caisson while musket balls fell like rain and the six-pounder cannons blasted away like thunder from hell's bowels. The second time was at Fort Brown on the Rio Grande, near Matamoros. The Mexican Infantry overran us. I lost this eye there. Your pa took a bayonet in the side before killing his attacker with his musket, bayoneting another, and hauling my useless carcass off to safety in the thick brush of an arroyo. He got the bleeding stopped or I woulda died. We became blood brothers then, as far as we both was concerned. After the war, we ran with our tails up—him an' me. Yeah, we did some stupid things. Crazy things. I won't go into it, but we was outlaws, your pa an' me."

"Our pa?" Reno said in astonishment.

"Me longer than him. He went back home, married up with your ma, found the Lord, moved out here to Kansas Territory. This was all Kansas back then. I'd written to him. Or..." Mando cleared his throat and gave a wry grin. "I reckon I should say I had a purty young lady"—his smile broadened, his eyes flashing bawdily—"write it for me since I couldn't read nor write back then, though I've learned a few letters by now. Leastways, enough to write my name."

He chuckled again.

"Anyway, I wrote your pa, told him what a wide-open, free country it was out here on the high plains. As yet unsettled. Rich land in the bottoms. Plenty of game. Big herds to be brought up from Mexico for a pretty price. Injuns weren't so bad back then."

He cast a fond grin at his half-Indian children. "So he came out here to Kansas. The thing of it was, you see, your ma didn't go much for ole Ty Mando. I'd just opened this post at the junction of two Injun an' white man trading routes. And the Overland Trail, which splits off near here. I was distilling whiskey and drinking half myself, and cavorting with fallen women."

He glanced at his children again, and assured them, "This was before your mother, my sweet lil' Summer Night's Moon."

"Oh, yes, I love how you've given up drinking, Pa." Isabelle glanced at the wine glass before her father, and smiled. Her eyes danced. Even frowning, she was pretty. But smiling, she reached an invisible hand into Reno's chest and gave it one-quarter counter-clockwise turn.

He could have stared at her forever. Not eating. Not sleeping. Not using the privy. Just staring at her. Obviously, she loved her father very much. It reminded Reno of his love for his own father, gone now because of the marauding Confederates.

Mando snorted then turned back to Reno and Sara. "He came with your ma and one child."

"That would be Ben," Reno said. "The rest of us were born out on the farm near Baxter."

Mando nodded. "We seen each other a few times, John an' me. He took a drink with me for old time's sake, and that was the last one I bet he ever took. Next time I seen him was in Julesburg, and he explained how your ma set him straight after he'd confessed his transgressions, told as how him and me couldn't carry on like we did in the old days. Times had changed. At least, for him. He tried to put me onto the Good Book, and while I gave it a try, it didn't take. Even when I had a purty sweet thing read to me from it."

Another bawdy chuckle.

"I found my own good woman soon after, though. A Lakota goddess. Like I said, she's gone now these three years, the hardest of my life. I couldn't have endured it without her children here by my side, lending comfort. They give me a reason to live, my children." He smiled at Peter, who returned his father's affectionate gaze while stroking the little badger that had fallen asleep in his lap, purring like a kitten.

Mando kissed his daughter's forehead then brushed tears of emotion from his cheeks with one hand. He turned to Reno and Sara. He hardened his jaws, and his lone eye shone with terror and anger.

"What happened to my friend John Bass, children?"

SEVENTEEN

Reno took a walk after the supper Sara had helped Isabelle cook—an elk loin roasted in chokecherry wine with beets, new potatoes, wild onions and asparagus.

Reno hadn't eaten a good meal since the murder of his family, much less enjoyed one. He'd enjoyed tonight's meal immensely, even with the retelling of his family's tragedy still fresh in his mouth. In fact, he couldn't remember ever enjoying a meal so much. Isabelle was not only beautiful, but she could cook. Reno suspected her mother had taught her well.

Silently, he wondered at the ability of the soul and the heart to heal. The loss of his parents, brothers, and sister was still an open wound, but after only a few days, he could feel it already beginning to scab over. He'd buried the young woman whom he'd deemed the love of his life, Miss Cassie Bernard, only a few days ago, as well, and still over the supper he'd eaten hungrily and with great relish, he'd stolen glances across the table at Isabelle Mando, and felt his heart swell.

Was time such a great healer, or was he just fickle?

Or maybe he and Sara had been so distracted by going after their family's killers that they wouldn't feel the full impact of the tragedy until later, after the killers were dead.

They'd talked into the early evening about the killings and the men who'd committed them, and about John Bass's mandate of vengeance. No one had thought of supper until they'd begun to run out of words. Now it was almost good dark, just a few red streaks of sunlight left in the west, so Reno picked his course carefully along the narrow pale ribbon of trail that led out of Mando's yard to the west and, he hoped, the river.

He felt drawn to water, for some reason. Water had always soothed him, and he felt the need for a few quiet moments by a stream.

Apache followed him and so did Apache's new friend, the stout, affable Sabrina, both dogs occasionally stopping to leap for mice in the brush or to chase a peeping gopher.

The trail dropped down the side of the hill, threaded a fringe of willows, and disappeared at the water's edge. To the right of the path, revealed in the last, watery green light of the twilight, lay a small pile of deer beans and the upside-down heart-shaped indentations of deer tracks. Both looked relatively fresh. A deer had paused here for a drink from the river, and moved on. Possibly, it had fled when it had heard Reno and the dogs. The dogs busily sniffed the ground around the tracks, scenting the deer, then shot off through the brush downstream, hot on the chase.

Reno stared out over the silent, dark-brown water lightly brushed here and there with salmon and saffron. The water smelled gamey from the muddy compost of rot from which the river bulrushes and other water weeds grew. He didn't mind the smell. It smelled like life. He drew a deep breath.

Something thumped in the brush to his left.

He turned to it, heart quickening. Foolishly, he hadn't brought a gun. He knew that Indians still posed a problem in these parts, but Mando had told him over supper that he was friendly with most of the River Band of Lakota who lived around here, having married into a family of one of the band. Even so, Reno knew well enough that the world was a dangerous place.

He should have brought the Sharps.

Something thumped in the brush to his right.

He wheeled that way, his heart pumping faster, feeling naked without a weapon. He half expected to see a fletched Indian arrow sticking out of the ground, but he saw nothing. If an arrow was there, it was likely too dark now for him to see it.

Someone laughed. Something whistled through the air and struck his right arm.

"Ow!"

Reno gave his back to the river, staring in the direction from which what he now realized was a rock had been flung. Something moved—a human-shaped silhouette. Footsteps sounded. Running footsteps. Whoever had flung the rock was running away.

"Hey!"

Reno ran forward through the bulrushes then took off of upstream along the river. Ahead, the shadowy figure turned left into a thin stand of willows and cottonwoods. Reno followed. He'd run maybe a half-dozen yard through the trees, the river bottom sand grabbing at his boots, when something hooked his right foot, pulled it out from beneath him.

He flew forward, hit the sandy ground, and rolled.

Behind him, a girl laughed.

"Dumb boy coming out here without a gun." Isabelle stepped out from behind a cottonwood. She turned to face him wearing a red calico blouse and long wool skirt. She'd brushed her hair recently. The last rays of the dying sun glinted in the stygian-blue tresses.

"You followed me." Not a question.

"A whole war party could have followed you without you knowing, stupid boy. I didn't follow you, though. I was coming down to the river like I always do at sunset."

"You're lying."

"If I'd been a Lakota warrior, you'd be screaming right now." She'd pronounced the name in the Indian tongue: La-Koh-Tahh. "But not for long. After I'd finished having my fun with you, seeing how loud I could make you scream, I'd cut your throat." She leaned forward and dragged her right index finger across her neck.

Reno sat up, wincing at the scrape on his knee. Ignoring the pain, which didn't feel all that bad in light of who'd caused it, he said again, "You followed me. Admit it." He was puzzled. She'd ignored him all through supper. He'd looked at her many times, and she'd never once so much as glanced at him, not even when he'd asked her to pass the sourdough biscuits.

"I told you—ohh!"

Reno had whipped his right leg sideways, clipping both her feet out from beneath her. She flung her arms up, hair flying, and hit the ground on her butt.

"Ohh!" she cried again.

She rolled onto her belly, sobbing.

Reno scrambled to his hands and knees and hurried over to her. "Isabelle!" He placed his hand on her quivering shoulder. She pressed her left cheek to the sand; her black hair hid her face. "I didn't mean to hurt you!"

She sobbed, quivering.

Repelled at what he'd done, Reno lowered his head to hers. "Isabelle!"

She whipped around suddenly. "Ha!" she cried. Something flashed. Reno looked down to see the curved tip of a Bowie knife pressed against his lower jaw. The girl's two lake-green eyes blazed up at him in the near-darkness, lips stretched back from her perfect white teeth. "I kill you now, stupid white dog!"

Reno smiled. He closed his hand around her hand holding the knife, and shoved the knife away from his jaw. He lowered his face to within inches of hers. Slowly, her lips closed back down over her teeth. She gazed up at him, into his eyes. He was tumbling into the twin lakes of her gaze.

Tumbling.

Forever tumbling.

"You followed me. Admit it."

She was drawing quick, shallow breaths, her blouse swelling.

"I followed you," she said quietly, the anger gone from her voice.

Slowly, Reno lowered his face to hers. Even more slowly, gently, he pressed his lips to hers. They were warm and soft. He pressed his bottom lip to the crease between her own lips, closing both of his lips around her plump upper one. She did not rebuff him. She did not turn away. She pooched her lips against his, ever so slightly but enough that he knew she was returning his kiss.

He drew his head back, dizzy. His heart was a bird flying crazily around in his chest. She pushed him off of her and gained her feet. She picked up the Bowie knife and slid it into a sheath hanging from her belt, at the small of her back. She picked up a small stick maybe a foot long, tapped it against her palm, and regarded Reno speculatively.

Her mussed hair was lovely. A thick lock curled down around the left corner of her mouth. She shook it away as she turned and walked downstream, tapping the stick against her palm.

"What your pa told you to do isn't fair, you know."

Reno walked up beside her, frowning at her walking along beside him. They followed a game trail upstream, a thin screen of cottonwoods to their left, the bulrushes to their right. "What do you mean?"

"Sending you and your sister after a whole gang of full-grown men. It's not right." Isabelle stopped and turned to face Reno. "You'll die."

"Your pa said he'd show us how to shoot men. Lots of them. I trust him."

"My father is a braggart. He's also a drunkard. A big loveable drunkard, but a drunkard just the same. He lives in the past, when he was fighting the Mexicans and then right after, when he was playing outlaw, before opening the general store and marrying my ma. He's afraid of dying, you see, Reno. He's getting his second wind helping you and your sister learn to go after bad men, and to kill."

She shook her head. "It's a crazy dream. Your father was out of his head."

"It's something we have to do, Isabelle."

"I'll never see you again." Suddenly, he realized there were tears in her eyes. They shone in the kindling starlight.

"Whatever happens, it's god's way."

"Your white god is going to get you killed."

"Then I'll go to Glory knowing I at least tried to avenge my family. I'll rejoin Pa and the others, knowing I tried to save them and maybe even took a couple of those Confederate devils with me."

"Don't confuse your father with your god, Reno. Your father was a man. Just a man."

"Not just a man, Isabelle." Reno smiled at her, remembering his father fondly. "You didn't know him."

She pursed her lips, drew a breath. "How long will you stay with us?"

"Long enough for your pa to teach us to shoot the guns he said he'd lend us." In fact, Ty Mando had said he'd "bestow" upon them "sufficient firepower to blow the doors off hell" but Reno wouldn't take handouts. He'd pay the man for the weapons as soon as he and Sara managed to earn the money.

"Meet me here tomorrow night, then. The same place."

Reno smiled. He reached for her.

She turned away and headed back the way they'd come. "That's enough, farm boy. Don't get your blood up." She glanced coquettishly over her shoulder at him, her long eyes slanting as she smiled. "Or anything else."

***

"Pa!" Mary Louis cried. "Pa—help me!"

Guns blasted.

Horses whinnied.

Men whooped and hollered.

Ma screamed and bolted out of the cabin as three graybacks grabbed Mary Louise and threw her to the ground. "No!" Ma cried, running through the melee of galloping horses and men shooting pistols and rifles. "Leave her alone! Leave my baby alone!"

"Mary!" Pa bounded up from behind the rain barrel off the cabin's front porch and, with his Springfield carbine in one hand, ran toward the men swarming over the sobbing Mary Louise. "Alta, get back in the cabin!" he shouted at Ma. "I'll get her!" He glanced at Benjamin and James and shouted, "Sons, cover me!"

He took only one more running step before a marauder's bullet clipped him across his right temple. Just a nick, but it was enough to drive Pa to the ground, where he was soon hidden in the roiling dust of the horses of the intruders swarming around the farmyard like Indians on the warpath.

Reno ran toward the farm, wanting to help. But it was as though he were running through quicksand. He tried to call out to his family, but his mouth seemed to be filled with rocks. Anguish clamped a tight fist around his heart.

"Reno!" The voice was Ben shouting at him for help.

No, the voice belonged to James.

"Reno!" That time it was Ma screaming for him.

He tried to call back to her that he was trying to help her, but for the love of him he couldn't get his mouth to form the words.

"Reno!" That time the voice was unfamiliar. It belonged to a woman. "Reno, wake up! Reno!"

Someone was shaking him.

Reno opened his eyes. He blinked. Sweat and tears dribbled down his cheeks. He blinked again. Behind the tears obscuring his vision like isinglass a pretty, copper-skinned, hazel-eyed face gazed at him from only inches away.

That pretty face was framed by long, straight, velvet-black hair. Reno knew he knew the girl's name, but it took him several more seconds for his brain to latch onto it.

Isabelle.

He blinked again. The dream dissolved slowly

behind the sifting smoke and gunfire. He was at Ty Mando's General Store over a hundred miles west of the farm. He'd been dreaming. Only a dream. Still, terror clung to him like skunk stink to a dog.

It was tempered by the face gazing back at him. Isabelle's brows were ridged with concern.

Embarrassment warmed Reno's cheeks and he lay back against his pillow. He glanced to his left. He'd slept with Peter, in Peter's upstairs bed, across the hall from where Sara had bunked with Isabelle. Peter's side of the bed was empty, the covers thrown back.

"I'm sorry," he said, swallowing, still catching his breath. "I was—"

"Dreaming," Sara finished for him, sitting down on the edge of the bed next to Isabelle. She seemed very subtly to edge Isabelle aside. She was fully dressed in her blouse and duck trousers and boots. "It was just a dream, Reno. I get them, too." She glanced at Isabelle, and Reno noted a crispness in her tone as she said, "I'll tend him."

Isabelle opened her mouth to speak, but Sara, putting even more of an edge on her voice, said, "He's my brother. I'll tend him."

Isabelle gave her a hard stare.

"Sara," Reno said, cajolingly.

"It's all right." Isabelle rose from the bed. "I'll be downstairs. Breakfast is ready. Pa's been calling for you two."

Reno frowned. "Calling?"

"Hear that?" Isabelle rolled her eyes toward the second-story room's single window.

Reno did hear it, then. He realized suddenly that he'd been hearing it for a while. Gunfire. Maybe that was had spawned his dream. Someone was shooting a short gun not far from the house. Make that two short guns. Some of the reports were nearly simultaneous.

"Pa and Peter are out giving their Colts a workout. Pa's way of calling you." Isabelle gave Reno a grim smile. She looked at Sara but offered no smile.

Though they'd spent the night in the same room—the same bed, even—a coldness hovered around the two young women. It was almost as though they were jealous of each other, though Reno could think of no reason either should feel that way. Sara was no threat to Isabelle. He and Sara were sister and brother.

Isabelle walked to the bedroom door. She stopped, cast Reno a furtive wink over her shoulder, then grinned and left the room.

EIGHTEEN

"She's pretty." Sara rose from the bed, slid a lock of Reno's hair out of his eye. "But just remember…"

"Yeah, I know—pretty don't feed the chickens."

"It also doesn't extract blood from your enemies."

"Ah, Sara!" Reno threw his single quilt back and swung his feet over the side of the bed.

"Don't 'ah, Sara' me, George Washington Bass." Sara planted her fists on her hips and stood over her brother, glowering. Her heart-shaped face flushed with anger, and her blue eyes sparked. "Don't you go fallin' for that pretty half-breed. Love will cloud your brain as well as your aim. It'll get you killed. Stay focused, Reno. We are here to get guns and ammunition and a few tips on killing. That's all."

"I am focused, Sara," Reno complained, reaching for his trousers.

"You better be. We made a promise to Pa." She

shoved his shirt at him. "Now, get dressed. You heard Isabelle. Ty Mando is callin' us with his Colts, and I for one am ready to fill my hands with some iron and get after that Bad Old Man and Black Bob."

She headed out the door, admonishing over her shoulder, "Don't dawdle!"

"I ain't dawdling, Sara!" Reno said, shaking out his shirt.

That sister of his was going to be the death of him yet.

He washed quickly with the cold water in the pitcher sitting atop the wash stand, fingered water through his hair, growing longer now from the lack of attention of Mary Louise's sewing shears. He shoved both his Confederate pistols behind the belt looped around his overall-clad waist, left his room just as Sara was coming out of the room across the hall.

Sara looked freshly scrubbed, her own hair damp from a wet brushing. They'd been on the trail several days now, and he'd almost forgotten what Sara looked like behind the trail dust she'd wiped away, and her thick blond hair freshly brushed down over her shoulders. Of course, her own Colt Navy .36 and the Confederate pistol they'd taken off the dead graybacks bristled from behind the wide brown leather belt she wore around her own lean waist, on the outside of her sack trousers.

"Feels good to get a good night's sleep in a real bed

again, don't it?" Reno asked her, repositioning his pistols.

"Don't get used to it." Sara swung away from him and headed down the stairs.

Reno rolled his eyes, shook his head, and followed her down to the first story. Isabelle stood at the range, an apron tied around her waist. She glanced at Reno and Sara, then plucked bacon from a cast-iron skillet.

She broke the bacon into pieces and placed the pieces on the open faces of two sliced and buttered sourdough biscuits. She closed the biscuits, making two lumpy, greasy sandwiches, set the sandwiches on a plate, and set the plate on the table, near where she'd already poured two stone mugs of steaming coffee.

"Breakfast," she said. "It's not much, but—"

"We overslept," Sara said, though it was barely dawn. "No time for breakfast."

***

Outside, the yard was murky with gray light. The handguns continued popping sporadically. Reno could see the flashes off to the east of the windmill and the main corral.

Sara grabbed her ragged felt hat and went out, leaving the door open behind her.

Reno gazed at her, frowning, then he looked at the greasy sandwiches. His stomach growled, and his mouth watered. "Sara, hold on!"

He peered at Isabelle standing on the other side of the table, and shrugged. "I for one don't intend to let good food go to waste. Thanks, Miss Isabelle." He quickly plucked both sandwiches off the plate. He shoved one into a pocket of his trousers, and took a big bite off the other one. He picked up one of the coffee cups, and, chewing, winked and grinned at Isabelle.

She looked down with a faint blush rising in her copper cheeks.

Reno wheeled and walked out onto the Mando cabin's broad front porch.

"Sara, hold on, galldangit!" Reno said as his sister angled across the yard to his left, toward where Ty Mando and Peter were both shooting the pistols at what appeared airtight tins set on posts—a makeshift shooting range in the grass at the edge of the yard.

Reno ate the sandwich in his hand in two big bites, chewed as quickly as he could without choking, then slugged half of the coffee, wincing at the burn as the hot, black liquid followed the biscuits down his throat and into his belly. He set the half-empty cup on the porch rail then hurried down the porch steps and broke into a run.

He caught up with Sara just as she was approaching big Ty Mando and the more diminutive Peter, a quiet though affable lad whom Reno really hadn't come to know even though he'd spent the night in the young man's bed. Even if Peter had been given to talk, which he didn't seem to be, Reno had been so tired after the long ride that he'd succumbed to sleep even before his head had hit the pillow. He hadn't even taken the time to recite his bedtime prayer, a rarity for him.

Both men ceased fire and raised their pistols. They stood before a bench constructed of halved pine logs propped on beer barrels, bark sides up. The logs were covered with guns and ammunition.

"Kind of early for shootin', ain't it?" Reno said, glancing at the sky in which a few stars still flickered faintly.

"The men you're hunting won't care what time of day it is, Master Reno." Ty Mando grinned and, holding a pistol with one hand, beckoned Reno and Sara with the other hand. "Come over here, both of you. I want to introduce you to the fine presents I am about to bestow upon you and with which you will avenge your sainted father and mother and the rest of your hallowed family."

"What do you have there?" Sara said eagerly.

Mando displayed the gun he was holding in both his open hands.

"This here, my sweet child, is the Remington Army Pietta Model 1858. Constructed of steel, it's considerably lighter that those old iron hoglegs you two are carrying. It is chambered for the .44-caliber ball with a nice long, eight-inch barrel. It's one of the most accurate and durable percussion pistols on the market today, capable of considerable power with muzzle velocities in the range of five hundred to twelve-hundred-plus feet-per-second, depending upon the size of the charge you load it with. In other words, this big popper can blow a hole through a two-inch privy door an' darn near blow the head off the man squattin' inside."

He laughed. Reno blushed at the off-color joke. Sara likely hadn't heard it. She stared at the gun, eyes blazing.

"That's what we want, all right," she said, a little breathless, as she stared down in wide-eyed eagerness at the pretty, long-barreled, darkly blued, walnut-gripped pistol residing in Mando's open hands.

Mando chuckled.

"See that long steel top-strap there, running over the top of the cylinder?"

"I see it," Reno said, admiring the beautiful weapon.

"That design makes the gun stronger and less prone to frame stretching than the Colts. The internal lockwork of the Remy is simpler, too. Less to go wrong when firing. But what I like best about these pretty, deadly ladies is that they allow for easy cylinder removal, a quick reload with a spare pre-loaded cylinder. See here?"

With a couple of quick movements with his fingers, he slipped the cylinder out of the pistol. He set it on the bench, grabbed another one, and, with a few snaps and clicks, slid the fresh cylinder into place and spun it. It buzzed like a well-oiled saw.

Mando grinned. "See how easy that was?"

"Wow," Reno said, shaking his head in awe. He'd never seen such a handy feature. He'd grown up with old muzzle-loading rifles that even after he'd become good at reloading, he could still shoot only three rounds per minute with. But with this gun here—if he had two cylinders, he could snap off twelve rounds in that much time…

He was feeling as light-headed as Sara obviously was.

"See how accurate this pretty lady is…even with a one-eyed old man doing the shooting."

Mando turned to the posts poking up in the brush at various distances from the bench. They were also set at various levels, some six feet and a little higher with several as low as two, three, and four feet. Peter had just set fresh tin cans and bottles on all dozen of the posts, and, leaning on his cane, had limped back to stand behind the bench near his father.

The growing light now shone in the brown glass of some of the bottles.

Mando raised the gun in his right hand, clicked the hammer back. He drew a breath, held it, and released it. Reno watched his right index finger draw back on the trigger, and he jumped with the gun's loud roar. Orange flames and white smoke lapped from the barrel.

A bottle shattered atop a post roughly twenty feet away.

Mando clicked the hammer back again, fired again.

Again, Reno jumped a little at the heavy blast. He watched, grinning, as a tin can went sailing off a post roughly thirty feet from the bench and off to the right of the one the bottle had been on.

Mando shot four more times, the bullets pinging into tin cans or shattering bottles. After the sixth shot, he lowered the smoking weapon to the bench, removed the smoking cylinder, replaced it with another loaded one, and snapped off six more shots. Cans flew and bottles shattered.

Mando lowered the Colt and turned to Reno and Sara, who'd been watching in hang-jawed awe.

"What do you think of that?" he asked, laughing proudly.

"Yep," Sara said, nodding and glancing at Reno. "That oughta do the trick, Mr. Mando."

"Please, call me Ty."

Sara smiled up at him. "Pa sent us to the right place. We don't know how to thank you, Ty."

"Oh, I'm not done yet."

Mando set the pretty Remington on the makeshift

bench. Smiling at Reno and Sara, he stretched an arm out toward his son, and said, "Peter, a little brass, if you will?"

"You got it, Pa."

Peter picked up one of two rifles Reno had seen lying atop the bench. He handed it stock first to his father, who took the long gun in both his hands, and turned to display it to Reno and Sara. "This here, children, is the first successful lever gun."

"Lever gun," Reno said, half to himself, letting his admiring gaze run down the long, dark-blue, octagonal barrel, across the smooth brass receiver and then on down the shiny walnut stock to the end of which was snugged a shiny brass plate.

"Watch this."

Peter stepped back and poked his fingers in his ears.

Mando raised the rifle to his shoulder, worked the lever attached to the gun's underside, and pulled the trigger. The rifle's report was even louder than that of the Remington. Mando worked the cocking lever again quickly, and fired.

He worked the lever again, and fired.

Again, and fired.

Again, and fired.

He kept firing the rifle until Reno found himself sharing another shocked look with Sara. He'd lost count of the number of times Mando had fired the weapon by the time the hammer pinged benignly down against the steel action. Pale smoke smelling of rotten eggs wafted on the growing morning breeze.

"For crying in the miller's ale," Reno intoned, staring down at the rifle Mando was again displaying in his hands, "how many rounds does that long gun hold, anyway?"

"Sixteen, boy."

"Sixteen?" Reno and Sara exclaimed in unison.

"Fired in less than a minute." Reno couldn't wrap his mind around the improbability of that.

"Watch." Mando set the long gun on the bench, near a tin can filled with almost finger-sized, shiny brass cylinders. What appeared cone-shaped bullets were seated on the tops of the cylinders.

"Metal cartridges," Reno said under his breath, watching Mando pluck one of the cartridges from the can. "My brother James told me about those. Least-ways, that he thought rifles would be firing them someday in the future, instead of lead balls with caps 'n' powder 'n' nipples an' such."

"The future is here, my lad. See this little tab right here." Mando placed his finger on a little metal half-circle attached to the underside of the gun, where the rifle was seated against the breech. He slid the tab up along the underside of the barrel, nearly all the way to the barrel's end. He turned the tab and about two inches of the barrel twisted out to one side, causing the barrel to separate and to expose an open tube.

He showed Reno and Sara the bass cartridge he was holding between his thumb and index finger then dropped the cartridge, conical bullet pointing up, brass cartridge pointing down, into the opening at the end of the tube. They could see the cartridge drop down the tube through a slight, vertical slit running up and down the tube's underside. Inside was a long spring sitting the length of the tube.

Mando dropped another cartridge down the tube. The second cartridge sat atop the first, at the bottom of the tube. Mando continued dropping bullets down the tube until sixteen bullets sat snugly atop each other, all with the conical lead heads pointing up. He flicked the brass tab into place near the top of the barrel, closing the tube, and extended the rifle to Sara.

He winked at Reno. "Ladies first."

Sara took the gun, staring down in fascination and appreciation. Reno didn't blame her. The rifle was the most beautiful long gun he'd ever seen. Its lines were clean and simple, as no-nonsense as a Sioux arrow. The varnished walnut stock shone in the lemony light of the sun now rearing its head above the eastern horizon.

"Where'd you get such a beautiful rifle?" Sara asked.

Mando glanced at Peter, who stood to his left,

leaning an elbow atop the bench. Peter looked at his father and grinned, his brown eyes glinting behind his round spectacles.

"Uh, well," Mando said, chuckling. "Let's just say a friend of a friend…who owes me a coupla favors… saved these little beauties—an entire crate of 'em, in fact—from being delivered to the cavalry at Camp Rankin." He wrinkled his nostrils. "Soldiers don't know how to care for long guns like these. Besides, they'd only blow the hell out of the Lakota with 'em, shoot what's left of the buffalo for sport, or shoot themselves in the foot. Nah. I got 'em here to sell to my special friends."

"We don't have any money," Reno said in shame.

"Your pa already done paid for two rifles and four Remington Piettas and ammunition for both. Along with enough pocket jingle and trail supplies to get you started. Yes, when you leave here, you'll each be armed with one Henry rifle and a coupla boxes of .44 rimfire cartridges, two Remingtons, and two spare cylinders. You'll be able to shoot all day and deep into the night, if need be."

Mando gave a sly wink at the twins.

"Yessir, your pa paid for all this a long time ago when he saved my rancid, foolhardy young hide down along the Rio Grande. Paid for these and a whole lot more. Now, it's time for me to pay him back by outfit-tin' his children so they can ride off and avenge him and the rest of his family. You don't owe me a damn thing, children. I only ask that you remain here for a few days—long enough for me to teach you to master these weapons. Fair?"

Reno and Sara shared a conferring look. Reno could tell Sara was chomping at the proverbial bit to get on the trail of the Bad Old Man and Black Bob. But fair was fair.

She and Reno nodded.

"When you two can shoot a bottle out of the air with both a Remington and a Henry, I'll give you your leave." Mando wrung his big hands together eagerly. "Now, then—Peter, why don't you set the cans and bottles atop the posts for the princess here?"

When Peter had accomplished his task, taking cans and bottles from a nearby pile and setting them atop the posts, Sara loaded the Henry under Mando's guidance. She levered the first round in the chamber, raised the rifle to her shoulder, and squeezed the trigger.

NINETEEN

Shooting a lever-action repeating rifle after so many years horsing around with single-shot muzzle-loaders and breechloaders and cap-and-ball pistols was a rarefied thrill.

Bang-bang-bang—one shot after another blasted from the barrel.

At first, it was hard to slow down and concentrate on each target. There was something about having all that ammo at the tip of the trigger finger that made the shooter feel in a hurry to snap off the shots. To feel the satisfying kick and hear the roar. But over the course of that first day, when he introduced the twins to their new "toys," Mando tutored Reno and Sara well on the finer aspects of shooting lever-action rifles, as well as the powerful Remingtons.

By the end of that first day, they were shooting all of the cans and all of the bottles off the posts with both the Henrys and the Remys. After that, Mando let them practice on their own, with only Peter's guidance and help setting up targets, while Mando repaired to his store. Occasionally he wandered out onto his porch to watch briefly and to yell advice, usually with a jug and a smoke in his hand.

While Reno and Sara blasted away at their targets over the course of the next three days, Peter limped around on his cane, setting up fresh cans and bottles or sitting on a log, patting the dogs and smiling his affable smile, occasionally offering advice. Reno knew the young man was gone for Sara, for he rarely took his eyes off of her, and she was the one at whom he directed most of his advice.

For her part, Sara mostly ignored the young man. She concentrated her attention on shooting cans and bottles, though Reno knew she was really seeing the faces of their family's killers atop those posts.

Meanwhile, Apache and his new friend, Miss Fox-ie, played in the yard or took sojourns to chase rabbits and flickertails. Isabelle remained in the house, doing her daily and near-constant chores, but also going into the general store section of the building when Mando needed help.

The store saw quite a bit of business during the day, with local men and even a few women riding or driving wagons up to the place for supplies. At night, market hunters, wood cutters, itinerant government and railroad surveyors, and a few cowboys from area ranches came in to drink in the saloon section off the back of the store. Mostly, they helped themselves to beer and whiskey, tossing coins into the tobacco tin behind the bar as per Mando's honor system.

Mando often joined them after supper. He enjoyed his clientele, most of whom were old friends—husky or stick-skinny, bearded, weathered men who'd lived in the West since long before the war. They were farmers or ranchers or river men—men who ferried supplies across the South Platte on rafts or up or down the river in keel boats. One spoke with a thick accent Reno learned was Prussian.

Some were former soldiers who, like Mando, had married squaws.

Even a few women came at night to Mando's saloon. Such women were as tough as the men, or tougher, and from a short distance away could even be mistaken for men. They certainly equaled the men's ribald senses of humor and salty tongues. They could also put away just as much beer and whiskey as the men, too. One even arm-wrestled one of the men and won, which seemed no big surprise to the other clientele.

Mando sat and gambled with his customers or joined in the long-winded and often raucous discussions. Sometimes he played the fiddle. When they heard the fiddle's first strains at night, Reno and Sara and Isabelle and Peter crossed over from the living section to the saloon. Reno and Isabelle danced and clapped to Mando's raucous strains and foot-stomping and loud, toneless singing while Apache and Sabrina played under the tables, snarling and growling in pretend skirmishes, or barked and nipped playfully at the dancer's ankles.

Sometimes a couple of the old salts joined them. One skinny, bird-like woman who had a mustache and a penchant for chewing snus insisted Reno dance with her. She always asked him when he was going to marry her and finally make an honest woman out of her. Reno always blushed and glanced at Isabelle sitting with Sara and Peter. The beautiful young half-breed frowned from beneath her eyebrows at him, in mock castigation, but also smiled a little while clapping her hands to the rhythm of her father's fiddle.

During the days, Reno and Sara continued practicing with their new weapons.

Of course, Sara was the first to blow a bottle out of the air. That put pressure on Reno, because now Sara was ready to leave. But they couldn't leave because, under the conditions of their agreement with Mando, they couldn't depart the trading post until they'd both shot a bottle out of the air.

Now it was Reno's turn.

The night of the day Sara shot the bottle, Reno climbed a rocky bluff near the river. He gained the top of the bluff, breathing hard from the stiff climb. He looked into the hollow atop the bluff, and smiled. Isabelle sat staring off to the west, where the setting sun was painting the cloud-strapped sky all the colors on a painter's pallet.

Apache and Miss Foxie lay nose to nose near Isabelle's feet, exhausted from another long day of flirtatious play. Apache looked up at Reno and whined a greeting then returned his snout to the ground. Miss Foxie thumped her tail then turned her head to nibble a tick bite.

Isabelle sat with her back to the hollow's chalky wall, her knees drawn up to her chest, her calico skirt draped over them. She sat with the toe of one of her black half-boots planted atop the toe of the other one. She rested her chin on her knees around which she'd wrapped her arms. The light-breeze, spiced by the pungent growth along the river as well as by the autumn-changing cottonwoods and native prairie grasses, turning red and brown now as the fall deepened, made her black hair flutter back behind her face.

She glanced up at Reno just for a second then returned her gaze to the sunset. Her expression was pensive, even sad.

Placing his hands on the butts of the two Remington Piettas snugged behind his belt—Mando had him and Sara taking the guns with them everywhere they went, getting to know them so that they felt like parts of them—Reno descended the rocks into the hollow where'd they sometimes built a fire, if the night was cool. This night was warm, and Isabelle had built no fire. Reno sat down beside her, leaning back against the chalky wall, and looked at her again, a frown of concern furling his blond brows.

"What's wrong?"

"You'll be leaving soon."

"Well…" Reno chuckled dryly. "Not until I blast a can or a bottle out of the air, like Sara."

"You'll hit it soon. She drives you, that sister of yours."

"She does, at that." Reno sighed. "But in good ways, mostly."

Isabelle continued to stare without expression toward the west. "She and my father are going to get you killed."

"I'll have some say in it." Reno had meant the comment as a joke, but Isabelle wasn't laughing. He stretched his arm around her shoulders, gently squeezed her. They'd met here on this butte near the river every night since Reno's first night here, and here they'd shared their dreams, secrets, and niggling worries. In short, they'd fallen in love. "I'll be back, Isabelle. I promise."

"Don't." Isabelle looked up at him, her eyes glinting with the colors of the sunset. "Don't make promises you don't know you can keep."

"I'll keep that one. I love you, Isabelle."

"Then how come since that first night you haven't tried to do anything more than kiss me?"

Reno frowned and pulled his head back in shock. "Why, because we're not married! I wouldn't be proper!"

His comment made her smile. She pressed her forehead against his chest. "You're so good, Reno. Please don't let anything bad happen to you. I know you shouldn't make promises you might not be able to keep, but promise me, anyway, will you?"

"All right, then." Reno caressed her slender back. "I promise."

Reno felt her shudder a little against him. He looked down to see a tear roll down her left cheek, glistening in the sun's dying rays. He brushed the tear away with his thumb. She lifted her head from his chest and gazed affectionately into his eyes. He returned the look then pressed his lips to hers.

A gun popped in the distance.

Reno pulled his head back from Isabelle's with a start.

"What was that?" she said with a gasp.

"Gunshot." Another pop sounded from the direction of the general store. "There's another one!"

A man shouted. Then more men shouted. A horse whinnied.

Both dogs were on their feet, ears cocked, looking

to the north. Miss Foxie gave an anxious bark.

Reno climbed to his feet and extended his hand to Isabelle. "Come on, Isabelle. That don't sound good. Not one bit!"

He scrambled up out of the hollow and turned to offer his hand to Isabelle. She waved him off. "Leave me, Reno! Go! I'll be behind you!"

Reno swung around and, adjusting both of the pretty Remington Piettas behind his belt, broke into a run to the northwest. Both dogs scrambled up out of the hollow and gave chase, overtaking Reno and running ahead. Reno ran hard as more gunfire sounded from the direction of the general store. Men continued shouting.

He followed the slender path through the brush and trees lining the river bottom. When he struck open ground, he ran harder, following the path angling out before him, pale in the twilight against the dark purple of the grass and sage. He couldn't see the general store from here, for it was up the rise and beyond another thin screen of willows and cottonwoods, a couple of hundred yards away.

He climbed the rise and made his way through the trees. On the other side of the trees, he paused to catch his breath, bending over with his hands on his knees. The dogs barked and ran ahead but Reno called Apache back. When Apache returned to him, Miss Foxie did as well, both dogs panting.

Apache mewled anxiously. The shepherd dog was no doubt remembering the raid on the Bass farm and was wondering if something similar were happening here.

Hearing the continued shouting, louder now that Reno was closer to the buildings, Reno wondered the same thing. Had the Devil's Horde circled back to hit what they'd missed when they'd swung north into Nebraska? Or maybe the Bad Old Man had come gunning for the kid who'd drilled the bullet into his arm, and had heard Reno was holed up at Ty Mando's General Store.

That must be it!

And Sara was there in the store.

Fighting back his dread and fear, Reno took off running again. As the buildings came into view, silhouetted against the oil pots burning in the yard around the store and the Mando residence, Reno heard a man shout, "Where is he, dammit, old man? Where is that kid, or so help me this rock-worshipper son of yours is gonna stretch some hemp!"

Sure enough. The Devil's Horde was back for Reno...

He ran up to the rear of the main barn hulking darkly before him. Again, he paused to catch a breath, and then walked to the barn's west rear corner and edged a look up the break between the barn and the blacksmith shop, which doubled as Peter's leather-working shack, toward the main yard. The yard was lit by the flickering red flames of the oil pots.

The eerie orange light revealed several horseback riders trotting angrily around the yard, shouting and cursing. At first, Reno thought the men he glimpsed from his vantage at the barn's rear corner were, indeed, the graybacks led by the Bad Old Man and Black Bob themselves.

But then he realized that these men were not wearing Confederate gray. They wore the dark-blue of federal soldiers.

"I wanna know where that kid is, Mando! We heard he was stayin' here with you. I wanna know where he is an' where your purty daughter is!"

"They ain't inside," came another voice, not as loud as the previous speaker's. Boots thumped. Some of the bluecoats must have checked the house for Reno and Isabelle.

They were the soldiers from town. The ones who'd attacked Sara and whose clocks Reno had cleaned for their trouble. They were back for revenge.

Reno couldn't tell how many were there, but judging by the shadows he saw riding angrily around the yard and the number of raised voices, he guessed they numbered more than had been in town.

They'd brought reinforcements...

"Go to hell!" Mando bellowed. "You go to hell! You bluecoats touch a hair on my boy's head, there won't be nowhere for you to hide that I won't find you!"

They had Peter.

Where was Sara?

He remembered the gunshots he'd heard previously. Her voice wasn't part of the melee.

Quickly, Reno thought through his options. He looked at the pistols jutting from the belt around his waist. He had a hand wrapped around the grips of each. He considered moving up through the break before him, and going to work with the pretty Remingtons. He nixed the idea. He needed the Henry, which he'd left inside the Mando's living quarters, leaning against the kitchen wall.

He hoped one of the bluecoats hadn't taken it when they were inside.

Footsteps sounded behind him. He turned quickly with a start, and his heartbeat slowed when he saw Isabelle approaching with both whining dogs on her heels.

"Reno," she cried softly. "What's happening?"

Reno took her hand and squeezed it. "Those soldiers from town."

She placed a hand over her mouth in shock.

Reno squeezed her hand again. "You stay here with the dogs. Keep them quiet. I'm going to circle around the house and go in the rear. I need the Henry."

Isabelle stared at him darkly, her lips parted as she breathed. "Be careful."

"I will."

Reno crept away from the barn and made his way along the rear wall to the east. Keeping low and hoping the darkness would conceal him from the soldiers, he moved quickly from the barn and around behind the corral and the target range. He continued circling the yard until he found himself, maybe eight minutes later, moving up to the rear of the living quarters.

He stepped inside through the back door and hurried to the kitchen. Relief washed over him when he saw the brass-framed Henry leaning against the wall, partly concealed by the many coats and other garments hanging from pegs. The federal soldiers likely wouldn't have known what the long gun was if they'd seen it, for with its lever action and long, slender barrel, it only vaguely resembled the old Enfields, Sharps, and Springfields they were familiar with.

Reno picked up the Henry and turned it so that he could look into the loading tube through the slit running up its bottom side. Fully loaded. He racked a round into the chamber and moved to the door.

TWENTY

"That does it!" a man shouted from the yard outside. "Hang that rock-worshipper son of the old man's!"

"Don't you dare!" Mando bellowed. "Leave my boy alone, you two-bit peckerwoods!"

Quietly, Reno tripped the front door's steel latch. The door shuddered free of the latching bolt. Reno drew it inward slowly, wincing as the hinges squawked faintly. When the door was open about six inches, he peered through the crack and into the yard.

Mando lay on the ground to the right, clutching his arm and bellowing curses at the three men who had dropped a lariat hondo around Peter's neck and were leading the young man to the barn. Peter sat on a horse. The three soldiers walked along beside him, one holding the coiled rope. Two other saddled horses stood near the windmill, nervously switching their tails.

Two other soldiers stood over Mando, all three

holding Colt revolvers on him.

Reno looked around for Sara. When his eyes settled on his sister lying sprawled in the dirt to the left of the windmill, his stomach flip-flopped. One of the soldiers knelt beside her inert body. He was fingering something in his hands. As the firelight glinted off the bluing coating the steel hogleg, Reno knew the man was admiring one of the Remington Piettas he must have found on Sara.

Reno's heart raced. He drew a breath to calm himself, telling himself that Sara might not be dead. Just because she wasn't moving didn't mean she was dead.

Meanwhile, the three soldiers stopped Peter's horse in front of the barn. One tossed the coiled rope over the hay hook hanging about a foot below the open loft doors.

Reno's heart thudded faster as he opened the door farther and stepped out onto the porch. He hoped the shadows beneath the porch's roof would conceal him long enough for him to do what he intended to do.

"Your son's gonna hang, Mando!" shouted one of the three men standing over the wounded general store proprietor who still bellowed blue curses. "One more time—where's your daughter and the big blond? The one with the anvil fists?"

Reno recognized the speaker. He was the big sergeant who'd been trying to savage Isabelle, the man whose face Reno had ruined with his fists. He sported white bandages over one ear, around the top of his head, and over his nose. In the light of the dancing orange firelight from the oil pots, Reno could see that both of the man's eyes were black and swollen.

"Go to hell!" Mando shouted shrilly. "You cut him down or I'll—"

Mando groaned as the big man with the ruined face kicked him in the belly.

"Slap that hoss, boys!" the big man shouted at the men by the barn. "Let the gimpy half-breed hang!"

Reno dropped to a knee. He lined up the Henry's sights on the rope trailing straight up from behind Peter's neck to the hay hook. He could barely see it against the barn's shadow. In the glinting, flickering light of the oil pots, it appeared a very thin, tan ribbon touched with crimson.

One of the soldiers slapped the horse's left hip. As the horse lunged forward with a whinny, Mando shouted, "Oh, you dirty dogs!"

Reno fired as the horse bounded out from beneath Peter, and the young man dropped suddenly. Peter stopped with a jerk as the rope drew taut.

Reno muttered a rare curse as his first bullet only nicked the rope.

Quickly, he racked another round into the chamber, aimed again, and fired.

The bullet cleaved the rope. Peter dropped straight down to the ground and landed with a grunt.

Only two seconds had passed between Reno's first and second shots. Too quick for the soldiers to comprehend what had just happened. They all looked around, crouching anxiously, whipping their heads this way and that, trying to figure out who'd fired the two shots.

"What in the hell?" yelled the man who'd been kneeling beside Sara. He leaped to his feet, swinging his head and wide eyes, glistening in the light from the oil pots, toward Reno. As he did, Sara suddenly moved. She raised her left hand. A gun shone in it.

"Take this, you wretched devil!" Sara wailed.

She'd been playing possum, most like.

The gun in her hand bucked and popped. Flames leaped from the barrel and onto the shirt of the man standing before her. The man cried and flew backward, his shirt on fire.

The big man whose face Reno had ruined turned toward the trading post, raising the Springfield in his hands. Reno ignored him for the moment, concentrating on the three men standing around the front of the barn, where Peter lay in a writhing heap on the ground.

Reno picked out one man of the three—they were all crouching anxiously and looking around desperately to understand what in the blue blazes was going on—and shot him. As that man flew back against the barn, the big sergeant's Springfield roared. Reno felt the hot wind of the bullet pass close to his neck before hammering the front of the log building behind him.

Reno drew a deep breath, keeping his wits about him, and swung the Henry toward the big sergeant who'd just shot at him. He levered a round into the Henry's action, quickly lined up the sights as the big man dropped his single-shot rifle to the ground and reached for the twin Army Colts holstered on his broad waist.

He didn't get either hogleg out of its leather before the Henry roared.

The .44-caliber rimfire round punched through the center of the sergeant's forehead, nipping the bottom edge of the bandage wrapped around the top of his head. His head jerked backward and then the rest of his body followed his head to the ground. He was so dead, he didn't even try to break his fall.

On her knees now, Sara had gone to work with her own Remington, shooting another man who stood by the barn, the Remington popping and flashing just ahead of Reno and to his left. As the other two men standing over Mando and the now-deceased big man, raised their own rifles and aimed at Reno, Reno triggered the Henry again. He knew he'd pulled that shot wide even as the bullet was on its way.

The .44 bullet plumed dirt just behind his target.

As the man's own slug ripped into an awning support post in front of Reno, Reno lined up his sights again. He hurried the next shot, too, and sent the soldier pin-wheeling with a bullet in his leg. The soldier cursed, dropped to the ground on his knees and whipped around toward Reno, bellowing another shrill curse as he unholstered one of his big Colt Dragoons.

As he raised the pistol, Reno lined up the sights on him, drew a breath, held it for one-quarter second, then released it. He squeezed the long gun's trigger. The soldier gave a shocked grunt as the bullet turned his right eye to jelly and blew out the back of his head along with a considerable amount of brain and bone.

He, too, was dead before his head slammed against the ground.

"Reno, one left!" Sara cried.

Reno glanced at her. She was scrambling to her feet and running to her right, trying to see around the windmill. Beyond the windmill, toward where the trail entered the general store's yard, the last surviving soldier was clumsily mounting his horse. The horse was curveting and whinnying, and the soldier was jumping up and down on one foot while trying to thrust his left foot through his saddle stirrup.

Reno ejected his last spent cartridge, which flew straight up out of the Henry's open breech to clank onto the porch floor around his boots, and tried to plant a bead on the fleeing soldier. He could let him go, but why? So he could make more trouble for the Mandos?

Reno shifted the rifle sights around, trying to lay

them on the soldier. The man ran along beside his fleeing horse for about twenty feet and then leaped into the saddle just as the horse reached the mouth of the trail. Horse and rider were at the very edge of the light from the flickering oil pots.

Reno had time for only one shot.

Our father who art in heaven…

Just before the man and the horse—rather, man-and horse-shaped silhouettes shifting against the dark night yawning beyond the yard—Reno released his held breath and gently squeezed the trigger. As he did, the night consumed the horse and rider. Reno heard only the thudding of the fleeing horse's hooves, the squawk of the saddle leather and the jangle of the bridle chains.

He thought he'd missed. But then, after the horse had taken about three more lunging strides, there came the hard thump of a body hitting the ground and the continued, softer thumps and crunching of that body rolling through grass and scrub.

Hallowed be thy name.

Five minutes later, Ty Mando said, "I'll be hanged boy." He looked up from where the soldier who'd been trying to flee lay in the scrub brush fifty yards beyond the yard. "You drilled that son of Satan a third eye right smack dab in the back of his head!"

Mando toed the big wet spot on the back of the soldier's hatless head where he lay belly-down, arms and legs stretched wide, in the night-dark grass. The man's horse was long gone.

Reno's heart raced. He lifted the Henry, which he still held in both hands. They were shaking. He couldn't have been shaking that badly when he'd shot at the soldiers, or he wouldn't have been able to kill them. The shaking had come later—along with the realization of what he'd done—the men he'd killed.

Men who would not see the next dawn.

Mando winked at Reno, wrapped his good arm around his broad shoulders. "It's all right. You'll get used to it."

Reno looked at the arm hanging slack at Mando's side. "You gonna be all right, Ty?"

"This here?" Mando looked at the arm. He gave a strained grin. "Hurts a mite, but it's just a flesh wound. Isabelle'll wrap it for me shortly."

Isabelle stood on the other side of her father, staring down in mute amazement at the dead man. Both dogs, Apache and Miss Foxie, were off snorting around in the brush. Sara and Peter stood on the other side of the dead man, both staring at the carcass, as well. Sara's shirt was torn, and her hair was badly mussed. She had dirt on her face. A short, shallow cut bled on her right temple.

"You all right, sis?"

Sara nodded. She hadn't said anything since she'd called Reno's attention to the fleeing rider. Now she stood holding both of her Remingtons down against her legs. She nodded. "One of those soldier vermin took me by surprise. I ran into the yard when I heard Peter yell. The soldier plowed me right over with his horse." She turned her head to one side and spat dirt from her lips. "I'll be all right. Just got a headache's all. I wasn't really out. Just pretending."

She stared at her brother and said with quiet awe, "That was some amazing shooting, Reno."

Peter stared at Reno, too. The young man was smiling. Rope burns shone on his neck, but he appeared otherwise unharmed. Leaning on his cane, he said, "That first shot nearly cut the rope clean through. The next shot did the trick." He laughed, shaking his head. "I've never seen anything like it."

"And you gave this fella a third eye," said Mando, gazing down at the dead man before them.

He had. He really had. Reno's mind was slow to understand what he'd done. It was as though he hadn't really thought about it. His mind had gone very quiet, and he'd just done what had needed to be done.

Without thinking...

"Now if I could just shoot a bottle out of the air," he said with a wry chuckle.

"Forget it, son." Mando drew a deep breath and looked sidelong at Reno. "You're ripe and ready to hit the vengeance trail, or I'm a one-legged, humpbacked Mormon preacher!"

TWENTY-ONE

Reno might have been physically ready to hit the trail, but he wasn't sure if he was mentally ready.

The night after he'd shot the soldiers he couldn't sleep even after saying several heartfelt prayers, begging for forgiveness. He was sure god forgave him, for he'd only done what was right. He was ridding the earth of scum. Those bluebellies would have hanged Peter and killed him, Reno, and who knows what they would have done to Isabelle and Sara?

No, that was wrong. Reno knew exactly what they would have done to Isabelle and Sara. And they'd probably have killed Ty Mando, too, before setting fire to the place, ridding the yard of the evidence of their transgressions, and ridden on to continue their depredations elsewhere.

Once men got the taste of blood, Reno believed, they became wolves. They couldn't get enough of it.

Now they were gone. Others were safe.

Still, Reno couldn't sleep. He was glad when, the next morning, Ty demanded he and Sara stay one more day at the general store. He was bringing in a couple of good horses for Reno and Sara, and they wouldn't arrive at the general store until noon. He was trading for them with a nearby horse rancher who'd trapped the wild horses in the Monument Butte country of western Kansas and gentled them himself. They were fast, hardy, well-trained mounts. Better than any Mando currently had in his own remuda.

Besides, Sara was still woozy and achy from her run-in with the devil-soldier's horse.

They didn't train that day. They let their weapons rest. Ty set them up with new clothes. "Riding and fighting clothes," he told them.

Mando outfitted Reno in gray striped wool trousers with a flannel shirt and suspenders along with a canvas jacket and a new pair of black leather boots with pointed toes. Mando pulled a hat off a rack in the store and smiled as he set the broad-brimmed, sand-colored hat on Reno's head. The hat was crisp and fresh with newness. In fact, all the clothes were new. Reno had never worn anything new before. All of his clothes had first been worn by his brothers.

Mando bestowed upon Sara black cotton trousers with suspenders, cream linsey shirt, black felt hat with a neck thong, and a buckskin jacket hand sewn by his late wife and trimmed with Indian beads. Sara also received a new pair of black leather boots. She and Reno only balked politely at the gifts, for they couldn't pay for them. On the other hand, the clothes they'd worn when they'd ridden to the general store were now rags. They desperately needed new clothes. Anyway, they knew Mando wouldn't take no for an answer, so they shyly but gratefully accepted the gifts, and after long hot baths, they put them on, feeling like whole new human beings.

Just after noon, the rancher arrived with the two horses.

On receiving the clothes after the beautiful weapons Reno and Sara felt like royalty. Western Kansas royalty, but royalty just the same. When they saw the two horses Mando had brought in for them, they stared at the two fine beasts—a rangy buckskin gelding named Jack and a coal-black mare named Grace—in hang-jawed, tongue-tied shock. Mando assured Reno and Sara that he would give Coyote and Old Otis a good home right there at the general store, with plenty of time to frolic in his pastures.

The twins spent the balance of the day getting to know and gently riding their new mounts while Peter watched from his perch atop the corral rail and Mando and Isabelle watched from their hide-bottom chairs on the main building's broad porch. Isabelle looked sullen, sad.

Despite all the gifts Isabelle's father had bestowed up him and Sara, Reno felt the same way. He took no joy in leaving Isabelle. She'd stolen his heart, just as he had captured hers.

But Reno would return for her, and they would marry, and all would be right with the world.

That night after supper, Reno met Isabelle at their usual secret place in the hollow atop the bluff overlooking the South Platte. She sat at the edge of the hollow, her legs dangling over the ledge, facing the river that was turning spruce green in the dusk. He knew she heard him approach, because her head turned to one side before she turned it back forward to stare at the darkening river again.

Reno climbed down the rocks and sat beside her, letting his own legs dangle over the ledge. She didn't look at him but only stared at the river.

Reno kissed her cheek and held out a book to her. "I have something for you."

"What is it?"

"A book of poems by a fellow named Keats. My teacher introduced me to him. He's really good. I could read him all day—after the Good Book, I mean." He paused. "Can you read?"

Isabelle nodded as she studied the cloth-bound tome in her hands. "I know my letters." She ran her index finger over the single word written in gilt letters on the cover: "Poems."

"I marked a page and underlined a couple of lines. It's as if he wrote those words from me to you."

Isabelle opened the page Reno had marked with a scrap of notepaper.

She studied the words for a time, moving her lips. Her eyes glazed slightly. She cleared her throat and read: "'You are always new, the last of your kisses was ever the sweetest.'"

She looked up, blinking tears away.

Reno recited, "'Now a soft kiss—Aye, by that kiss I vow an endless bliss." He turned her head toward his and pressed his lips against hers. As he kissed her, he felt against his cheeks the wetness of her flowing tears.

When he pulled his lips from hers, she sniffed, brushed her cheeks with the backs of her hands. "I'm never going to see you again, Reno. I know I'm not."

"I promise, Isabelle."

"You can't promise me that, Reno." She studied him closely, sadly. She'd been holding a small bur-lap-wrapped object in her lap. Now she unfolded the burlap to reveal a small, stamped-leather box. "I want you to keep this with you. To remember me by. Open it at night and think of me."

Reno took the slender box. It was outfitted with small, delicate gold hinges and a gold latch on the edge. He tripped the latch and opened the box with a slight creaking sound. Isabelle's face stared up at him from the box's gilt-edged, velvet lining.

"Pa had us each sit for our ambrotypes in Julesburg last year. We each had one taken alone and then all three of us together. I want you to have this one of me."

Reno smiled down at the picture. Isabelle looked so formal, sitting in a brocade parlor chair with ornate wooden arms. Her thick, black hair was pulled up in a bun. She stared off, with just the hint of a smile on her lush lips, somewhere over Reno's left shoulder. She wore a polka-dot dress with a fancy lace collar and cuffs.

Reno swallowed a knot in his throat as he closed the box and wrapped it in the burlap. "I'll keep it close to me at all times."

"Be careful with it." Isabelle leaned toward him and pressed her sweet lips to his. "It's fragile. Just like my heart." She smiled from beneath her brows at the sentiment, no less sincere for being syrupy.

Reno drew her close and kissed her.

***

Reno didn't sleep much again that night.

His heart felt twisted inside his chest. He wasn't sure what caused the sensation—an eagerness to get back on the trail of his family's killers, his fear, or his deep sadness and reluctance to leave Isabelle, whom he was sure was his life's one true love. Miss Bernard had been his one true love, but she was gone now, and he had to move on. Isabelle had filled the empty space in his heart.

And now he was leaving her.

But he would be back. She might not allow him to promise her that, but he did so silently just the same. And he promised himself, as well.

Isabelle's sadness was so palpable in the kitchen that morning as she made and served breakfast, that hardly anyone spoke more than two or three words, and those were mainly to ask for the biscuits or the salt and pepper to be passed, or something like that. And even those were spoken in the hushed tones of a funeral.

After breakfast, Reno and Sara went out to saddle their horses—Grace and Jack. Mando and Peter followed them out. Isabelle had doctored her father's bullet-torn arm, and it hung now in a sling.

Silently, with Mando and Peter watching through the corral rails, Reno and Sara bridled and saddled their mounts. Peter opened the corral gate. As Sara let her black mare out of the corral, Peter limped up to her, and smiled. He held a double rig of black leather holsters in his right hand. They hung on a black leather cartridge belt filled with what appeared to be .44-caliber, rim-fire cartridges. An empty knife sheath hung from the belt, as well.

Sara looked at the young man in her frowning, grumpy way, glanced away, and then turned back to him. He stood where he'd been a second ago, smiling and holding up the gun rig.

Reno, standing just behind Sara, glanced at Mando. Ty stood leaning against the corral's gate post, smiling from Sara to Peter and back again. He glanced at Reno, winked, then returned his gaze to Sara and Peter.

"I don't get it," Sara said, still frowning, glancing at the handsome leatherwork. "For me?"

Peter's smiled broadened, and his dark Indian features turned a shade or two darker. "I made it myself. Leather from the last bull we butchered."

"He's been stayin' up late and gettin' up early, workin' on it," Mando said.

Since it didn't look like Sara was going to do anything more than stare at him in mute silence, wrinkling the skin above the bridge of her nose, Peter took a couple of tentative steps closer to her, and slid the cartridge belt and twin holsters toward her.

"Go on," Peter said. "They don't bite."

Sara glanced at Reno. She looked at Peter again, then at the belt. Stiffly, she reached out a gloved hand for the gun rig and took it from the young half-breed. She drew it to her slowly, looking for all the world as though it was really a rattler in her hands. She looked it over carefully. She peered at Reno and then turned the rig so he could see the front of both holsters. Each was adorned with a silver cross.

"It's not real silver, of course," Peter said. "But the metal nickeled up right nice to look like silver."

Reno felt a lump grown in his throat. If Sara did, as well, she did a good job of hiding it.

She turned to Peter and said, "I didn't get anything for you."

"I didn't expect you to. Just be safe out there. And… come back, if you've a mind."

Sara removed the twin Remington Piettas she wore wedged behind the plain brown leather belt around her waist. She shoved each revolver into each holster, snapped the keeper thongs over the hammers, and wrapped the rig with the two Remys around her waist. She slid her long knife, also a gift from Ty, into the sheath. She buckled the large, square, nickeled metal buckle and tied the thongs dangling from the holsters to her thighs.

"Rub mink oil into 'em from time to time," Peter advised. "That'll keep the leather from drying out. You can even rub some wax into them for a better draw."

Sara nodded. "Obliged."

Peter only smiled then limped back to stand near the gate post and his father.

Mando stepped up to Reno. He extended his big hand, and Reno shook it.

"Farewell," Ty said. "Go with your god, boy."

"I can't thank you enough, Ty. If I lived a thousand years…"

"If you lived a thousand years, I wouldn't want you to do anything more than kill that Bad Old Man and Black Bob and all the rest of that rebel scum."

He walked over to Sara. "Honey, would you shoot me if I gave you a hug?"

"I reckon you won't know till you try." Sara almost smiled.

Mando hugged her. Sara wrapped her arms around his back and pressed her forehead briefly against his shoulder. When she pulled her head away, Reno thought he noticed a faint sheen in her eyes. It disappeared quickly as she turned away and swung up onto the mare's back.

Reno mounted Jack and followed Sara into the yard. He looked around for Isabelle. She stood on the porch, staring at him pensively from over the railing. She had one arm on her chest. With the other hand, she fingered a lock of her long hair hanging against her neck. She gave him a brief smile. Reno pinched the brim of his new hat to her. Isabelle turned and walked into the cabin.

They'd said their goodbyes the night before.

"That girl's tumbled hard for you, boy," Mando said. "You come back and marry her, now, hear?"

He winked.

Reno grinned. "Yes, sir."

Hooves thudded to his left. He turned to see Sara galloping on out of the yard, heading west.

"Enough lollygagging for her," Mando said, chuckling.

"I reckon so." Reno looked at Apache. The shepherd lay next to Miss Foxie nearby, both dogs staring at their owners skeptically. "You ready to hit the trail 'Pach?"

The dog glanced at Miss Foxie and moaned.

"I think your dog's in the same boat as you are, boy," Mando said, grinning.

"Come on, Apache," Reno beckoned to the dog. "We'll be back. I promise."

Again, Apache looked at his sweetheart and moaned. Miss Foxie looked back at him, tilting her head dubiously.

Reno laughed and swung the buckskin across the yard. He yelled over his shoulder, "Thanks again for everything, Ty...Peter. We'll see you again soon!"

Reluctantly, Apache leaped to his feet and ran after Reno, barking.

As he rammed his heels into Jack's loins and the gelding lunged into a hard gallop, Reno wondered if he and Sara really would be back here again, or if he'd just told a lie that would one day come back to haunt him.

He remembered last—him and Isabelle in their love nest atop the bluff overlooking the river...

TWENTY-TWO

Lamar Humphries from Ringgold, Georgia, woke out of a dead sleep, sitting bolt upright. He tried to scream, for his neck was burning. He brought both hands up and instantly felt the oily slickness of what he knew right away, with a shrieking horror inside his head, was blood.

A face moved up close to his. The light of the low-burning coffee fire—Humphries' and his two partners' fire—flickered across the right cheek and glinted in the blue eyes of the pretty blond girl crouched over him. A broad- brimmed black hat shaded the upper half of her face from the afternoon sun. Still, the blue eyes blazed into his from the darkness beneath that hat brim.

From the dark shadow inside the girl's soul.

"Do you know what woke you, Reb?" she asked softly.

He looked down and saw blood spurting out from what he imagined in his speechless horror to be a long gash stretching across his neck.

The girl—a pretty little thing, but with the flat eyes of a cold-blooded killer—held up the wide-bladed knife from which blood dribbled onto Lamar Humphries' belly. He tried to speak, to ask for help...to beg for mercy, as though the wound wasn't so bad that either one would help...but he could work no words up through the blood flooding his throat.

Only blood oozed from his throat. He coughed it out, and it ran down over his chin, down his neck. He gasped for air, but choked when he breathed only blood, felt the strangling sensation of the blood filling up his lungs.

It was everywhere. He was drowning in it.

Oh, god, he thought, panting as panic rose in him, his heart racing, the screaming growing louder and shriller inside his head. Oh, god...oh, god...I'm dyin'! This pretty little blonde done killed me!

That horror-stricken thought had barely made its way through his brain before he flopped back against his saddle, dead.

***

Reno stood frozen, staring at his sister crouched over the dead man. He held the Henry repeating rifle in both hands across his thigh, squeezing it.

Sara straightened, looked over at Reno. She frowned then reached down to clean her knife on the gray trousers of the dead rebel lying before her. "What?"

Reno stared into her questioning eyes. Only then, as she gazed back at him, did Sara return to him. The young woman whom he'd watched slide the knife across the grayback devil's throat had been someone altogether different. Someone he had never seen before. Someone he did not know. It was as though he'd been riding with a stranger who only resembled his sister.

But then he supposed that back at Ty Mando's General Store, when he'd been killing the federal soldiers, he'd appeared a mere shadow of his own former self. A stranger inhabiting young Reno Bass's body…

"I thought we were going to try to take him alive," Reno said.

"I couldn't do it."

"Huh?"

"I said I couldn't do it." Sara pulled one side of her buckskin jacket back to slide the knife back into its sheath. "When I got up close to him, I remembered seeing his face at the trading post. That pinched-up rat's face. And I thought about that face maybe being the last face Mary Louise ever saw on this earth, and…well, I just couldn't do it. I had to kill him."

"We might have found out from him where the other two are, Sara."

"We know where the other two are, Reno. We heard the rifle shot earlier. They're out hunting. They left this fella here to recuperate by the fire."

Again, she glanced at the dead man. A blood-blackened felt bandage was wrapped around his thigh. According to the farmer they'd met down the river to the west a few miles, the dead man and his two compatriots had spent two nights in the farmer's barn a couple of nights back. The now-dead man had been wounded, and the other two, being cousins of his, had held back with him to help him recover.

That the trio was part of the Devil's Horde, there was no doubt. They were all dressed in Confederate gray, or at least scraps of Confederate gray, and were heavily armed with Confederate-model rifles and pistols. These three had come along behind the gang's main body, which had sacked a few more farms earlier, but was continuing west more quietly than before.

The farmer had said the horde had stopped at his farm but only for food and water, grain for their horses. Then they'd continued west along the South Platte, pushing deeper into the newly established Colorado Territory, likely intending to lose themselves in the mountains.

The farmer believed they were running low on guns and ammo. Also, the leader of the pack, the Bad

Old Man, had been severely wounded in his arm. He'd looked ghostly. He'd been sweating profusely and appeared in great pain. He'd asked the farmer for laudanum. When the farmer had reported he'd had no laudanum, Montgomery had demanded "squeez-in's'". All the farmer had was a crock jug of wild cur-rant wine; he'd turned it over to the colonel, who'd wrapped it carefully in cloth and stowed it in his war bag.

The Bad Old Man had also inquired about a doctor in the area, and the farmer had told him the nearest sawbones he knew about were in Denver City farther west along the South Platte.

The gang had left, taking only food for themselves and their horses, cloth for bandages for the old man, and the wine. They hadn't fired a single bullet. They'd pulled their horns in for the time being.

The three cousins, including the wounded man, had come along a day and a half later, and holed up in the farmer's barn until the farmer had grown peevish over how they'd ogled his eldest daughter. Getting the drop on the three of them early one morning, armed with a brace of Baby Dragoons and a percussion shot-gun, he and his stout Danish wife had ordered them to leave, which they'd done while cursing him and his wife up one side and down the other.

Earlier in the day, their third day of travel west of Ty Mando's store, Reno and Sara had picked up the trio's

AVENGING ANGELS: VENGEANCE TRAIL

trail in the farmer's yard, and followed it here, finding only the now-dead man asleep and sweating from the blood poisoning in his leg, most likely. They'd heard a distant rifle shot as they'd approached, and that's why they believed the other two were in the area, probably hunting, for there was little food in the three killers' makeshift camp.

"They'll likely be back soon," Reno said, casting his gaze into the grassy distance.

"And we'll welcome them with open arms." Sara retrieved her Henry from where she'd leaned it against a tree, levered a cartridge into the action, then off-cocked the hammer. "What did you do with the horses?"

"Tied them back in the trees. Left Apache back there, too. With orders to stay."

"The horses can't be seen from a distance?"

"No, they can't be seen, Miss Persnickety Britches."

"Just checking. Can't be too careful, with your head in the clouds."

"My head isn't in the clouds."

"You are distracted by Isabelle."

"No, I'm not."

"Yes, you are. I've seen it in your eyes."

Reno's cheeks warmed with embarrassment. He supposed he did think about her a lot. But he certainly didn't let thinking about her cloud his thinking about what he and Sara were out here to do. No, sir. He was as determined to avenge their family as Sara was.

He turned to the dead man and felt his insides re-coil. The man lay there staring up at the sky, his eyes wide in surprise. "We just gonna let him lay there?"

Sara was staring off toward the southwest. It was from that direction, off across a sea of fawn-colored grass, yucca, and prickly pear they'd heard the shot when they'd been riding up to the camp. "What else would we do with him?"

"I don't know. He just seems so exposed."

"Forget about him."

"I think we should say a few words over him."

Sara whipped her head toward Reno, her eyes bright with exasperation. "Say a few words over that demon spawn? The devil's progeny? He probably des-ecrated our sister, Reno!"

"Yeah, but..."

"What? You wanna pray for his soul?" Sara marched over and glared down at the dead man. She brought her right foot back then jerked it forward, burying the toe of her black leather boot in the dead man's side, making the body jerk—the body a little out of sync with the head. "I'll pray for his soul!"

She leaned forward, hardening her jaws and red-dening her cheeks. "May god send you to hell where you belong, you filthy, murderous vermin!"

Again, Sara kicked the dead man. The man jerked but kept staring at the sky.

Reno stared at his sister in shock.

She turned to Reno and said, "There, I said a few words over him. Now get your head straight and help me keep watch for the two other devils. They should be along soon."

She walked out a way from the camp and dropped to her knees in a patch of tall grass growing up out of a low area that must contain a seep, for some of the grass was green as though freshly watered. Reno turned back to the dead man. He might be vermin but he was still a man. Didn't god create every human being? Didn't he also love every human being, despite their failings?

Wasn't it a sin to kill? Only good men, he reminded himself.

To appease his obsessive thoughts on the subject, Reno silently muttered a quick prayer, asking that the man's soul be given a shot at salvation no matter how undeserving, then walked over to the left of Sara. He hunkered down in the grass beside a box elder tree, facing his sister who knelt staring toward the southwest, though from to time she turned her head to survey the whole area.

Reno found himself worrying about her. He'd been anxious about her off and off for a long time now. Ever since their family was killed, anyway. He hadn't really put his finger on what worried him about Sara until now.

But now he knew what troubled him.

He worried about her soul.

He wondered if she'd lost her religion. Her belief in god. If she no longer believed in god, she would go to hell when she died. The possibility nagged at Reno. He couldn't let that happen.

Sara was a good, sweet, decent person deep down. At least, she had been before the killings. Now, Reno wasn't certain. She might have not only lost her faith in god but her faith in humanity, as well.

Somehow, he had to bring her back around to their father's teachings. Back to god. Reno loved his sister more than anyone or anything else on earth, and he could not let her go to hell.

Besides, her hot-bloodedness wasn't always practical. They had to learn where the Bad Old Man was headed, and they could learn that from the other two men who'd camped out here—if he and his sister left at least one of them alive.

"Sara, you let me take down the next two," Reno said. "I'll put a bullet in 'em, but I don't want to kill 'em. We have to learn where Montgomery and Hobbs are headed."

"We know where they're headed," Sara said, still looking into the distance, her senses as keen as a deer's. "They're headed for Denver City."

"At least they were a week or so ago. They might have moved on from there now. I heard Denver City's big, and we won't be able to track them out of there."

"I'm betting they're still there. You winged Montgomery pretty good, sounds like. He'll likely be laid up for a while. I heard that after Colorado became its own territory and gold was found along Cherry Creek, Denver City became seven kinds of a hellish sewer.

"Even after the rebellion started down south, and a lot of the northern men left. A lot stayed. Miners and saloon men and freighters, mostly. And hurdy-gurdy girls, of course. Montgomery's men will love it. They're likely stomping with their tails up right now, tipping back the devil's juice." Sara stretched her lips back from her white teeth in a cold, eager grin. "We'll be able to shoot 'em down like ducks off a mill pond."

"Just the same, Sara—let me ambush these two. I want to take one alive. Will you please humor me for once in your life, sis?"

Sara turned to him and smiled. "All right. Here comes your chance."

Reno frowned. "Huh?"

Sara canted her chin to indicate due south. "They're heading this way."

TWENTY-THREE

Reno swung his head sharply left and stared out over the long grass growing by the seep, out to where the shorter grass grew with the yucca and the prickly pear, the grass out there now cinnamon-colored with the fall.

Two horseback shadows moved toward him and Sara. They were probably a half a mile away, a little larger than stick figures from this distance. Stick figures silhouetted against the horizon stretching away behind them, under a high-vaulting sky in which the sun hung at around the two o'clock position. Cloud shadows swept over and around the riders, like smoke from chimney fires being shepherded along by a fast wind.

Dread touched Reno. More killing.

Two more men, alive now, would be dead soon. Reno had killed several men by this time, but he wasn't accustomed to it. Killing repelled him. He supposed that was a good thing. But he had a job to do. And being repelled by killing people didn't make it any easier.

"Let me have 'em," Reno said, slowly levering a round into the Henry's breech.

"They're all yours, brother."

Reno scuttled forward until he sat at the very edge of the high grass. He was further concealed by scraggly wild plum shrubs growing at the edge of the seep, the plums red, but some beginning to ripen toward purple. He off-cocked the Henry's hammer and sat back against the heels of his new boots, which were still uncomfortably hard, not having been broken in yet, and rested the cocked Henry across his thighs. He caressed the hammer with his gloved right thumb, flicked his right index finger up and down the slender, crescent trigger.

He looked around, judging how hard the wind was blowing and from which direction. He picked up some dirt and sand, held it high, and let it sift through his fingers. The wind was blowing from the west. Not hard, but he'd have to allow for it.

The riders continued moving toward Reno and Sara. They were walking their mounts, spaced roughly twenty feet apart, occasionally moving a little closer together then apart again. At one point, they rode around the west side of some obstacle before them—maybe a patch of prickly pear or possibly a coiled rattlesnake. Then they came straight on again.

Slowly their silhouettes grew against the horizon, until finally Reno could see that one wore a collarless striped shirt and suspenders and dark trousers. The other was bare chested, wearing only suspenders holding up his old, torn gray cavalry trousers. He was skinny and his skin, including that of his long, hawk-nosed face, was bronzed by the sun. Gray, sunken-topped Confederate kepis with square visors topped both men's heads.

One of the horses whickered and blew, shaking its head, rattling the bit in its teeth. Reno could hear the sounds clearly now, which meant it was time for him to go to work.

Our Father who art in Heaven, hallowed be thy name…

He raised the Henry, adjusting the sliding sight just ahead of the breech, pressed the brass butt plate against his shoulder, and flicked the hammer back with his thumb. He let the sights hover over the man riding on his left.

Your kingdom come, your will be done, on earth as it is in heaven…

He compensated for distance and wind, and steadied the barrel.

Give us this day our daily bread…

He drew a breath, took up the slack in his index

finger, and drew back on the trigger.

The Henry thundered.

And forgive us our trespasses, as we forgive those who trespass against us...leastways, those who didn't murder our family...

Reno drew a breath and watched as the man he'd aimed at jerked sharply to one side and fell back in his saddle. The man's legs flew up; his hat blew away on the wind. The man's yell, muffled by wind and distance, reached Reno's ears only after the man had tumbled over the tail of his horse and struck the ground behind it. The horse whinnied as it lurched forward and ran off to the west, buck-kicking.

And lead us not into temptation...

Quickly, Reno levered another round into the Henry's chamber and slid the rifle toward the other man, who stared at his fallen partner in shock. He was close enough, within fifty yards, that Reno could see his mouth hanging open. Reno aimed for the man's shoulder, squeezed the trigger.

But deliver us from evil...

Just as his index finger drew back against the trigger, the man swung his right leg over his saddle horn. The bullet hit him right as he started his leap to the ground, drawing two pistols from the holsters on his hips.

He wailed and fell forward and rolled in the grass. Reno wasn't sure where he'd hit the man, but he was pretty sure it wasn't in the shoulder.

"Hellfire! Let's go!"

Reno leaped to his feet and strode quickly forward, angling slightly left, toward the man he'd first shot. Sara made a bee-line for the second man, who just then leaped to his feet, clutching a hand to his neck. Blood spurted from between his fingers. The man shouted a wretched profanity when he saw the young man and woman walking toward him and his fallen comrade, and said, "Who the hell are you, and why'd you shoot me, blame it?"

"Put the gun down," Sara told him.

The man held a revolver down against his right leg. It appeared to be cocked. Sara extended both of her big Remingtons straight out from her shoulders as she strode toward the Confederate, her long blond hair and the flaps of her buckskin jacket blowing behind her and to one side in the western wind.

"Drop the gun!" she repeated when the man only stared at her, crouching and clamping his hand against his neck.

"I asked you a question," he said, his voice shrill with pain and anger. "Why did you shoot me, you little polecat?"

"You killed my family. Put the gun down."

Reno watched warily as Sara approached the neck-wounded man, who still held the gun down by his side. Reno walked over to where the man he'd wounded in the arm flopped around in the grass before him, twenty-five feet away. Reno was closing the distance as quickly as Sara was closing the distance between her and the neck-wounded Confederate.

The neck-wounded man stumbled backward. "You followed us?" he screeched.

"That's right. We followed you. And we are going to kill each one of you scurvy devils."

The man cursed again and raised the gun in his right hand. Reno stopped dead in his tracks. His heart lurched. But Sara didn't let the neck-wounded man get his gun leveled on her. She shot him again. The bullet tore into his right shoulder. He howled and flew backward, hitting the ground and rolling.

He clambered back to his feet, looked at Sara over his shoulder, and screamed, "You're loco as a peach orchard sow!"

He ran stumbling off to the south.

Sara glanced at Reno and sighed. Reno looked at the man running away from her. They weren't going to get anything out of that one. He did not begrudge his sister the bullet she sent hurling into the back of the fleeing man's head. When the neck-wounded man had hit the ground and rolled and lay still, Reno turned his attention back to the man on the ground before him.

The man clutched his right arm with his left hand. He was no longer thrashing but lay on his back, staring up in anger and terror at Reno, who now stood over him. Reno was surprised at how young he was. He appeared even younger than Reno. Maybe by as much as two years. He was skinny with long, greasy, dark-red hair and a long, angular, hollow-cheeked face. His sunburned cheeks wore a patchy red down. The shirt he wore was relatively new. So were his trousers and black leather shoes. He'd plundered the clothes from a man he'd killed, most likely.

Reno looked at the kid's eyes. They were wide and round and filled with more fear now than anger.

"I...I'm sorry," the young Confederate said, haltingly. "About your...your family, I mean..."

Reno drew a sharp breath to calm himself. He tried not to look into the kid's eyes anymore. He wouldn't be able to do what needed to be done if he looked into his eyes. His guts writhed, and he spat to one side, trying to keep his anger up.

He said, "Where's your gang headed? The Devil's Horde. Where they headed?"

"Look at what you done to my arm!"

"Do you remember what you did to my family? No, you probably don't. There's been too many you've massacred to remember only five poor souls."

"I need help here! I'm in miserable pain!"

Sara stepped up on the other side of the skinny Confederate. "You're gonna be in a whole lot more pain if you don't tell us where the rest of your grayback slime is headed."

"This is awful! Look how I'm bleedin'!"

Sara raised one of the Remys. Both were still in her hands. She angled the barrel toward the sobbing rebel and drilled a bullet through his other arm, just above the elbow.

"Sara!" Reno said.

The skinny Confederate screamed shrilly as he fell back against the ground. He looked down at his second wounded arm in wide-eyed, hang-jawed shock.

"Where are they headed, you miserable piece of dung? Where are they going after Denver City?" Sara asked, her voice ominously calm as she again clicked the Remington's hammer back. She gazed down the barrel at the red-faced kid's head. "The next one's gonna go through your left knee if you don't tell me. The one after that—"

"I don't know!" the kid screamed at Sara, forked veins bulging in his forehead.

"Tell me!" Sara aimed at the kid's left knee.

"I told you—I don't know where the colonel an' the major is headed! They just said we was gonna ride west and kill us some more Yankees and live high on the hog on the Union spoils! We was gonna rob us some Union banks and become rich on Union wealth, and then we was gonna go back home and run all the federals an' the northern bankers an' the carpetbaggers out of the south, and we was gonna rebuild the

Confederacy!"

"All right," Sara said. "Thank you."

"Sara!" Reno screamed when he saw what she was going to do next.

She didn't even blink as she put the next bullet through the skinny Confederate's head.

"What?" she asked Reno, frowning, as Reno gazed at her in open shock. "We got what we wanted out of him." She holstered each pistol in turn, shoving them down snug in the black leather holsters trimmed with the nickeled crosses Peter had made for her. "I'm gonna run down his horse. I think I saw a deer tied behind the saddle. Suppertime soon."

She walked away.

Reno stared at her back, then turned to stare down at the skinny Confederate staring up at him through half-shut lids.

For thine is the kingdom, and the power, and the glory, forever and ever. Amen.

TWENTY-FOUR

Sara did the cooking that night, so after supper Reno took the dishes down to a creek curving east of the camp, within a thin sheathing of fall-painted river birches and cottonwoods, and gave them a good scrubbing with handfuls of pebbles and sand.

The sun was not yet down, but the light was soft and shadows were long. An autumn chill was building. As he scrubbed out a cast-iron skillet he'd found in the gear of the two dead Confederates, along with several gold and silver coins plundered from Union shops and banks, Reno felt chicken flesh rise across his back.

Suddenly, he didn't feel alone out here. He looked up suddenly, and apprehension closed its cold fist around him. He hadn't brought the Henry with him, for he'd been packing the dishes and the skillet. But he had both Colts. He wore them now in both the

flap-top holsters he'd taken off the two dead Confederates, for they no longer had need of the scabbards.
He wore one for the cross-draw on his right hip, the
other in the same position on his left hip.

He was about to drop the pan he'd been cleaning
and reach for the pistols but forestalled the move
when he saw that the man sitting a tall, roan stallion on a bluff on the other side of the creek was not
wielding a weapon of his own. The man appeared
tall and rangy. He was a Negro fellow in buckskins
and a broad-brimmed, leather sombrero with a neck
thong dangling down his chest. He wore high-topped
Indian moccasins. A rifle in a buckskin scabbard decorated with many colorful Indian beads was strapped
to his saddle.

As Reno gazed up at the man, who sat sideways
to him, and the man stared back at him. They studied each other for a long time, Reno's heart beating
quickly. Finally, the man raised one brown-gloved
hand to his hat and touched two fingers to the brim
in salute. He touched his heels to the roan's flanks and
rode on down the bluff's opposite side, slowly sliding
from Reno's view.

Reno felt as though he'd seen a ghost. The man had
been there, and then he was gone. There was only the
salmon-tipped top of the bluff staring back at Reno
now.

He quickly finished washing the skillet, the two

plates, the two cups, and two spoons, piled every-thing atop the skillet, and hurried back into the trees where his and Sara's fire flickered. Inside the woods surrounding the fire, darkness had fallen, relieved only by a patch of luminous green in the sky above.

He found Sara sitting by the fire, running a clean-ing patch down the barrel of her Henry repeater. Apache lay curled up beside her, tired from the long day's journey, but he thumped his tail when Reno entered the camp. Both of Sara's Remington Piettas were laid out before her, on a clean felt cloth.

She'd taken them apart and cleaned and oiled them. That's what she'd been doing when Reno had left the camp. She'd cleaned them every bit as careful-ly and lovingly, her tongue pressed to the top of her bottom lip, her eyes sort of hazy with affection, as she was now cleaning the Henry. They were like babies to Sara. Only Sara likely wouldn't show nearly as much as affection to babies as she did her guns.

"Hey, sis—guess what?" Reno set their utensils down near one of the two canvas war bags in which they carried their cooking gear.

"What?"

"I just seen a man. A Negro."

Sara glanced at him, frowning. She stopped run-ning the rod, tipped with an oiled cotton patch, down the Henry's barrel. "A black man?"

"Yeah, I was down by the creek. I just looked up

and there he was. A black man in buckskins sitting a
fine-looking roan stallion."

Sara let her gaze flicker off, repeating Reno's
words quietly, moving her own lips. She looked at
Reno again, and asked, "Did he see you?"

"He saw me before I saw him."

"Did he look like trouble?"

"Well, he was armed. Had two pistols and a knife
strapped around his waist, had a rifle of some kind in
a saddle boot. He didn't threaten me with any of 'em,
though. We studied each other for a time and then he
just waved and rode away."

Sara regarded her brother critically for a time. "Are
you sure you saw a black man on a fine roan stallion,
Reno?"

Reno scowled, incredulous. "What—you think I'd
lie about somethin' like that?"

"No, but I do know your mind takes fanciful turns
now and then. Sometimes I wish Miss Bernard never
taught you to read. It was after you started reading—"

"He was real, Sara." Indignantly, Reno began drying the utensils he'd washed, and shoved them into a
war bag. "My fanciful turn of mind didn't make up no
black man on a fine roan stallion."

"All right, all right—don't get your drawers in a
twist." Sara resumed thoughtfully cleaning her rifle.
"I doubt he's with the Devil's Horde. No black man
would ride with the Bad Old Man and Black Bob,

since they're all Confederates and they been rebelling over freeing the slaves."

"Nah, he wasn't with them devils, all right. Seemed like he was just passin' through."

"Since he's got his own fine horse, I reckon he's not after ours, either. Unless he wants them to sell."

"I doubt it. He didn't seem like trouble. I think he was just passin' through. Just gave me a shiver, though—seein' him up there of a sudden. I reckon if he'd wanted to, he could have shot me. I mean, if he was one of the Devil's Horde."

Sara gently leaned the clean Henry against a tree and opened one of the four boxes of .44 rimfire cartridges Mando had given them—two for Reno and two for Sara. One hundred rounds total. "I reckon we're gonna have to be more careful. I mean, we're far from home. Not that we have a home anymore. But we're out here in the wide open frontier."

"Meaning what?"

"Meaning that there are more men than just the Bad Old Man's men we have to worry about. Like Pa said, many men came west to escape the law back east because out here there's dang few laws. At least, dang few lawmen to enforce them."

"Meaning what?" Reno repeated.

"Meaning we both have to keep our heads clear and our eyes and ears skinned on our back trails as well as on the trail ahead of us." She paused for affect then added, "Even when we're scrubbing dishes."

Reno heard his sister's admonishing words. He also heard what she did not say. At least, not out loud. She'd also reminded him to stop pining for Isabelle Mando, because pining when the chips were down might get him killed.

He knew she was right. Still, after they'd bedded down and let the fire go out, in case the black man returned or any other bad men came, Reno waited until he could hear Sara breathing deeply, regularly, indicating she was asleep.

Then he reached quietly into his saddlebags, pulled out the burlap wrapped ambrotype Isabelle had given him, and admired it in the remaining amber glow of the nearly dead fire.

Reno thought he remembered Miss Cassie Bernard saying one time how all roads once led to Rome, which was a city far away across the ocean and existed a long, long time ago, before the barbarians sacked it. Sort of like how the Devil's Horde sacked so many farms and little towns in western Kansas, Reno supposed.

Anyway, all the trails out here in the newly established Colorado Territory seemed to lead to Denver City. At least, that's how it appeared the closer and closer they got to the town on the banks of the South Platte and Cherry Creek. More trails intersected the main one—the one they'd been following for the past three days. They knew the wide trace cut through the buck brush, buffalo grass, yucca, and sage lead to Denver because occasionally they'd seen a crude wooden signed marked DENVER CITY with the distance in miles painted beneath it or to the right of it. The older signs still said KANSAS TERRITORY, while the newer signs said COLORADO TERRITORY.

They hadn't started to see other folks using the trail until a day ago, the day after they'd killed the three Confederates and confiscated their deer and a few of their cooking supplies and gold and silver coins, which would come in handy when they needed trail supplies. The twenty-five dollars Mando had given them wouldn't last forever.

Around noon yesterday, they'd started to meet farm or ranch wagons on occasion, and men on horseback. Some of the pilgrims came up from behind Reno and Sara and passed on by. Some were soldiers, but most of the riders were dressed like ranch hands—some better than others, but most wearing mustaches or full beards and wearing a saddle gun or two, and sometimes a sheathed Sharps or Springfield rifle. Almost all were men, though a couple of the farm wagons carried dour-looking women in drab dresses with stovepipe collars.

When most of the men met Reno and Sara or passed them along the trail, they nodded politely or touched fingers to their hat brims. But there were a few who looked a little too long at Sara. She stared stonily straight ahead, ignoring them. When two such men passed them, Reno heard them muttering to each other and snickering. He looked back once to see one man, well older than Reno and Sara, looking over his own thick shoulder at Sara, a lewd expression twisting his mustached lips and glinting in his otherwise dull eyes.

Reno gritted his teeth and steeled himself against pulling his Remingtons from the soft leather holsters on his hips and blowing two rounds through the back of the guttersnipe's head.

Sara had been right. It was wide open out here. There were few laws. At least, few that were obeyed. It seemed to be that way with the laws of personal propriety, as well.

A nice distraction from pondering the darkness of men was the nearly solid wall of mountains that grew larger and larger as Reno and Sara continued following the trail along the river to the southwest. Reno had never seen mountains before. He had never seen anything larger than the chalky sandstone and limestone bluffs poking up from the prairie grass in western Kansas. The sight before him now made his stomach feel light as air. The mountains vaulting up out of the distant western prairie were like the teeth on a giant saw blade. Some teeth, worn down by time, were smaller than others. Some loomed above the others; these were tipped with white.

Reno couldn't help staring at that vast ruggedness, trying to imagine what the mountains would be like if he rode up into them, if such a thing were possible. But he'd heard it was possible, for gold had been discovered high in the Colorado Rockies. That the mountains formed a solid stone wall must be an illusion caused by distance. There must be gaps between those tall peaks, and at least some of those gaps had to be threaded with trails.

He'd like to see for himself one day.

"Reno." Sara's voice nudged him out of his reverie.

He looked at her. She'd stopped her horse on a low butte above a dry creek.

"Get your head out of the mountains," she scolded him. "Look there."

She turned her gaze to the south and west, where a giant city sprawled among the shallow, grassy bluffs. Reno halted his buckskin. He'd been smelling the overfilled-privy odor of the city—or of what he figured was the stench of the city, for what else could it be?—for a good hour now, but he hadn't caught sight of it until now. Denver City was almost as impressive as the mountains pushing up beyond it in the west, forming a natural stockade from north to south.

"Holy moly," Reno said. "That's even bigger than Julesburg."

"Must be three, four times as big," Sara said. "Stinks to high heaven, too."

"Yeah." Reno wrinkled his nose at the stench. "Hope the Lord don't mind." The reek wasn't just from privies but from stock, as well. And coal and wood smoke. Maybe even from the mingling of a great crowd of unwashed humanity. Whatever caused it, it wasn't pleasant.

"How could he not?"

"I never did see such a place," Reno said, still staring in fascination as a big Pittsburg freight wagon rumbled past him and Sara on the trail they'd learned from other wayfarers was called the Southern Cutoff of the Overland Trail. They'd been seeing more and more such freight rigs as they'd neared Denver City— big, stout-wheeled wagons piled high with freight covered with dirty white tarpaulins and pulled by anywhere from four to ten mules nearly as big as buffalo. The freight was likely being hauled from Kansas City or St. Louis to Denver City or the gold camps cropping up in the mountains farther west.

Such wagons were driven by stocky, bearded gents in canvas pants, suspenders, and wool shirts, floppy hats shading their eyes from the burning western sun. Reno had heard some of them talking and yelling at their mules in foreign tongues. The men were well-armed against Indian attacks, for now in the late 1860s, the Sioux, Cheyenne, and Arapaho were intent on keeping the growing herds of "pale eyes" out of their ancestral homelands, which the whites seemed intent on appropriating and desecrating.

Reno was glad he and Sara hadn't seen any Indians. So far. Passing freighters—those who spoke English—had warned him and Sara of the dangers.

Apache sat a few feet ahead of where Reno and Sara sat their horses. He'd briefly, sportingly chased the last freight team that had passed but he'd returned to his master and mistress soon thereafter to sit now, regarding the sprawling city on the prairie before him. His ears were up—at least, as far as they would go, for the tips always curled down slightly—and made a low moaning sound deep in his chest.

"I know what you mean, Apache. A city that size kinda gives me the fantods, too. Especially after seeing the perdition that Julesburg was."

"Yeah, well, the Devil's Horde headed here," Sara said. "So I reckon we're headin' in to mix with perdition dwellers. No time like the present."

She clucked the black mare forward, and Reno did likewise to his buckskin. To Apache, he said, "Climb on up here, 'Pache." He leaned back to pat the horse's rump behind him. "Safer up here as we ride through town."

Apache did as he'd been told, settling himself atop

Reno's saddlebags and bedroll, around which he'd wrapped his canvas jacket.

"You really think they're here, Sara?" Reno asked as they rode toward the sprawling town. "Seems like they'd avoid a town this size. There's gotta be law in Denver City."

"Yeah, but there's a sawbones here, too. Probably more than one. And since the Bad Old Man needed a doctor on account of you, I'd say they're here, all right. At least, they were. We'll find out soon, I reckon."

"If they were here, the townsfolk would know about it. It's not like them graybacks don't stand out."

TWENTY-FIVE

Reno and Sara followed the main trail past the town's ragged outskirts comprised of old shanties and miners' shacks sulking in the brush, and stock pens and large wooden warehouses. A little farther along, the trail became a very wide, dirt-paved street, which a wooden sign identified as Market Street. It was lined on both sides by the largest buildings Reno had ever seen.

Many were only one or two stories but still impressive, for special care had been taken in their construction. Some were three and four stories high. Whereas most of the buildings in Julesburg had been constructed of raw planks, or whipsawed wood frames or logs or a mixture of both as well as of tent canvas, many of the structures here were of brick. Not merely mud adobe bricks but real oven-baked clay.

Reno and Sara simply rode for a while, swinging their heads from one side of the street to the other in amazement at the extraordinary structures surrounding them, as well as at the variety of humanity teaming in every direction. Seemingly, all the races of mankind abounded here, moving along the wooden sidewalks and crisscrossing the busy streets. He saw all manner of wheeled contraption, as well. In addition to buckboards and drays, there were leather buggies and carriages of all shapes and sizes. Some were driven by men dressed to the nines including long black coats and stovepipe hats.

The blond twins and their dog passed a large brick structure boasting an ornate wooden balcony stretched across its second floor and out front of which men in three-piece suits and armed with brass musical instruments were boarding a wagon. They all wore big smiles and a jubilant air. Staring up at the building, Reno saw the words DENVER ATHENAEUM stretched across a masonry slab near the very top of the place, just beneath the roof. A wooden ladder-sign mounted on the boardwalk fronting the structure's many arched front doors announced: CURRENTLY APPEARING: MADAM DIDELOT'S PARISIAN DANCE COMPANY.

"Well, I'll be hanged," Reno said as they passed the rollicking band boarding the wagon. "Must be a show house of some kind. Or a dance hall."

"A theater, I believe, is what they call it. You'd know that if you had actually listened to Miss Bernard instead of only sniffing her perfume and ogling her pretty dresses."

Reno wrinkled his note at his colicky twin.

Awhile later they passed a smaller brick building housing the HOLLADAY OVERLAND MAIL & EXPRESS Co., which a heavily loaded stagecoach was just the pulling away from, being jerked along by a six-hitch team of wild-looking horses. They rode on and paused before the hulking Methodist Episcopal Church, easily the largest building they'd seen in town so far, and that was saying something.

Reno tipped his head far back to stare up at the massive structure. "For the love o' ole St. Pete, would you get a load of that steeple?"

"They put a lot of work into it, that's for sure."

"At least, there's good Christian folks in these parts. Makes me feel a little better."

"Well, if there are, I sure haven't seen any I'd call good Christians. The language I've been hearing is not in the vocabulary of good Christians. Not even Catholics talk like that. And while we've come across one church, and a big one, at that, I've so far counted twenty-one drinking establishments and other establishments which I'm sure serve drinks, though they appear to specialize in other sundry delights of the vilest kind."

Reno's cheeks warmed. He'd seen those, too, but discretion had prevented him from pointing them out to his sister. He hadn't thought she'd noticed. But, of course, she had. Few things slipped past Sara.

"It does give me hope," Sara said.

Reno frowned. "What do you mean?"

"Hope that the Devil's Horde is still here. A perdition like this one, and of this size, with this many drinking establishments as well as houses of pure wickedness no doubt grabbed a'hold of the Bad Old Man and Black Bob's crew. Also, I think they'd fit in better than we suspected they would. Why, there's folks of all stripes on these streets. While the Confederates would stick out, they wouldn't stick out that far. And they might be trying to fit in."

Sara was looking around, narrowing her eyes. "I just bet they're still around here...somewhere. It might take us some time to find them, but find them, we will."

"I reckon we're gonna have to start inquiring."

"I reckon we are."

"Let's put our horses up. I think we'll be spending the night."

"That we will. Maybe a couple of nights, though I'll take no pleasure in it." Staring at a couple of bare-chested men wrestling out front of a saloon, in an area marked off by ropes and surrounded by cheering men, Sara wrinkled her nose. "Animals."

"I saw a livery barn a ways back," Reno told her, and swung the buckskin around.

They rode half a block back in the direction from which they'd come and pulled up at HANS JOHANS-SEN LIVERY & FEED. A man in canvas trousers and sack shirt under a black sack coat sat whittling a stick, leaning his chair back against one of the barn's open doors. A couple of hostlers worked in the paddocks stretching off each side of the barn, and a tall young man in suspenders and collarless shirt worked inside the barn directly behind him, applying soap to dried out tack hanging from a peg.

"Excuse me, sir?" Reno said.

The man lifted his head, and the brim of his cloth immigrant hat rose to reveal two steel blue eyes and a thick, black, handlebar mustache badly in need of trimming. His face was long, and pocked flesh sagged off the high cheekbones. He let his eyes flick from Reno to Sara then back to Reno.

He let the front legs of his chair drop down to the ground. "Ja? How can I help you, young folks? You want to stable your horses. Octar Lever, they look worn out!"

"First things first," Sara said before Reno could re-spond. "How much for stabling, feeding, and a good rubdown?"

He pointed at the prices written on a shingle tacked to the barn's front wall, between the doors and a sashed window. "Seventy-five cents per horse for stabling and feed. An extra ten cents for a good rubdown."

"What?" Sara said, astonished.

"This is Denver City, young lady. My prices are as cheap as you'll find, and I fill up quick this time of day. Men come in from the mines to stomp with their tails up." The man whom Reno assumed was Hans Johanssen swung his arms and stomped his feet in a bizarre pantomime of dancing.

The liveryman grinned.

He narrowed his eyes at Sara, and they flashed in appreciation. "But you're a pretty one, though. For you and your brother—jah, you're brother an' sister, all right, Ich kann die Ähnlichkeit sicher sehen!—I'll knock off five cents from the stabling and feed. That would be ninety cents, then. Best prices in town!"

Sara scowled at him. "If you knock off five cents, that would be eighty cents."

Johanssen furled his shaggy black brows laced with gray. "It would?" He looked up, counting on his sausage-sized, crooked fingers. "Octar lever—you're right!" He grinned again. "All right, all right. Eighty cents it is."

Sara gave Reno a sour look, rolled her eyes, and sighed.

She and Reno and Apache dismounted. Apache saw a cat poke its head out from a break between two buildings, and ran off to chase it despite Reno's admonition to stay.

"Don't worry," Sara told him. "That vermin cur will be back to continue to share his fleas."

"Apache don't have fleas!" Reno said, indignant.

Ignoring her brother, Sara gave her reins to Hans Johanssen and said, "You haven't seen a gang of Confederates pull through Denver City—have you, Mr. Johanssen? The Devil's Horde?"

"The Devil's Horde? Ach du meineGüte!"

The young man working in the barn paused in his work to cast Reno and Sara a dubious look. He wore a frayed bowler hat, and he had a long, lumpy nose and pimple-spotted cheeks.

"No, I haven't seen any gangs called the Devil's Horde. Are you sure they came this way? Why are you looking for them?"

"They killed our family," Sara said, shucking her rifle from her saddle boot.

Reno pulled his own Henry from its scabbard. "I shot the gang's leader, and last we heard, he was looking for a sawbones."

"Ach du meineGüte!" the liveryman repeated, shaking his head. Reno translated the expression as something akin to: "Holy cow!" Or, possibly: "What is the world coming to?"

"If this Devil's Horde is in town, I haven't heard about them or seen them. Around here, it's best to mind your own business. To look away from trouble, because there's plenty enough around that you don't want to get involved in." Johanssen, holding both sets of reins now, glanced at the young man with the long nose working in the barn. "Eddie, come and take these mounts inside for tending then turn them into the north lot."

When Eddie, glancing shyly at Sara, who ignored his bashful glance, had retrieved the horses and led them through the open double doors, Johanssen turned to his young customers again. "How many are in this gang?"

"Probably only a dozen or so by now," Sara said proudly. "We've been whittling down their numbers a little at a time."

"Is there no law after this Devil's Horde?"

"There were, back in Kansas, but they turned chicken."

"We don't think the law is quite cutout to deal with the likes of the Devil's Horde," Reno explained.

"Oh?" asked Johanssen. "And why would that be?"

"Because they're a big bunch, and dangerous. And for most of the badge-toters, it's not personal." Sara glanced around the street, looking for the men she and Reno were after. "It's easier to give such dangerous devils a wide berth when you got no dog in the fight." She glanced at the liveryman again. "So to speak."

Reno said, "We promised our father we'd avenge him and our ma and brothers and our older sister, Mary Louise. We don't take promises lightly, Mr. Johanssen."

"We're going to kill them all," Sara added. She looked off again. "And the sooner we can find them, the sooner we'll do just that. Buck them all out with lead, send them to hell, and close and bolt the smoking gates behind them."

Johanssen stood regarding them as though they'd each sprouted two heads. He rubbed his jaw and said, "Echt? Where do you two come from, anyway?"

"Western Kansas," Reno told him. "Baxter, Kansas, to be exact. Leastways, a farm near there."

Johanssen nodded slowly. "This must be quite a country, this Baxter, Kansas, to have bred up such a determined pair of man-hunters. A young pair of twins who'll hunt down killers the law is afraid of..."

"I don't know about that," Reno said. "But we are, all right."

TWENTY-SIX

Johanssen gave Reno and Sara the name of a nearby hotel that wouldn't break their bank.

It was called the Platte, and they found it—a three-story, white-painted frame building—on Fifteenth Street. The room wasn't much, but it would do. When Reno had dropped his rifle on the lumpy bed covered in a wash-worn, faded quilt, and opened the window to freshen the stale air, the low roar of the city infiltrated his and Sara's temporary sanctuary.

He didn't mind the noise or even the stink of trash and slop buckets that had apparently been emptied right into the street or into the alleys flanking the buildings. He'd never seen anything like Denver City before. He found the constant activity heady, intoxicating. The bustle of people and the variety of shops they swarmed around, like bees in a hive, was endlessly fascinating. He hadn't been able to stop looking from here to there and to over there since he and Sara had first ridden into town.

He drew a deep breath of the relatively fresh air. As he looked around at the town over which shadows were stretching, he saw the Athenaeum Theatre one block over to the north. He could see only from the balcony up from his vantage here in the Platte's third story room, at a rear corner of the building. On the balcony now were four or five colorfully attired ladies lounging around, smoking cigarettes from long holders, leaning forward against the balcony rail and waving and calling down to the street below them.

"Come on in, boys," Reno heard one of them call, her high clear voice ringing above the city's din. "Shows runs every hour after seven. You're going to want to see them all, because they get better as the night wears on—don't they, Daphne dear?" she asked, turning to the tall brunette clad in purple silks and black feathers on her left.

The brunette leaned forward and shouted something into the street below but the other woman's pronouncement had evoked a series of whoops and yells so loud that the brunette's words were drowned.

Still, they echoed inside Reno's head: "You're going to want to see all three, because they get better as the night wears on..."

What had she meant by "better"? Just what kind of shows was she—?

"See him?" Sara said behind him, startling him.

"What's that?"

Sara stepped up beside him and looked out the window and into the street. "I assumed your critter was what you were looking for."

"Oh, yeah," Reno said, feeling a little chagrined. He'd hoped to seen his beloved dog on the bustling streets below the Platte, maybe having followed their scent, if Apache could pick out Reno and Sara's scent from the potpourri of aromas wafting through the city. They hadn't seen the shepherd dog since he'd taken off after the cat at Johanssen's livery barn. However, the ladies—if you could call them that— over at the Athenaeum had distracted Reno from his endeavor. "Uh...no, no, I don't see him, doggone it."

He yelled the dog's name. The word "Apache" got him more than a few dubious stares from passersby, all of whom looked from the young man shouting "Apache!" from the Platte's third-story window toward the lurking or possibly rampaging redskin in question. Reno supposed it wasn't a good idea to shout such a name at the tops of his lungs on the wild western frontier, even in a city. He knew the Apaches were southwestern Indians—farther south and west than Denver—but Indians all across the west were raising hob with the pale eyes' western expansion. Reno doubted they'd attack a city the size of Denver, but he'd obviously put the fear-evoking possibility into a few heads down there on the street.

"I reckon I'd better go out looking for him," Reno said, turning from the window.

"We'd best get something to eat first."

Sara lay belly down on the single bed that appeared a little under double-sized. The mattress listed to the top left. He'd end up with that side, Reno supposed. The lady who'd been working the front desk had looked a little funny when Sara had asked for a single room and a single bed, since two rooms and even a single room with two beds would have cost them more.

It hadn't felt funny to Reno and Sara; they had shared a bed as well as a room for the first twelve years of their lives. When they'd turned thirteen, Pa had moved Reno into James and Ben's room, though his two older brothers had made Reno pay heavily in physical anguish for his incursion into their domain.

Reno supposed the woman at the desk had seen all kinds here in a booming cow and gold town like Denver City. The city was home to the Athenaeum, after all. The woman hadn't done anything beyond raising a skeptical brow. Reno wondered what she would have said if they'd brought Apache with them. He wasn't sure what he'd do with the dog once he found him. He just hoped he found him.

Apache was all he and Sara had left of their family. Apache was part of their family, as far as Reno was concerned. Sara might not have seen him that way, but Reno knew she thought more of the dog than she let on.

"We still have some venison from last night," Reno said, glancing at the war bag Sara had thought to tote from the livery barn.

Sara was counting their money—the twenty-five dollars Ty Mando had given them to get them started on the vengeance trail as well as the coins they'd confiscated from the two dead Confederates. The graybacks' money had likely been stolen from folks who'd worked hard for it, but there was no way Reno and Sara could return the gold and silver to its rightful owners. It was theirs now. They'd soon repay the folks who'd likely died before they'd been robbed. They'd repay them in bullets delivered to their killers.

Bullets or knives or stick and stones. Whatever it took.

Sara counted several coins into her hand, and shook it. "We have jingle to spare on a good cooked meal. Let's go find a restaurant. On the way there and back, we'll look for that mutt of yours."

She scrambled off the bed, which pitched and rolled like a boat on a choppy lake.

***

The woman at the Platte Hotel's front desk told them

that the Buckhorn Restaurant, on the corner of Sixteenth and Larimer, had good food for cheap, so Reno and Sara headed that way.

The traffic on the streets had greatly decreased since they'd entered town, after dusk had fallen over the city. Many of the shops were closed but the saloons and hurdy-gurdy houses were taking up the slack in business, for most of the streets' activity seemed to be hovering around these "dens of damnation," as Sara so bitingly called them.

As they walked, Sara asked several passersby about the "demon graybacks who might have ridden to town on blown horses a couple of days ago." She received only blank stares or single head wags.

Reno whistled and called for Apache, though he used the dog's cut-down nickname, "'Pach," so as not to rile the populace. They hadn't found the dog by the time they reached the Buckhorn, and Reno was getting nervous. The only town Apache had ever visited was Baxter. He'd always ridden in the supply wagon when the Mando family, or part of the family, had made a supply run. But Baxter was hardly larger than a single block of Denver. There was a good chance the beloved shepherd was lost, or worse...

Reno kept an eye out the Buckhorn's window for the dog as he and Sara ate pork chops with pepper gravy, boiled potatoes, a cob of corn apiece, and buttered carrots. Reno was still hungry enough after the main meal that he asked Sara if he could have a slice of the peach pie listed on the menu card.

"It's only an extra three cents," he said, a juvenile plea pitching his voice. He felt silly having to beg his sister for a piece of pie, but there it was. They hadn't discussed who would take charge of their finances, but Sara obviously had. That was all right. She was the more level-headed of the pair, so it was only right that Reno felt a little tied to her apron strings, so to speak.

He'd keep watch over their souls. Sara would make sure they didn't go broke.

Sara sipped coffee while Reno devoured the pie mantled by a liberal dollop of fresh-whipped cream in four bites, and licked the sugary, creamy remains from his wooden-handled, three-tined fork, groaning.

Sara watched him skeptically, quirking one corner of her mouth with her customarily wry half-smile. "Men are a crude lot, gluttons all." Immediately, her mouth straightened, and a pensive gaze washed over her eyes. Reno knew why. Sara had merely repeated what she'd often said at home after watching her three brothers devour their meals with the unabashed delight that Reno had just devoured his with now, so far away from home.

It was almost as though Sara were waiting for her mother's customary scolding, "Oh, Sara, how you go on!"

Sara turned her head to look out the window. Tears blurred Reno's vision. He waited to see if he'd see any tears in his sister's eyes. For a few seconds there, he thought he saw a growing wetness. But then it was gone and Sara studied the street stonily.

Reno sniffed, brushed tears from his cheeks with his hands.

Ignoring him, Sara said, "Let's mosey." She slid back her chair, rose, and carefully counted coins onto the table.

It was nearly dark now, just a little light silhouetting the high mountains in the west. As he and Sara headed back toward the hotel, Reno called for "'Pach" again, but he was starting to feel hopeless. There was no sign of the dog.

When they returned to the Platte, he told Sara he was going to keep looking for the dog. Sara said she was going up to bed. She was feeling a little hopeless, too, Reno could tell. Not because of Apache but because she hadn't gotten any good leads about the Devil's Horde. She'd asked a couple more men about the gang but they'd coldly ignored the question while favoring her a little too boldly with their drink-bleary eyes.

She was starting to worry she and Reno wouldn't pick up the killers' trail again.

Reno thought they would get on it again soon, somehow, but right now he was more concerned about Apache than the grayback devils.

As he turned to leave Sara in front of the Platte, he looked back at her when she said, "Hey, Reno."

"What?"

She narrowed an admonishing eye at him. "You stay away from the Athenaeum, hear?"

Reno felt his cheeks warm. "What would I want with the Athenaeum?"

She gave a droll snort then turned and walked into the hotel. Reno stared after her, anger burning in him. Chagrin did, as well. How could she read his mind so clearly? How did she know that the Athenaeum had been nibbling away at the perimeters of his consciousness when even he hadn't been aware of it himself?

Damn that sister of his, he thought, then instantly prayed for forgiveness, assuring god he had not meant it. What would he do without his sister? Without his sister and Apache? They were all he had left in the world.

He continued walking the streets lit by occasional burning oil pots and the glows from saloon and hurdy-gurdy house windows. He was so desperate that he started calling Apache by his full name though not as loudly as before. Anyway, there weren't many folks on the streets. Most were in the saloons or parlor houses or gambling dens, all too numerous to count.

Worry was driving a rusty blade into his belly by the time he'd walked for nearly an hour, covering most of the streets in the town. At least, most of them outlying the business district. He morosely headed back in the direction of the hotel. As he did, he heard a great commotion—the rumbling of a sizable crowd accompanied by muffled band music and women singing.

Following the din, he soon found himself standing off a front corner of the Athenaeum.

Of course, the din had been coming from the dance hall. Or theater, as Sara had called it. Whatever it was, it was doing a hopping business. Brightly and scantily clad young ladies were again milling around on the second-floor balcony, calling bawdily down to the men lined up on the boardwalk fronting the theater. The men—all shapes and sizes and wearing all styles of attire—filed into the building through two separate doors. The lines moved quickly as each eager man paused briefly outside of each door, paying entrance fees to two big burly gents in three-piece suits.

One of the "ladies" on the second-floor balcony turned to Reno and smiled brightly, the white line of her baking powder teeth showing between her lips in the illumination of a nearby oil pot. "What're you waiting for, sugar?" the "lady" called, beckoning. "Come on over and join the party. I guarantee you won't be sorry!"

TWENTY-SEVEN

"Oh, yes, I will," Reno said with an ironic chuff and started away from the theater.

"Hey, you!" The voice had come from near the end of the line. A tall young man in an ill-fitting suit coat, baggy duck trousers, immigrant cap and suspenders beckoned to him. "Come here!"

Reno frowned. He almost started on his way again, ignoring the young man's call, but there was something vaguely familiar about caller. Reno felt he'd seen him before but he couldn't remember where.

"Come over here—I want to talk to you but I can't leave my place in line!" Again, the young man beckoned with his long, thin arm. "Come on over! It's about your dog!"

The words instantly piqued Reno's attention. "My dog?" He hurried over to the young man. As he got closer, he remembered that he was the tall young man with the long, lumpy nose and pimple-mottled cheeks who'd been working on the tack in Johanssen's Livery& Feed Barn. "Hey, you're…"

"Eddie O'Brien." He had a faint Irish accent. "I work at—"

"I know," Reno said. "Mr. Johanssen's barn. What this about my dog? I've been lookin' all over—"

"Don't worry," said Eddie O'Brien. "I got him tied up over at the barn. He's inside, safe and sound. No need to worry. He came back about a half hour after you left and was sniffing around your horses, obviously lookin' for you and your pretty sis." He grinned with chagrin. When Reno saw the glitter in Eddie's eyes, Reno knew the young man had been drinking. His voice was a little thick. "You don't mind me sayin' she's pretty, do you, lad? I don't mean it in any kinda seedy way. She's just right pretty, sure enough."

"Nah, that' all right. Just don't tell Sara, though, or you'll likely get one of her knees where you'd least like it. For some reason, she don't take to compliments." Reno clutched the young man's arm in excitement. "So, you say Apache's at the feed barn?"

"Safe an' sound. I gave him a little jerky and a bowl of water. He'll be fine till you return for him in the mornin'."

Reno felt as though an anvil of worry had been lifted off his shoulders. "Eddie, I don't know how to thank you." As they'd been talking, they'd both been moving forward, following the line up to one of the two open doors before which stood a beefy gent in a three-piece suit and bowler hat, accepting payment from the men filing past him.

"Oh, that's all right. He seemed friendly enough."

"Well, thanks again, Eddie. I'll let you get on inside." Eddie was almost to the beefy gent by the door.

As Reno started to turn away, Eddie grabbed Reno's arm. "Hold on, hold on. Uh...what's your name, anyway?"

"Oh, I'm Reno. The pretty sourpuss is my twin sister, Sara."

"Why don't you join me inside, Reno? I got more to tell you and"—Eddie glanced at the long line that had formed behind him—"I don't want to give up my place in line."

Eddie glanced at the beefy gent by the open door and then up at the half-naked girls enticing the men from the second-floor balcony. "Oh, no, I..."

"It's about them Confederate killers. The ones who killed your family. They were here. In Denver." Eddie kept his voice down, as though what he was saying was a secret.

"They were here? Where they headed?"

Eddie had stopped beside the beefy gent in the suit and was fishing coins out of his pocket. "Come on inside, Reno. I'll tell you inside. Besides." Eddie grinned as he gave a couple of coins to the big man. "You'll enjoy the show, believe me."

"Oh, I can't."

"Come on!"

Reno hesitated, his heart racing. He glanced up at the balcony again, at the girls showing way more flesh than seemed prudent on a cool autumn night. He could hear his better angels whispering in his ears. But at the same time, he felt the firm hand of his own curiosity pushing him up toward the beefy gent standing by the door. Grinning devilishly, Eddie beckoned from where he stood from just inside the theater's open front door.

"Ah, heck…I'm gonna go to hell for sure, but…how much is it?" he asked the beefy gent.

He could hear the men behind him growing impatient.

"Come on, kid," one of them said. "Pay or get out of the line. We want to get inside!"

"Hold your horses," Reno said.

"Fifty cents," said the bored-looking beefy gent from his perch upon a stool, hooking his thumb at a large placard clearly marked in large numbers: CURRENT SHOWING: 50 Cents.

Fifty cents? Why, fifty cents could buy him a pair of good wool socks! Fifty cents would buy him a whole sack of coffee! Their room had cost only fifty cents more! And Sara would kill—

"Kid," the beefy gent said, impatient now as more

and more men were yelling at Reno from behind, "pay or get out of line!" He extended his thick hand and snapped his fingers.

"All right, all right." Grumbling but feeling a little light-headed with the anticipation of what he would see inside...and hear from Eddie about the Devil's Horde, of course...he dug two dimes, a five-cent piece, and a twenty-five cent piece out of his pocket and dropped them into the hand of the beefy gent, who tossed the coins in a spittoon at his feet and waved Reno through the door.

As Reno stepped across the threshold, a giant hand closed around his heart and squeezed. He felt as though he were passing through the smoking gates of hell itself. As though he were passing from the realm of light and goodness into the realm of darkness and sin.

His heart thumped with excitement. He was breathing hard and sweating, as though he'd run a long way.

And that's exactly what I'm going to have to do if Sara ever finds out where I've been. I'm gonna have to run a long, long way...

As he stepped into the wooden floored lobby, engulfed by the stench of tobacco and sweating men, the noises he'd heard outside grew louder—the band music, the women singing, and the whooping and hollering and boot-stomping of what sounded like a thousand men. Reno felt the reverberations of the cacophony under the soles of his new boots.

He and his new friend Eddie were ushered along by more beefy giants in suits stretched taut around their muscular physiques and through a door over which a sign announced: MAIN STAGE.

The door let on to a vast room filled with many plush-upholstered seats. The high walls to the left and right were decorated with large, gilt-framed paintings Reno couldn't see clearly because of the dim light. He didn't think he wanted to see them clearly, because what he could see painted there had likely earned the painter a one-way ticket to eternal damnation.

Balconies with ornate wooden railings looked out over the room from higher on both walls. The balconies hosted men much better dressed and bar-bered than Reno and most of the other men on the main floor. Such men, dressed to the nines, sat in what appeared brocade upholstered chairs in rooms partitioned off from one another with elaborately pa-pered walls. Many of these men weren't paying much attention to the stage below them. They were talking and laughing with the young women sitting beside them. In some cases, there were two young women to a man.

Most of the young women were far younger than the men they were with, which hinted to Reno that said women were possibly not the men's wives.

He doubted that said women were their daughters, either. No respectable lady, old or young, would ever enter the doors that Reno had been frighteningly easily lured through and at likely dear cost to his soul.

Still, he couldn't take his eyes off the main attraction—the dozen or so young women dancing atop the stage at the room's far end to the accompaniment of a small band perched in a sunken area between the stage and the first row of chairs. To the thundering piano, accordion, and horn music, punctuated by crashing brass cymbals, the ladies danced about in tandem with each other, kicking high their long, pale bare legs.

Yes, their legs were bare from the tiny little, lace-edged pantaloons they wore, right down to their high-heeled black or red shoes. The color of their shoes corresponded with the color of the rest of what they were wearing. Which wasn't more than Reno thought he could stuff into his mouth and still eat a full meal around!

Their upper torsos were covered with about as much cloth as that covering their lower unmentionable regions. They danced about, singing and swinging their arms and kicking their legs and keeping their smiling faces turned to the room filled with whooping and hollering and yowling men—miners and cowboys and everything in between. As they cavorted together about the stage, their sacred upper parts moved in such a fashion that Reno suddenly felt so woozy, he feared he would pass out and end up on the floor.

By now, Eddie had led him to a couple of open seats—about the last two open seats in the place. He hadn't been aware of sitting down, wedged into the crowd of hollering, clapping, stomping young men, until now, so riveted was his sinful gaze. Somehow his main motivation for entering this perdition in the first place oozed up through the wash of other thoughts and feelings flowing through him, and he leaned toward Eddie and said, his tongue feeling swollen, as though from proscribed liquor, "Eddie, what were you gonna tell me about the Bad Old Man's bunch...?"

He swallowed then ran his tongue around his mouth, trying to moisten it. He felt like he was chewing sand. "You say they was here, didja? Or been through here?"

But just then Eddie, wide round eyes riveted on the stage, leaped to his feet and waved his arm high over his head, thrusting two fingers of his other hand between his lips and loosing and ear-rattling, high-pitched whistle.

"Sit down, ya dang hoople-head!" bellowed a man somewhere behind Reno and Eddie.

Another said, "Yeah, sit yourself down, you cork-headed dung swamper, or I'll blow a hole in ya wide enough to see the stage through!"

"Reno!"

The familiar voice chilled Reno right down to the bone. He'd just imagined it, though. No doubt his guilt was working on him. There was no way Sara would have entered such a place as this...

"Reno!"

Was there?

"Reno Bass!" Sara's voice rose again, even louder than before.

"Oh, god!" Reno lurched up out of his seat and swung to his left.

Again, he was sweating and his heart was racing. Fear and humiliation threatened to swamp him. When he saw the tall blonde clad in the beaded buckskin jacket striding down the aisle, hands cupped to her mouth and swinging her head from right to left and back again, his initial impulse was to try and make a run for it.

Did the Athenaeum have a back door?

Several men behind Reno yelled at him, but he only vaguely heard them. He stood frozen in terror as he watched his sister, her black hat snugged atop her blond head, her black, nickel-trimmed holsters sitting snug against her hips, moving along the aisle, still shouting his name. He felt a piece of rock candy or something akin to it smack off the left side of his head as a man yelled, "Sit down, ya blasted sodbuster!

You ain't a window, and I paid good money for this show!"

Just then Sara swung her head toward Reno. She stopped dead in her tracks. Both blue eyes bored into him. They burned like twin brands pressed to his cheeks. She stopped just for a second. Then she came toward him, moving through the crowd of seated men like a bull through a chute.

Reno just stood there beside the now-seated Eddie, who was tugging on Reno's right hand, trying to pull him back down in his seat before he took a bullet from the crowd behind them.

TWENTY-EIGHT

Reno wasn't much worried about taking a bullet. In fact, at this moment, he would have welcomed one.

He was far more worried about his sister, who was on him now like a duck on a June bug. Sara scrambled over the knees of about eight men trying to enjoy the show, grabbed Reno by his left ear, and pulled.

"We're out of here, brother!" she fumed as she wheeled and began dragging Reno over the men's knees, still holding on to his ear. She had such a firm, relentless hold, he was sure she was going to rip the appendage right off the side of his head. "Come on, Reno! Come on—we are getting you out of here!"

"Sara, gallblastit," Reno wailed, clutching at the wrist of the hand of the thumb and index finger she had clamped around his ear, "you're gonna pull my consarned ear plum off!"

A roar went up around Reno as Sara continued

to mercilessly pull him over knees toward the central aisle. At first he thought the men were merely enjoying the show on the stage. But then, as he and Sara reached the central aisle, he saw a dozen men pointing at him and laughing loudly, guffawing. He realized the show the crowd was now enjoying was not the one on the stage but the spectacle of his own lowly, humiliating predicament.

"You blew fifty cents on a lurid show involving naked girls?" Sara shrieked at the top of her lungs as she continued pulling Reno up the aisle toward the lobby by his ear. "You cork-headed peckerwood!"

The men around Reno and Sara laughed louder as Reno stumbled along behind his sister, crouched forward and wrapping his hands around her wrist, trying to work some slack into her iron grip. "Sara!" he cried. "Sara! Dang it, Sara—owww!"

That made the men laugh even louder. He wasn't sure, but he thought he even heard female laughter, which could only mean he'd drawn the attention of the "ladies" on the stage and that they were now laughing at him, too!

He was relieved when he and his ranting sibling pushed through the curtained doorway and he stumbled into the lobby. As he did, Sara released her death grip on his ear. As blood oozed back into it, it hurt even worse than before. Reno clutched it, grimacing, "Ach! Oh, Sara, you don't understand!"

"Oh, I think I understand very well, George Washington Bass!" Sara raged at him, red-faced, before stomping toward the door beside which the beefy gent now stood, looking down at the floor, as though he too was frightened of the raging blonde. "You threw fifty cents away on young women parading naked on a stage! In a house teaming with no-accounts and heathen miscreants, and dripping with unabashed sin!"

"Sara, let me explain!" Reno pushed past another dozen men waiting on the boardwalk for the next show to begin and followed his long-striding, stiff-backed sister out into the street. "Sara, wait!"

"Get back to the hotel, Reno! You and your lordly ways, praying over this and praying over that, and then I find you in there!" She stopped and swung around to point her arm and incriminating finger at the Sodom and Gomorrah from which she'd extricated her brother.

"How in blazes did you know I was in there, anyways?"

Sara sighed and, still fuming, turned to make her way down a dark alley, heading in the general direction of the Platte Hotel. "When you didn't come back, I figured you were there. I knew you were thinking about it. Those half-naked young ladies were praying on your mind. And...sure enough!"

She gave a furious groan as she strode into the alley, Reno following along behind her, holding his hat in his hands. He'd had to grab the felt topper earlier, during Sara's initial assault, to keep from losing it back in the theater.

"Fifty cents!" she added. "We could buy a bag of groceries for that amount of money!"

Reno ran up beside his sister, matching her stride. "Sara, won't you please stop and listen to me? I had a perfectly good reason for going in there. I was following Eddie O'Brien!"

"Who on god's green earth is—!"

A deep-throated shout sounded behind them. "Down, ya crazy pups! Hit the deck!"

Something flashed in front of Reno, at the far end of the dark alley. What could only be a bullet buzzed ominously through the air just over and between Reno and Sara's heads.

Sara must have heard the warning and seen the flash at the same time Reno did, because she and her brother flung themselves forward and hit the ground on their bellies simultaneously. There was another flash and a roar straight ahead of them. The bullet crackled into some trash behind them.

Another gun roared. This one spoke from behind, the same direction from which the warning had come.

The gun behind them roared again, again, and again. In the midst of the roars, Reno heard a man ahead of him give an anguished yelp. Another man grunted. There were two thuds as both men hit the ground.

Reno kept his head down, wincing. He discovered he'd reached over to his right to cover his sister's head with his hand, as though his flesh could somehow deflect a bullet. He had his hand clamped over the back of Sara's head pretty hard. She grunted softly then reached up with one of her own hands and removed his big paw from her head.

She looked at Reno. Her eyes were wide and round with shock. Reno gazed back at her. He assumed his eyes looked the same way hers did.

Stunned.

Silence hung heavy over the dark alley.

"Children, you go on back to where you came from!" rose the voice from behind them again. It was a deep, throaty, resonant voice. The man spoke with a southern lilt. "You hear me?" he said, louder, putting more steel in his voice. "You go on home an' leave the huntin' of them graybacks to the grownups!"

Boots crunched gravel.

Reno turned to see a big, man-shaped silhouette move across the alley mouth. The man wore a big hat and he appeared to be wearing buckskins, as well. He stopped just before he disappeared around the front of one of the buildings abutting the alley.

"Oh," he said as though in afterthought, turning to

face the alley once more. "You best stop askin' around about 'em, too. Blame fool thing to do. They got spies, don't ya know." He spat and then added crankily, "Go on home!"

He stepped up onto the boardwalk fronting the building on Reno's right, and was gone.

Reno stared after the man for a full minute. Sara did, too.

They turned to stare at each other. Sara's eyes were still wide with shock.

Reno's heart had been racing. Now it finally slowed a bit. Figuring he couldn't stay hunkered down here in the darkness of the alley forever, he gained his feet and then helped Sara up, as well.

Sara said, "Who...?"

"Yeah," Reno agreed.

Who were the two men at the far end of the alley?

Who was the man who'd saved their bacon? How had he known the other two would be waiting for them in the shadows?

There'd been something about their guardian angel that had seemed familiar to Reno, but he couldn't quite put his finger on what it was. He only vaguely considered the man now as he and Sara walked slowly toward the alley's far end, where it opened out on the street flanking the Platte Hotel. Fortunately, there was no one else on the secondary street this time of the night, but men's voice rose in the distance. Denver had law, as would any town of this one's size, and the law had apparently heard the gunshots and was trying to figure out where they'd come from.

"I don't know—I think from over that way!" a man shouted from somewhere to Reno's left.

Reno quickened his pace and soon found himself staring down at one of the two dead men as Sara stared down at the other one. Reno's dead man was dirty and sunburned. A cocked Confederate revolver lay near his open right hand. He wore a new suit coat, which clashed with the rest of his ragged attire. The only thing it didn't clash with was the new brown bowler hat lying in the dirt near his head from which long, thin hair trailed down to the man's shoulders.

The rest of the man's mismatched rags said he was one of the Devil's Horde, all right. There could be no doubt. The new coat and the new hat had likely come from one of his victims. Or maybe he'd bought them off a store rack with money he'd stolen from one of the many men he'd killed.

Whatever the case, this was one of the Bad Old Man's men. Which meant the gang was here in Denver City. Or close.

"Come on, Reno."

Reno turned stiffly to Sara. She stood over her own dead man—a long, unshaven, wiry man clad in a buckskin vest over a gray tunic with gold buttons and soiled gray trousers. Ambient light winked off his open eyes and off the blood oozing out of a hole in his leg and out of another hole in the man's chest clad in blue poplin.

Sara tugged on Reno's arm. "We have to get out of here. Someone's coming."

Reno heard it then, too—footsteps approaching from his left. He turned in that direction two see two man-shaped shadows moving toward him. Badges shone on their dark-blue uniform coats.

"Hold it right there!" one of the police officers yelled.

Reno and Sara wheeled and ran. They hadn't discussed it, but they both knew they couldn't let the law delay them. The Denver City Police would only try to interfere in their vengeance quest.

"I said it hold it, consarn it!" one of the officers shouted, louder and shriller this time.

"This way, Reno!" Sara turned sharply left, passing in front of her brother, and ran into another dark alley's mouth.

Reno followed. As he did, a gun barked behind him. The bullet spanged off a brick wall mere inches from his right shoulder.

He crouched as brick shards peppered his hat and shoulders, and ran faster into the alley, fear gripping him, knowing that if two Confederates had ambushed him and Sara, two more...or god only knew how many more...might be waiting for them at the end of this alley, too. They could be running right into the jaws of death.

The alley opened onto Larimer Street. Reno was relieved to see no one waiting for them. He followed Sara as she swung to the right and slowed to a fast walk as they made their way along a wooden board-walk, heading in the direction of the hotel.

There was more of a crowd here on Larimer, with several nearby saloons casting amber light onto the broad, hay-flecked dirt street. Men stood in groups outside of the saloons. Some of the saloons obviously doubled as "honey houses," for some of the men were accompanied by laughing women. Reno smelled the cloying odors of cheap perfume mixed with man sweat, the smell of oil from the burning pots, and alcohol. It was getting late, but Reno had a feeling downtown Denver City rarely, if ever, locked its doors.

The traffic on the street and boardwalks made it possible for him and Sara to return to the Platte without further harassment by local lawmen. If the policemen had followed the twins into and out of the alley, Reno, having glanced discreetly over his shoul-der a couple of times, hadn't seen them.

They retrieved their room key from the prissy, bespectacled young man who manned the front desk at night, and who gave both Reno and Sara a curious thrice-over as he retrieved their key from the pigeon hole behind the desk. Slowly, taking his time, he deposited the key into Sara's open hand.

He didn't say anything, but he was darned curious about the identities of these two tow-headed twins, boy and girl. They were dressed in trail duds now, and wore the Remington Piettas, but Reno suspected it was still obvious what they were—Kansas sodbusters.

Former ones, anyway...

Sara wrinkled her nose at the fancy dan, closed her hand around the key, and Reno followed her up the stairs to their room on the third floor. Reno closed the door slowly, anxiously pondering what had happened over the past hour.

A lot.

Silently, also deep in thought, Sara walked past the hurricane lamp on the dresser without lighting it and stopped at the window. She slid the curtain aside with the back of her hand, and peered down into the narrow, mostly dark side street flanking the hotel. That was the street on which the two dead Confederate devils now lay and where the Denver City police were probably milling, no doubt assuming Reno and Sara were the dead men's killers.

"See anything?" Reno asked.

Sara had her head shoved up close to the window and was gazing off to her right. "No. Too dark." She let the curtain fall back into place and gave her back to the window. "So...they know we're here."

"Yeah." Of course, she meant the Devil's Horde.

With uncustomary chagrin, Sara said, "I reckon it wasn't so smart—us asking all around town for them like a couple of stupid blabbermouths. Someone must have told them we were looking for them and the Bad Old Man and Black Bob sent a couple to find us."

"And kill us," Reno said, swallowing.

"Yep." Sara paused. As she walked over to the dresser, all Reno could see of her was her shadow with blond hair tumbling about her shoulders. She removed the mantel from the chimney with a glassy clink, and plucked a sulphur match from a small box beside the lamp. "I wonder where the rest of them are holed up."

As she dragged the match across the top of the dresser, igniting the sulphur-tipped head, Reno said, "Eddie might know."

Sara turned up the lamp's wick, touched the flame to it, then blew out the match as the lamp spread a watery, umber light around the room, nudging shadows this way and that. "Who's Eddie?"

"My new friend. Eddie O'Brien. You remember the long-nosed swamper from Johanssen's Livery and Feed?"

Sara nodded as she dropped the still-smoking lucifer into an empty airtight tin likely placed there to collect spent matches used in lighting the lamp. Frontier towns, many of which were constructed mostly of wood, were notorious for going up in flames. Folks had learned to take precautions against accidental fires.

"He's the one who pulled me into the Athenaeum."

Sara dipped her chin and gave a wry twist of her mouth. "He pulled you in? Against your will? When I found you, you looked plenty willing."

Reno's cheeks warmed.

TWENTY-NINE

"I had to follow Eddie into the theater so he'd tell me about the Devil's Hoard."

Sara just waited, chin down, one skeptical brow arched.

"He said he had some information about them," Reno said."Where they might be, maybe."

"And you had to follow him into the theater so he'd tell you. He wouldn't tell you outside the theater." It wasn't a question. She stated the implication as though to show Reno how absurd it sounded.

Reno sighed, removed his hat, and hooked it on one of the bed's rear posts. He sat down on the edge of the bed and stared up at his sister. "He was going in, following the line, and if I hadn't gone in with him, I never would have learned about the Devil's Horde."

"Likely story!"

"It's true, Sara!"

"Well," Sara said, blinking, "what did you find out?"

Reno winced. "Nothing."

"Nothing?"

Again, Reno sighed. "As soon as we walked into the theater, Eddie got all preoccupied with...well, you know..."

"With the naked, ahem, ladies."

"That's right," Reno said, staring down at his hands in his lap. His ears rang a little and he could feel a vein throb in his temple. "I reckon I did, too," he confessed, fidgeting with his hands. "All right—you got me, Sara. You caught me lookin' at naked girls. Or just about naked, anyways."

"Yes, they were just about naked, all right."

"You're not my mother."

"No, I'm not."

"I can do what I want."

"Yes, you can."

"You had no right pullin' me out of the theater like that." Reno brushed his hand against his ear. It was still sore. "They were all laughin' at me. Even the nearly naked ladies."

"Yes, the ladies were laughing, too."

Reno felt the burn of anger now. He was right. She had no right to do what she'd done. She'd overstepped in a big way, and she'd made a fool out of him, though he supposed he'd made a fool of himself by going into that sinful place, even if he had only been following his new friend Eddie.

Eddie. Some new friend he'd turned out to be. Reno was liable to go to hell now, because of Eddie. At the very least, he'd get a good chewing out by ole St. Pete at the pearly gates. How ashamed he was going to feel!

"I'm sorry, Reno."

Sara's words startled him. He looked up from his hands in his lap. She appeared to be the one now feeling ashamed. The anger had left her eyes. Her gaze was soft, contrite. He'd rarely seen a soft, contrite expression on Sara's face. It surprised him.

"Ah, heck, sis," Reno said. He chuckled. "I reckon it was some funny, lookin' back on it."

"From now on, you can do whatever you want to do. As long as it doesn't get in the way of our mission."

"It didn't get in the way of it. Well, maybe it did a little, since I didn't get anything out of Eddie after we got seated."

Sara sat beside Reno on the bed. "Do you think he really knows where the Bad Old Man and Black Bob are holed up?"

"If I remember right, he said somethin' to make me think they might have left town."

"I doubt it." Sara lifted her hand to brush some dust from Reno's thick shoulder. "Since two of them bushwhacked us, they must still be here. Or some of them, anyway. If it hadn't been for the fellow behind us, I reckon we'd be..." She let her voice trail off.

There was no point in saying it.

"I reckon."

"I wonder who he was, anyway," Sara said. "He sounded southern."

"I know. Somethin' seemed familiar about him but I didn't get a good look at him." Reno turned to his sister, his eyes grave now. "Maybe they know where we are—the Devil's Horde. Maybe that fancy dan downstairs or the other desk clerk told them devils we were here—the two sodbusters who've been lookin' for 'em."

Sara drew her mouth corners down. "Could be. I reckon we'd better take turns staying awake tonight. Listening...keeping watch."

"I'll take the first turn."

"All right." Sara rose, kicked out of her boots, shrugged out of her jacket, and plopped down on the bed, resting her head against the pillow and crossing her ankles. "Wake me in a couple of hours, and I'll spell you." She sat up and fluffed her pillow. "In the morning we'll go over to the barn, pay a visit to your friend Eddie, and see just what it is he thinks he knows about those southern devils."

"Sounds good." Reno smiled at her and placed his hand on one of her feet. "He found Apache, tied him inside the barn. We'll get him tomorrow."

"Wonderful. The fleabag's back." Sara yawned. "Boy, I'm sleepy."

"Go to sleep, sis." Reno rose and kicked out of his boots. He grabbed his Henry rifle from where he'd leaned it in a corner, pumped a round into the action, and off-cocked the hammer. He lay down next to Sara, leaned back against the bed's brass headboard, and rested the rifle across his thighs. "Good night, Sara."

"Good night, Reno."

Sara rolled toward him, wrapped an arm around his waist, and pressed her cheek against his side. "Next time you need to see a naked girl, why don't you just ask me?" She looked at him and smiled. "I'd be a whole lot cheaper."

Her smiled broadened, and she winked. Of course, she was only kidding.

Reno chuckled and tapped his thumb against the Henry's hammer.

He lifted his father's Bible from the chair beside the bed and flipped through it. He found a passage that his father had underlined. It was as though his father had underlined the passage just for him, Reno, for just such a night as this, when he was feeling such great shame. It was First Samuel 12:20: "'Do not be afraid', Samuel replied. 'You have done all this evil; you do not turn away from the Lord, but serve the Lord with all your heart.'"

He closed his eyes and prayed, asking for forgiveness for what he'd done earlier this night at the Athenaeum and for salvation from wickedness so that he could serve the Lord with all his heart.

✳✳✳

Reno didn't awaken Sara after a couple of hours. He had too much on his mind for sleep.

To get the images from the Athenaeum from flashing behind his retinas, he tried to prepare himself for his coming travails. He had a feeling they would soon catch up to the gang that had murdered their family. He sensed the Bad Old Man and Black Bob were close. He tried to imagine several different scenarios and how he would handle each one, both physically and mentally.

He prepared his mind and his soul for more killing and the possibility of death. He had almost died several times in the past weeks. He'd almost died this evening, as well. He'd known raw fear, and for seconds it had paralyzed him. Somehow, he had to master that fear in the future. If he suffered even momentary paralysis when confronting the Bad Old Man and Black Bob, he would die. Sara would probably die, too.

Their family would remain unavenged.

Even worse, the Confederate demon spawn would remain upon the earth to continue their depredations.

Why was it that every time his mind wavered from the Devil's Horde, images from the Athenaeum flashed in his mind?

He feared he was deeply evil. But then, was any man not evil? He reminded himself about original sin.

No, he didn't wake Sara. He stayed awake himself, listening for interlopers and enduring the assault of the untethered thoughts on his mind. Sara awoke just before dawn on her own and demanded Reno close his eyes and get at least an hour's worth of sleep. She took the rifle and the Bible out of his hands, set them aside, and drew the chair into the corner near the door. She unholstered her Remingtons, sat in the chair, and propped her stocking-clad feet on the edge of the bed.

Reno curled on his side, tried to sleep. He was surprised that when he opened his eyes again, sunlight was streaming through the window at which Sara stood, staring out. She'd slid the curtain aside, and the buttery light shone in her hair like spun honey.

"Whoa," Reno ground, rubbing his eyes with the heels of his eyes. "I musta conked out."

Sara turned from the window. She held a steaming tin cup in her hands. "You'd no sooner closed your eyes than you were snoring like Pa."

"Really?"

"Really. The Athenaeum must have finally released

its hold on you." Sara smiled.

Reno looked at her. "I'm bad, ain't I? You were right. I'd been thinking about that place ever since I first laid eyes on it."

Sara sipped her coffee, her blue eyes glowing in the lens-clear, high-altitude sunshine pushing through the steam rising from the cup. She swallowed and leveled a hard look at her brother. "You're not bad, Reno. In fact, you're the best person I've ever known."

Reno frowned. "Really?"

"Really."

"You don't think I have to worry about my soul?"

"No, but you should probably worry about mine."

Frowning again, Reno shook his head. "Why?"

Sara gazed at him for a few more seconds, pensive, then shook her head. "Never mind." She glanced at a crock jug sitting on the dresser. "I got us some coffee and biscuits. Drink and eat a little, and then let's go see your new friend Eddie."

It was Sunday morning.

Reno had lost track of the days, but he realized it was Sunday because the city's streets were deserted even at eight-thirty. On a weekday or a Saturday, they'd have been rollicking. Drunks lay in the street and along the boardwalks like dead men after a battle. The gonging of a church bell gave the crisp, early-autumn, sun-washed morning a funereal air, given the bodies.

The air smelled of urine and vomit and alcohol.

As he and Sara made their way along a boardwalk, stepping over passed-out drunks as they headed toward the livery barn, Reno said, "You know, Sara, I've wanted to visit a city for a long time, but now that I have, I don't reckon I'll be so eager to visit another one. I prefer it out in the wide open, personally."

Sara wrinkled her nose as they stepped over the legs of two men leaning back against the front wall of the Bullhide Saloon, out cold, their heads tipped together like two lovers enjoying a sunset together.

"I have to agree with you there, brother."

Reno slowed his pace as he and Sara approached the livery barn. "Doesn't look like Johanssen's open yet."

The barn's front doors were closed and no one except horses could be seen in the two corrals flanking the place. Reno hoped he'd find Eddie somewhere inside, though it being Sunday morning, Eddie might be sleeping in along with most of the rest of Denver City. Reno tripped the wooden latch on the man door to the left of the two stock doors, and stepped into the barn's musty shadows.

"Mr. Johanssen?" he called as Sara followed him over the threshold.

The only light was that slithering through a few small, sashed, and very dusty windows. The barn was mostly shadows and blurred edges. A man-shaped silhouette slumped in a chair to the right, leaning back against the wall near the door to a small side room.

"Mr. Johanssen?" he called again.

The man whom Reno thought was Johanssen didn't stir. Likely still asleep with the rest of Denver City after a long, raucous Saturday night.

Sara stepped up beside Reno and they both stared down the barn's long, broad alley foreshortening into still more shadows. Reno called, "Eddie?" He hadn't called loudly, but the barn was so quiet it sounded loud to his own ears. "Eddie, are you here? It's Reno... from last night."

A whimper sounded from the shadows ahead along the alley.

Reno glanced at Sara. They both frowned. Sara swept the flaps of her buckskin jacket behind the butts of her Piettas, and closed her hands over the grips.

Reno turned to gaze down the barn alley and said, "Apache? That you, boy?"

Another whimper. A shadow moved low to the floor and came toward Reno, sort of slinking along the floor.

"Apache?" Reno moved forward, frowning.

The dog gave a low mewling bark and then moved

more quickly toward Reno. It was Apache, all right. The dog was dragging a few feet of rope behind him. It appeared to have been chewed through. Apache kept low to the ground, whining and thumping his tail anxiously as he approached Reno, who dropped to one knee to greet the dog.

"Apache? What's going on, boy? What's got you so...?"

Behind him, Sara said, "Reno."

Reno patted Apache and said, "Hey, Sara, Apache's awful nervous about somethin'. Eddie had him tied up but it looks like he chewed through his rope."

Again, Sara said, "Reno."

"What is it?" Reno glanced behind him.

"Johanssen's dead," Sara said. "And we got trouble."

THIRTY

Apache's hackles went up and the dog crouched even lower, showing his teeth and growling as he glared at the front of the barn. Reno frowned as shadows moved behind him. Boots scraped across the floor, and then three men and Sara stepped into the barn alley. Apache growled louder, crouched low, butt in the air.

Reno grabbed the dog's rope collar, holding him back, as he stared in cold-blooded dread at Sara and the three men in Confederate rags mismatched with skins and furs and buckskin.

One of the men held Sara in front of him. He clutched a big knife against Sara's neck. With his other hand, he drew Sara back against him. He was a little taller than Sara—a scrawny man with a round felt hat and a moon face with a scrubby beard.

One of the other two men held Sara's Henry rifle

and grinned at Reno. Tall and bearded, he sported one lazy eye. The other man—short and stocky and wearing deerskin leggings and a Confederate sword, just then pulled both of Sara's Remington Piettas from the black holsters tied low on her thighs. He stepped back and faced Reno, raising both pistols, cocking the hammers, and extending the revolvers at Reno and Apache.

"I'm sorry, Reno," Sara said tensely, lifting her chin away from the point of the knife the moon-faced devil held taut against his neck. "They were in the side room. Grabbed me before I could call out."

"Nice guns you two got here," said the man holding the Henry, raking his eyes down the octagonal barrel to the factory-engraved brass breech, then glancing at the two Remingtons the short, stocky man was holding. "Nothin' but the latest Yankee shootin' irons for you two."

"Toss yours over here," said the moon-faced man holding the knife to Sara's neck.

"All right, all right," Reno said. "Just don't hurt her."

"Do as I say, and I'll think about not hurtin' her," said the moon-faced gent, stretching his chapped lips back to show widely-spaced, tobacco-brown teeth. He spoke with a slow-rolling southern accent. His eyes were brown, shallow, and mean. "And call that dog off or I'll shoot him. Don't wanna fire a shot so early on Sunday mornin', but I will."

He looked at Apache and raised his brows to show he was serious.

"Stay, Apache," Reno said, tugging hard on the dog's collar. "Lie down."

The dog lowered his hackles, glanced up at Reno. Whining deep in his throat, he sank to his belly and lay flat against the floor but kept his angry eyes on the three men with Sara.

Reno straightened. He held his Henry in his right hand. Now he tossed it to the man holding Sara's Henry, who caught the gun in one hand, looked at it admiringly, then leaned it against a ceiling support post to his right.

"Now the hoglegs," said the moon-faced fellow with Sara. "Nice an' slow."

Reno's heart tattooed his breastbone. He did not want to give up his guns and render himself defenseless against these proven killers, but what else could he do? If he didn't do as they demanded, Sara would die. If he did, Sara and he would also die. Still, he had no choice. He had to buy them some time.

He looked at Sara. Her blue eyes were wide and round with rage and fear.

He closed his hands over the Remingtons holstered butt forward on his hips. Just as he started to pull, he stopped when a low, tight voice behind him said, "I'm s-sorry, Reno..."

Reno turned his head. Eddie stepped out of a stall

fifteen feet away and moved slowly toward Reno, sort of dragging his feet. He moved stiffly, holding both hands over his belly. As he entered a shaft of lemon-colored light angling through a window, Reno saw his brown eyes were wide and glassy. His long face with its long, lumpy nose hung slack. He was powdery pale.

Reno glanced down at the young man's hands. The yellow light glinted on the blood and viscera oozing out of the young man's belly and through his fingers.

"I double-crossed you, Reno," Eddie said, stopping and grabbing a plank stall wall for balance. "They come around one night an' paid me to tell 'em if anyone came through here, askin' for 'em…" He looked from Reno to Sara then back to Reno. "Last night I went and told 'em…before I seen you again outside the theater." Shame shone in his pain-bright eyes. "I'm…sorry, Reno. I was gonna warn you after the show. Pr-promise I…"

He didn't finish the sentence. His knees buckled and he dropped to the floor like a sack of grain, jerking for a time before he lay still.

The moon-faced devil grinned and chuckled as he stared at Reno from over Sara's left shoulder. "We told most of the liverymen in town to let us know if anyone came around askin' about us handsome southern gentlemen. Told 'em if they told any law or anybody else about us, they'd die hard…very painful.

Might even be some money in it if they warned us of shadowers." He glanced down at the dead Eddie. "The kid came an' told us last night about you two. Described you to a 't'. Said you'd likely be over to the livery barn this mornin', since he had your dog. He wanted money for a girl of the sportin' variety. Well, he didn't get it, so he went away mad."

Reno stared at the man, fury blazing in his heart. He wondered if these men knew about the two Confederates his and Sara's guardian angel had killed last night. Those two must have followed Sara from the Platte. "You didn't have to kill him." But, of course, they'd killed him. He remembered how they—these very men standing before him, ragged, stinky, stone-eyed demon-savages fresh out of Satan's own hell—had killed his family.

"Come on, come on!" The tall, bearded man with the lazy eye gestured impatiently. "Toss the hoglegs over here, or Corporal Hill will cut your sister's throat!"

"Hurry now," said the moon-faced man called Hill. "The Bad Old Man, Colonel Montgomery, remembers you two very well. On account of how you, kid—his eyes blazed at Reno from over Sara's shoulder—shot his arm off. He's waitin' to see you. In fact, he's been waitin' to see you again for several weeks now. In fact, you're somebody he just can't get off his pain-addled mind. No, sir!"

Lying flat against the floor near Reno's boots, Apache growled loudly, showing his teeth.

"No, Apache," Reno ordered. "Heel, boy."

"The guns, kid!" Hill yelled, gritting his teeth and pressing the blade of his knife a little tauter against Sara's neck. She winced as a bead of blood oozed from her neck and onto the tip of the knife.

"Here you go," Reno said, shucking both Remingtons slowly and flipping them in the air, then grabbing their barrels. He tossed each one in turn, underhanded, to the tall gent with the lazy eye. "Ease up on the knife," he told Corporal Hill, seeing a drop of Sara's blood run slowly down the blade from the tip toward the hilt.

Apache growled again.

Corporal Hill glanced from Apache to the tall man with the lazy eye. "Shoot the dog. I'm tired of him lookin' at me like I'm a bone he wants to chew on."

"No shootin' unless necessary," said the short gent with the sword, snarling at Hill. "You heard the old man. A shot'll be heard all across town!"

"It's necessary!" said Hill. "Virgil!"

"All right, all right."

"No, I got him," Reno said, crouching and grabbing Apache's collar again.

"Get away, kid, or you'll get it, too!" warned Virgil, walking forward and cocking a big Confederate revolver.

Suddenly, Hill screamed. Reno realized that Sara had somehow nudged the man's knife away from her neck and rammed one of her feet down on one of his. That was Reno's call to action. He released Apache's collar and said, "Get him, boy!"

While Sara struggled with Hill and the short man, Reno leaped on Virgil, who'd turned his back on Reno to see what was happening with the girl. Reno drove Virgil to the ground. As Virgil cussed a blue streak, Reno grabbed the revolver out of his hand while Apache sank his teeth into the man's left shoulder, growling and snarling.

The gun roared.

Apache gave a shrill yip.

"Devil!" Sara shouted.

Her shout was followed by a smacking sound. Reno glanced up to see his sister fly backward and hit the floor hard. He was about to rise, but then he saw a rifle butt moving toward him from his left. That was the last thing he saw before the world exploded into a bright burst of pain followed by darkness.

✳✳✳

Reno woke to the drumming of hooves on wood.

The drumming felt like hammer blows to his head. Wincing against the pain, he opened his eyes to see light-tan horse hair and part of a leather stirrup fender. He could smell the musk of the horse the hair belonged to, and the leather of the fender. He realized he was hanging down the side of the moving horse at an odd angle.

The horse's movement and clomping sounds pained him. His wrists burned, as well. It was then that he realized, as consciousness returned, helped along by misery, that his wrists were tied to a saddle horn. His own saddle horn he saw, rolling his eyes to look upward and to his right.

His feet were tied to his stirrups.

He'd been tied to his own saddle. Unconscious, he dropped down over Jack's left wither.

Grimacing against the raw burn in his wrists and the hammer blows of the drumming hooves assaulting his head, Reno pulled himself upright on the saddle and looked around, squinting against the abrasive high-country sunshine. He and Jack were crossing a bridge spanning a shallow creek. They were almost across, only about ten feet to go. A man riding ahead of the buckskin held Jack's reins in his hand. He held either Reno or Sara's Henry right in his right hand, butt against his leg, barrel up.

Jack walked with his head down, rippling his withers uneasily.

"Reno." Sara's familiar voice sounded on his left.

Still squinting and wincing against the assault of the light on his eyes and battered brain, he turned to his left, felt the pain drop down into the back of his neck and spine. His sister rode her black mare, Grace, beside him. Grace was being led by the scalawag riding ahead of her.

"You all right, Reno?" Sara had a nasty cut on her right cheek. The skin was discolored around it.

Reno winced again, nodded. "Yourself?"

Sara shrugged a shoulder.

"Where we goin'?"

"Ask them." She looked at the three men riding ahead of them.

The man leading Sara's horse—the short, stout man with the cavalry saber—turned to glare at her over his shoulder. "Shut up."

They were leaving the bridge now and climbing a trail leading up the bank of the creek they'd just crossed. A wooden sign, marred by three bullet holes, leaned on a pine post on the trail's right side. AURARIA, KANSAS TER. was painted in Gothic black letters on the badly worn wood. Scrub buildings rose from the brush around them.

Reno endured the pain of swinging his head to look behind him. Apparently, they'd left Denver City to the north, crossed the creek on the southern perimeter of that less-than-fair city, and were now entering the nearby, much smaller and scrubbier town of Auraria.

Auraria wasn't much, Reno saw as they rode

down the main street—or what he took for the main street, since it was sheathed between a dozen or so false-fronted buildings, most of them log or adobe or a combination of both.

There were a few men on the boardwalks, Reno saw now as the wind rose and picked up some dust and swirled it around him. Most of those men—in fact, all—didn't look too happy about being out there, however. They stood cloaked by the shadowy doorways of sorry-looking saloons, or were half-hidden by awning support posts. They gazed into the street as the three Confederate devils led the two tow-heads down the street behind them.

"What're you looking at?" Virgil snarled at one man. The short, bearded old man in hitch-and-brace overalls standing between the partly open doors of a blacksmith shop, took one step back and to one side, concealing himself behind one of the doors.

The wind blew again, further concealing him behind a screen of sunlit dust and dead leaves.

The street appeared to end at a large, white-washed adobe brick building growing larger and larger before Reno and Sara now as they came to within fifty feet and continued approaching. It stood on the right of the street, across from a large barn, on the street's left side. Reno saw a sign tacked across the second floor of the large brick structure, identifying the building, fronted by a brush-roofed peeled-log front porch, as THE EL DORADO HOTEL. Another sign hanging from hooks beneath the porch's brush roof announced: SALOON above, in slightly smaller letters: ROOMS BY THE HOUR. On another, even smaller, sign were the words: FREE STABLING ACROSS THE STREET FOR THE PRICE OF FEED.

A lot of a half-dozen or so bedraggled men lounged atop the El Dorado's porch, some sitting with one hip resting on the unpeeled log rail, smoking briar or corncob pipes or cigarettes. A crock jug stood on a low table amongst them, and they seemed to be hovering around the jug like half-weaned pups around their mother. They'd all turned their heads to watch Reno and Sara and the three Confederate devils ahead of them.

One of the devils on the porch—a dark, hawk-faced man in a straw hat and gray Confederate tunic with the arms hacked off, revealing tattoos on the man's forearms and biceps, removed the pipe from his mouth, spat into the dirt below the porch and said, "I'll be hanged if the old man didn't have it right."

"He knew they were back there, all right," said the moon-faced Corporal Hill as he brought his bay gelding to a halt at the head of the five-horse pack, near one of the three well-worn hitchracks sagging in the street fronting the porch. He turned to Reno and Sara, leering, and said, "Said he could smell 'em. Said he could see 'em in his fever dreams. Especially the boy—the big blue-eyed towhead who'd drilled that ball through his arm. Grieved him somethin' awful," he appeared very happy to inform Reno.

"Corporal Hill!" a voice thundered from one of the El Dorado's open, second-story windows. "Quick your incessant gum-flappin' and bring 'im up here to me. I wanna see 'im up close!"

Hill and the other two devils on the street turned and lifted their gazes toward the open window. Hill said, "You got it, Colonel Montgomery, sir! Do you want the girl, too?"

"Yes, the girl, too!" came the thundering, resonant reply in a deep southern drawl, so that every word seemed to acquire an extra syllable or two.

Sara dropped her gaze from the window to Reno, curled her upper lip distastefully, and said. "Sounds like Old Beelzebub himself up yonder. Sure enough, we've been led right to the devil's lair."

THIRTY-ONE

"Shut up, little Yankee girl," said the tall, lazy-eyed man called Virgil. "That's Colonel Montgomery, and you'll call him Colonel, sir, or nothin' else—understand?" He showed her his big skinning knife, threatening her with it, then carelessly cut her the ropes tying her wrists to her saddle horn.

The moon-faced Hill cut Reno's wrists free of his own horn and then cut his feet free of his stirrups. Hill gave a caustic laugh then reached up, grabbed Reno's shirt, and pulled him out of the saddle. Reno hit the ground hard on his right shoulder and the side of his head. He rolled once then sat up, holding his head in his hands. His unceremonious meeting with the ground had kicked up the pounding agony in his head, and for a few seconds he felt so sick to his stomach, he thought he would vomit.

Virgil had pulled Sara off the black mare, though

not as violently as Hill had pulled Reno. She managed to stay on her feet, anyway. She cussed Hill savagely, using words Reno hadn't even known were in her vocabulary. Hill walked around Reno's horse and her horse and backhanded her, sending her pin-wheeling into the street.

"Corporal Hill!" Montgomery's voice thundered again. "If you can't manage the simple task of bringing those two young sodbusters up here posthaste, please turn the task over to someone who can! Perhaps the cleaning girl…?"

This evoked snickers from all of the devils except Hill. He flushed a little, glanced at Virgil and the stocky, moodily silent man with the sword, then drew his big Confederate pistol, stepped back, cocked the weapon, and waved it toward the El Dorado's front door, propped open with an iron heating brick.

Reno and Sara shared a glance. A dark one. One that said far more than words could have. One involving apologies for the fate that had befallen them, regrets, and reassurances that no matter what happened next, they'd be together, at least. Reno glanced at the three men standing in a ragged semi-circle around them then stepped forward. Sara fell into stride beside him.

Her eyes were cold and hard, her face expression-less.

Their hands weren't tied, so Reno considered his options. It looked likely only the three who'd brought them here from the livery barn were going to accompany them into the hotel. The others appeared comfortable right where they were on the porch. They evidently felt their assistance was not needed. Reno and Sara were just two relatively harmless sodbusters, now that their guns had been taken away.

Could Reno somehow manage to grab a gun off one of the men flanking him and Sara as they entered the dark shadows of the El Dorado?

He glanced briefly at Sara. She was wondering the same thing. She wasn't beaten yet. Not by a long shot. She might have been as afraid as Reno was. How could they not both be afraid in such a situation? But she wouldn't give up until her last breath left her lips and her soul was mounting a cloud for the pearly gates and the golden hallway.

Reno wouldn't, either.

"To the stairs at the back," Hill snarled behind him.

Reno swerved slightly toward the stone staircase at the rear of the dimly lit saloon. There were two more Confederates in here—thick-set older men with salt and pepper beards. One had a patch over his left eye and a bloody bandage over his ear. He wore a sergeant's chevrons on the sleeve of his ragged shirt. The other man was smoking a long, black cheroot. He wore a salt-stained kepi with a torn leather bill, gray breeches, a dirty red undershirt, and suspenders. On his feet were brand-new, brown leather boots.

A cottony gray kitten sat on his shoulder, which he seemed to be feeding from bits of jerky piled on the table before him. The kitten looked at him expectantly, tilting its little owl-like head with tiny gold bb-gun eyes, meowing each time it opened its mouth, wanting more jerky. This man and the sergeant—maybe they were both sergeants, older noncoms—were playing chess at a small, square table.

They'd paused in their play to regard Reno and Sara with narrow-eyed interest as the blond twins crossed the room to the rear, Hill and Virgil and the stocky devil following from about ten feet behind. Side-by-side, Reno and Sara mounted the stairs. As they approached the second floor, Reno started to smell a foul, sour odor. As they reached the second floor, Hill behind them said, "Turn right an' walk back toward the front of the building."

Reno and Sara turned right and walked down the dim hallway, the odor growing stronger with each step they took. The hall was lit by a couple of bracket lamps. A sour carpet runner muffled the clomping of boots as the party moved along the hall toward the end facing the street. Three men stood in the hall, some holding rifles, all wearing pistols, smoking.

There was a more formal air about these three, though Reno couldn't quite put his finger on what gave him that impression, because they were no better attired than the rest of the devils downstairs. Like the others, their clothing had clearly seen years of war and the violent trek west. Some of their original uniforms remained, like relics, while the rest had been replaced by more western-styled gear plundered from farms and ranches.

But even most of that was dusty, sweat-stained, worn. Maybe the formality lay in the fact that these three somehow seemed more alert, less drunk than the others. Possibly, since they were older, in their thirties as opposed to their twenties, they were officers. They leaned silently against the walls, their dark, bony, mustached or bearded faces grave.

Noting the stench again, which was overpowering this close to the end of the hall, Reno realized these three were holding a death vigil for the old devil himself—the Bad Old Man.

Montgomery was dying.

As Reno and Sara approached the partly open door at the end of the hall, Reno heard a man's slow drawl say: "...we pulled foot an' headed to Mexico, Major. Tomorrow, for sure. You'll like Mexico. You didn't have the experience I did down there in '46, but the senoritas..." A raspy chuckle. "They're some special, Major. Yessir, some special, they are. All that brown skin and sparkling brown eyes..."

The raspy chuckle became a cough.

"We'll go when you're ready, Colonel," said another man in the room with Montgomery. "When you're ready, we'll pull out."

"Gotta go soon, Major. We might have the local law cowed. But they've sent for the bluecoats. I'm sure of it. We don't have time. The Union scourge will be here soon. Must head to Mexico posthaste."

"Like I said, Colonel…"

The Major let his voice trail off when Hill stepped around Reno and Sara to tap lightly on the door.

"Come in," said the voice Reno now recognized as belonging to the Bad Old Man.

Hill pushed the door wide, strode into the room, then stepped to one side, turning to Reno and Sara and raising his brows darkly, jeeringly, and silently announcing: "Well, here it is, sodbusters. The end of the trail."

Reno and Sara walked into the room side-by-side. The room with its whitewashed adobe walls was large but nearly empty except for a large bed to the right. The bed was so big that the old devil Reno and Sara had been chasing for the past month—the bib-bearded Confederate demon who had loomed so large in their lives—appeared swallowed by it. But it wasn't really that the bed was so large, Reno realized now, as he stared, stricken, at the gray-bearded old man who lay upon it.

It was that the Bad Old Man, shrunken to a virtually mummified skeleton. He barely made a lump in the sheets and quilts drawn up to his bearded chin.

The face peering at them from the pillows propped at an angle against the spools of the brass headboard was as pale as the bedding it sank back into.

The eyes, drawn far back into their bony sockets, were as dark as coals. Only one arm lay down over the bedding, resting along the Bad Old Man's bony frame. The bedding where the other arm should have hung down from the shoulder was stained dark-red with fresh blood.

The arm was gone. Cut off.

The stench lifting off the dying man's withered body wafted like a hot wind from hell over Reno and Sara, making Reno's eyes burn. Even Sara made a rare reaction. She drew a shallow breath then lowered her chin and shook her head against the cloying odor of rotten flesh. Reno heard her gulp.

Apparently, the Bad Old Man's arm hadn't been taken off in time. Blood poisoning had invaded his body, and the rest of the Devil's Horde was merely waiting for him to die so they could continue south to Old Mexico. However, before the Bad Old Man breathed his last breath, they were going to give him one last gift—the young man who, for all intents and purposes, had shot his arm off, and the young man's sister.

Major "Black Bob" Hobbs sat in a chair in the room's front corner, beside the colonel's bed. He wore a full Confederate uniform complete with gray greatcoat, as shabby and sweat-stained as it all was. Two rows of gold buttons ran down his chest. A battered gray slouch hat was hooked on a crossed knee. His gray leather trousers were shoved into high-topped black cavalry boots. The toe of the left boot was torn, revealing the tip of the man's stocking-clad foot, which in turn was torn, revealing Black Bob's big left toe.

His forehead bulged. His deep-set black eyes smoldered out from well-like sockets. Coal-black hair, lightly streaked with gray, was combed straight back over his head. It curled down around his ears. His black beard, thick as a mink's coat in winter, was as black as his hair, owning fewer touches of gray. Near the right corner of his mouth, the beard was streaked with fresh chaw that glistened in the light from the window overlooking the street. Black Bob wore two pistols on his hips. A saber rested across his lap. He had both hands on it.

A bottle stood beside him, on a low table, along with a white stone mug.

He stared at Reno and Sara, his eyes cold and hard and glistening with drink. A faint, oblique smile tugged at his mouth corners.

The Bad Old Man stared at Reno and Sara from his mounded pillows. He cleared his throat, his spindly chest rising and falling slowly beneath the covers. "Who are you?" Oddly, in sharp contrast to his withered countenance, his voice was still strong and clear.

Reno opened his mouth to tell the man his name, but before he could even begin to speak, Sara leaned slightly forward at the waist and screamed, "Go to hell, you filth!"

The tall, lazy-eyed man flanking Sara, holding her Henry in one hand, stepped forward to smack Sara's head with his other hand. "Don't you dare talk like that to the colonel, you foul-mouthed Yankee trollop!"

Montgomery held up one pale, wrinkled hand. He stared at Sara without expression, though his eyes blazed with indignant rage. He looked at Corporal Hill standing behind Reno, poking one of Reno's own revolvers against his back. Sliding his gaze back to Reno, the Bad Old Man said, "Take this one out an' hang him. Blow his arm off first. Then hang 'im!"

"No!" Sara screamed, lunging toward Montgomery.

Virgil grabbed her coat collar and pulled her back.

Montgomery looked at her. "That one—she's got some fight in her. You men can have her. Do to her what you will, then take her down to Mexico. Sell her to the Mexicans. They'll finish her off in their own special way." He laughed, but choked and convulsed with coughing.

"You got it, Colonel!" said Virgil. He pulled Sara back again by her hair, harder this time. He laughed and nuzzled her neck then tossed her to the stocky man.

"Get your hands off my sister!" Reno was about to launch himself at the stocky man but just then he felt Hill press the barrel of his own revolver against his arm. The man intended to blow his arm off right here, right now.

Reno whipped around, throwing both arms wide. As he did, the Pietta in Hill's arm roared.

The bullet sliced across Reno's side. Flames from the gun spread to Reno's shirt. As Reno fell back against the foot of the colonel's bed, slapping at the flames biting into his skin, Hill raised the Remington once more and cocked the hammer. He smiled coldly, his eyes glinting like the devil's eyes as he aimed the gun at Reno's arm again, narrowing one eye.

"Not in here, you fool!" roared Black Bob Hobbs, rising from his chair, holding his saber in one hand. "You'll hit the colonel!"

Hill had just started to turn toward the major when his head exploded.

The Remington in the corporal's hand bucked and roared once more, the bullet hammering the wall to the right of the colonel's bed. Hill dropped the gun as what was left of his head jerked sharply toward the room's open door. His feet sidestepped in that direction as well.

He turned sharply, then fell like a suit of clothes dropping from a hanger.

Virgil and the stocky man with the saber froze.

So did Sara, pulling free of the stocky man's grip. All eyes went to Virgil, covered in the bone, brains, and blood that had been blown out of Corporal Hill's head. Virgil's lower jaw hung in shock. He looked around wide-eyed, peering down at Hill and then at the blood staining his shirt. It dripped down his long face, as well.

He raised a hand to his bloody face just as a bullet smashed into his forehead, blowing out the back of his head and splashing it into the hall behind him, where the five other Confederates stood, staring into the room, frowning curiously, still trying to wrap their minds around Corporal Hill's sudden, puzzling demise.

THIRTY-TWO

Reno had patted out the flames on his shirt. Eyes stinging from the smoke wafting around him, he turned to peer through the open window facing the street.

A man lay on the gently sloping roof of the barn across the street. He was just then poking a cartridge into what appeared to be a Sharps .54 carbine like the one Reno had used before he'd replaced it with Ty Mando's Henry.

The men on the veranda below the window were shouting and cursing, boots thudding as they scurried for cover.

"There he is!" one of them shouted. "On the roof yonder! Git him!"

The shooter was a good sixty yards away, but Reno still recognized him. He was the big, black, buckskin-clad man he'd spied when he'd been washing cooking utensils at the creek. The man had set his sombrero on the roof beside him, and he again gazed down the barrel of the cannon in his hands.

Smoke and flames blossomed from the .54-caliber's barrel. A man's scream rose from the veranda, and the Sharps' heavy, echoing report was quickly accompanied by return fire.

Only about six seconds had passed since the first shot had blown apart Corporal Stock's head. Now the other men in the Colonel's room and out in the hall were shaking off their shock and were reaching for their weapons. Reno did, as well, scooping one of his Remingtons off the floor where Stock had dropped it then leaping onto Stock and ripping the other revolver from the holster on the moon-faced devil's left hip.

In the periphery of his vision, he saw Sara crouch to retrieve her Henry rifle from the floor near Virgil, who lay with the upper half of his body in the hall, the lower half still inside the room. A hole the size of a silver dollar gaped in his forehead, just beneath his hairline. He stared straight up in the ceiling as though in wide-eyed fascination at his sudden, grisly annihilation.

Guns popped around Reno now. Men in the hall were shooting into the room at him and Sara. A bullet sliced across Reno's right ear as he swung toward the stocky gent whom Sara had apparently kicked in a lousy place for a man to get kicked. He was on the floor but recovering from the assault, his fat face puffed and red with anger, raising both of his Confederate revolvers.

Reno shot him, the Pietta thundering in the close confines.

The man winced, lowered his hoglegs, then cursed and started to raise them again.

Reno shot him again, and he fell flat against the floor.

In the corner of his left eye Reno saw Black Bob leaping toward him, swinging the bayonet. Reno ducked. The bayonet whistled through the air where his neck had been half an eye blink before.

More bullets stitched the air as Reno extended one of his Remys at Black Bob, whose own slashing momentum still had the major turned sideways to Reno, preparing the bring the blade back forward from behind his left shoulder. He seemed intent on decapitating the blond Yankee.

Reno fired the Remington. He could barely hear the revolver's blast above the roar of the Henry rifle, which Sara was firing and levering and firing again at the five men in the hall. As Black Bob flew back in his chair with his guts on fire, Reno dropped to a knee and glanced into the hall. Two men were down, but two more were crouching on each side of the hall, exchanging fire with Sara, who angled her Henry around the door's right side.

She'd taken back the Henry Virgil had confiscated. The other one lay on the floor between the stocky gent, who'd appropriated it for himself, and a washstand. Reno grabbed the fine sixteen-shooter, cocked it, and dropped to a knee off Sara's left shoulder. From here, he could see through the door and into the smoky hall.

As Sara drew her head back behind the door frame, the man crouching on the left side of the hall drilled a bullet into the frame. The bullet blasted slivers of wood onto Sara's left shoulder and her hair. Reno quickly aimed at the man, and shot him in the upper chest. As the man jerked back against the wall, Sara shot the man on the right side of the hall.

Reno's shooter bellowed curses and tried to raise both his pistols again.

Again, Reno shot him, this time in the left cheek. The man dropped both guns and curled up on the floor at the base of the wall as though it were time for a nap.

The other man got to his feet unsteadily. Mewling like a trapped coyote, he ran down the hall, tripping over his own boot toes, away from the colonel's room. When he turned to start down the stairs, Sara gained her feet, stepped into the hall, raised the Henry again, and shot the man in the neck.

He dropped the single pistol he was holding and stood wobbling before he fell forward. Reno heard thumping on the stairs as the man's dead body tumbled toward the main saloon hall below.

From down there came the sound of a small battle. Guns roared. Men shouted back and forth and scuttled around, boots thumping on the wooden floor, kicking tables and chairs this way and that. From outside rose the heavy belching sounds of the Sharps .54.

Reno smiled. His and Sara's guardian angel was still going after the Confederate devils with the carbine.

However, the Sharps was a mere single shot with paper cartridges. He was going to need a little help of his own.

Sara lowered her smoking Henry and turned to Reno, frowning curiously, listening to the gunfire issuing from below and outside. "I don't get it." She shook her head as she looked down at what was left of Corporal Stock and Virgil. "Who shot…"

"Our guardian angel from last night." Reno gained his feet. "Shall we give him a hand…?"

"Hold on." Sara was looking down at the floor behind Reno. "One last rat to kill up here."

Reno followed his sister's gaze to see Colonel Montgomery crawling toward him on the floor. The Bad Old Man wore only a night shirt, the tied-up left shoulder dark with blood. His skinny, hairless white legs were bare. He crawled silently toward Reno. He looked like a white, bearded worm or a giant hatch-ling chicken. It was an awkward maneuver, given that he had only one arm, and his body was filled with rot. It was made even more awkward by the fact that he clutched a revolver, which he must have taken off of Black Bob slumped dead in the chair, in his spidery right hand.

The Bad Old Man was bad right up to the end.

He stopped a few feet from Reno. His dark-blue eyes blazed like stormy light off a choppy sea. He raised the revolver and winced, several muscles in his sweat-washed face twitching, as he tried to ratchet back the hammer.

"Let's rid the earth of this demon scourge once and for all, brother." Sara took a step forward, poked the barrel of her Henry rifle into the old man's mouth. It clicked against its teeth.

The colonel's eyes bulged as he looked up at Sara in glassy-eyed terror.

Sara slid the rifle's maw far back in the old man's mouth, tipped his head back then shoved his entire body back flat against the floor. She smiled down at the old devil as she said, "Goodbye, Old Beelzebub. The burning seas await. I hope you can swim or at least dog paddle, because you're gonna be awash in the unholy fires of hell for a good, long time."

The old man stared up at her, choking on the iron barrel shoved down his throat. He convulsed and grabbed desperately at the barrel with his lone hand.

Sara squeezed the trigger. The Henry leaped. The blast was muffled by the old man's head, which cracked open like a melon split by an axe.

Sara lifted the dripping barrel and turned to Reno. "All right, then. Let's go downstairs and finish the eradication."

Reno stared down at the Bad Old Man's head for a moment, vaguely surprised not to see little black snakes slithering out of the ruined skull. He swing-cocked his own Henry and followed Sara down the hall, stepping over dead devils as he went.

He descended the stairs behind Sara, both of them crouching and peering forward, into the saloon hall. It was dimly lit and smoky, but Reno saw the half-dozen men crouched near the broken-out front windows on either side of the door.

Five or six lay dead on the floor or draped over tables or atop overturned chairs. The coppery smell of fresh blood mixed with the rotten egg odor of powder smoke.

The shooting had tapered off. Now only one man was firing his pistol, triggering lead at the barn across the street. When the hammer clicked on an empty chamber, he lowered the weapon and turned to the man kneeling beside him.

"I don't see him. Either we got the blue-gum devil with the Sharps, or he's just out of ammo."

"I say we go drag that black snake out of its lair," said another.

All six of the men froze.

They stared at each other tensely. They'd all sensed the towheaded sodbusters standing behind them, side by side at the bottom of the stairs, wafting powder smoke enshrouding them.

Reno squeezed the Henry in his hands. Sara did the same.

Reno's heart thudded. Here they were in the devils' lair. Most of the vipers were dead. There were only six left.

Suddenly, one of the killers snapped his head around to stare back at Reno and Sara. His dark eyes glinted fearfully. The others turned then, too. They held pistols or single-shot rifles. They saw the brass-breeched Henrys in the sodbusters' hands. The old-model weapons the devils wielded were no match for the sixteen-shooters. They seemed to sense that.

They stared, speechless, at Reno and Sara.

Reno, however, was not speechless. As though of their own accord, words from Deuteronomy fairly exploded from his lips when he held up his left fist and shook it as he spoke:

"'Because you did not serve the lord your god with joyfulness and gladness of heart, because of the abundance of all things, therefore you shall serve your enemies whom the lord will send against you, in hunger and thirst, in nakedness, and lacking everything. And he will put a yoke of iron on your neck until he has destroyed you.'"

They killers stared, blank-faced.

One second passed. Two...

A couple of them wailed as they turned full around, raising their weapons. Only two got off errant shots before Reno and Sara's bullets tore into them, blowing three out the windows and one through the front door.

One slammed against a ceiling support post, blood pumping from his chest, while the last one flew back atop a table, sighing as he died, flopping his arms and legs until Reno and Sara each drilled one more round into him, silencing his caterwauling forever.

Reno and Sara strode slowly forward, glancing around at the dead devils spread out around them, blood from a couple of bodies draped over tables or chairs dripping onto the floor. Again, words issued from Reno's mouth, as though from the lips of god himself:

"'Even though I walk through the valley of the shadow of death, I will fear no evil, for you are with me; your rod and your staff, they comfort me. You prepare a table before me in the presence of my enemies; you anoint my head with oil; my cup overflows.'"

A man on a table to Reno's left still breathed, making slight strangling sounds. Reno shot him again. The bullet drove the man off the table to the floor.

EPILOGUE

Reno and Sara stopped at the front of the room, near the open door. They turned around to admire their handiwork—a den full of Satan's dead soldiers.

Reno didn't know when he'd felt more pleased. More fulfilled.

More at one with god.

Footsteps sounded behind him. He and Sara whipped around, raising their Henrys once more. They turned to see a tall black man in buckskins standing before them. He was a handsome man with a mustache that trailed down both sides of his mouth. On his cheeks was a three- or four-day beard shadow. Reno had never seen a Negro up close before. He found himself staring with keen fascination.

The black man nudged his leather sombrero off his forehead with the barrel of his Sharps and said, "All clear in there?"

Reno and Sara nodded dully.

The black man stepped up onto the porch. The twins each took a step apart, making room, and the black man stepped over the threshold. He strode slowly forward, looking around, his Sharps cradled in his arms. He walked to the back of the room and when he got to the stairs, he turned around and strode forward again.

Ten feet from the door, he stopped and tilted his gaze upward. "The Bad Old Man? Black Bob...?"

"Satan's head has been cut off," Sara assured him.

He looked at her and didn't say anything for a moment. He looked at Reno then nodded slowly, pursing his lips. "Fine, then. Fine..."

Reno said, "You saved our lives last night."

The black man smiled. "You saved mine today. All I got's this single-shot and two revolvers. Fact is, I expected to die when I finally met up with the Devil's Horde. Like you, I reckon, I figured someone had to do it...since the law wasn't up to the task."

Sara said, "They did to you..."

"What they done to you, most like. Burned my farm. Killed my family. I still got a boy. We was in town buyin' supplies when the Bad Old Man and Black Bob rode through, cut around the edge of Coldwater, Kansas, hit my farm. Burned it. Murdered my wife...two daughters—Princess and Queen Virginia."

Tears glazed his liquid black eyes. He blinked

them away, sleeved one from his cheek, then extended his big open hand to Reno. "I'm Norman Withers. Freeman. Been free since just after the war started. Pulled my wife and my daughters out of Louisiana and headed to Kansas to farm. Aggie, short for Agamemnon, was born a year later."

"We're from Baxter," Reno said, shaking the man's hand. "I'm Reno Bass. This is my sister, Sara."

"Please to meet you, Miss Sara," said Norman Withers, shaking Sara's hand. He looked at the Henry in her hands and pointed to it. "Do you mind?"

Sara held the rifle out to him.

Withers leaned his old Sharps against the wall, took the Henry from Sara, and held it up to inspect it with glassy-eyed admiration. He worked the lever, then depressed the hammer while squeezing the trigger, off-cocking it. He ran his hand down the long, octagonal barrel. "So that's the Tyler Henry. I've heard a lot about it. Never expected to see one." He smiled at Sara. "Never expected to have one save my life."

He looked at Reno. "I reckon I'm glad you didn't take my advice and go home."

"We never could have done that," Sara said.

"No." Withers nodded. "It's time now, though. Time for all three of us to go on home. Me? I got a boy to raise. I left him with the parson's wife. Didn't expect to see little Aggie again. I do now, though." He grinned broadly, showing large, white teeth. "And I can honestly say I can't wait to pick him up, give him a big hug, and start over."

He handed the Henry back to Sara.

"Farewell, both of you." Withers pinched his hat brim to Reno and Sara, then swung around and walked back out onto the porch. He stopped halfway down the steps, turned back and said, "Oh…your dog's right over there." He tilted his head to indicate north along the main street. "He followed me followin' you from Johanssen's Livery, trailin' his rope. I tied him to a hitch rack over there to keep him out of harm's way."

Reno stepped outside and saw Apache sitting near a hitch rack on the other side of the street fifty yards away. The dog gazed toward the El Dorado, anxiously shifting his weight from one foot to the other and quietly yipping. Folks were beginning to surface from shops and the breaks between buildings, gazing curiously, apprehensively toward the El Dorado Hotel. Reno and Sara's horses had run off when the shooting had started. The buckskin and the black mare stood now with the dead killers' mounts near an alley mouth on the other side of the street.

"Take care, now," Withers said, and began walking along the street, heading to a horse tied to a hitch rack near Apache. It was the only horse on the street—a big roan stallion.

Sara came out of the saloon to stand on the porch

with Reno.

"Well, that's done," Reno said.

"Yes, it is."

"What now?" He looked at her. "Go home? Start over, like Mr. Withers?"

"We don't have anyone waitin' on us at home like Mr. Withers does," Sara said. She turned her head slowly to Reno. "I don't, leastways. You have Isabelle."

Reno felt the weight of sadness return to his shoulders. He felt Sara's loneliness. All the pain of the past month had settled on both of them once more. Reno once again became aware of the pain of his injuries. Only battling evil seemed to relieve his misery.

He loved Isabelle and would return to her one day. One day...

Until then, god had more work for Reno and Sara.

Hooves drummed in the west. Guns crackled.

The twins swung their heads to gaze beyond where Withers was just then mounting the roan. Five or six riders galloped toward the El Dorado.

They were running hard, whooping and hollering like wolves on the blood scent, triggering pistols into the air. As they galloped past the El Dorado, shooting and yelling and laughing, Reno saw bulging saddlebags laid over the backs of two of the gang's horses. One of the riders saw Sara and shouted something lewd, making a depraved gesture with his hands.

When the riders had passed, their dust sifting

thickly behind them, Sara turned to Reno and said, "I got a feelin' those fellas are up to no good."

"I got a feelin' they robbed somethin' over in Denver City. Maybe a bank, say. Possibly a brothel. Maybe killed people. They have that look about them."

"I got a feeling you're right, brother," Sara said. "I also got a feelin' that what we did here today was a good start." She glanced into the saloon behind her then turned to Reno, arching one brow.

"But just a start," Reno said.

They reloaded their Henrys then moved off into the street. Reno untied Apache then mounted his horse. The Avenging Angels galloped off toward Glory.

Let your faith be like a shiel•, an• you will be able to stop all the flaming arrows of the evil one. Let go•'s saving power be like a helmet, an• for a swor• use go•'s message that comes from the Spirit.—Ephesians 6: 16-17

A LOOK AT: AVENGING ANGELS: SINNERS' GOLD

SADDLE UP FOR BOOK TWO OF THE HEART-POUND-ING, BULLET-BURNING, BIBLE-THUMPING WESTERN SERIES!

After avenging the brutal slaughter of their family at the hands of Hell-spawned cutthroats, twins Reno and Sara Bass continue their quest to purge the West of the Devil's minions who prey on the vulnerable and unsuspecting.

When they reluctantly accompany the hapless Brenda Walon to Hatchet, Nebraska, it quickly becomes clear Brenda is in deadly danger. The seemingly quiet town of Hatchet has many dark secrets—including the legend of hidden gold and the greedy desires of those willing to kill for it!

Sara and Reno realize not all of the Devil's horde ride roughshod and bloody in the open. Now it's up to the Avenging Angels to protect the innocent by flushing out Hatchet's human demons and sending them back to Hell.

AVAILABLE OCTOBER 2019 FROM A.W. HART AND WOLFPACK PUBLISHING

ABOUT THE AUTHOR

Peter Brandvold grew up in the great state of North Dakota in the 1960's and '70s, when television westerns were as popular as shows about hoarders and shark tanks are now, and western paperbacks were as popular as Game of Thrones.

Brandvold watched every western series on television at the time. He grew up riding horses and herding cows on the farms of his grandfather and many friends who owned livestock.

Brandvold's imagination has always lived and will always live in the West. He is the author of over a hundred lightning-fast action westerns under his own name and his pen name, Frank Leslie.

READ MORE ABOUT PETER BRANDVOLD HERE:
https://wolfpackpublishing.com/peter-brandvold/

Made in the USA
Coppell, TX
08 November 2024

39861975R00215